Jack touched her shoulder.
"Desiree, I'm sorry...."

She flinched. "Please, Jack. Don't say anything. Just go."

"Desiree." The word was a whisper. His eyes were gentle.

Please, please, she begged silently. *Don't let him look at me like that.* "Good night, Jack." She opened the front door.

"We can't pretend this didn't happen."

"We *will* pretend this didn't happen." She didn't add *or else.* He was smart enough to understand.

She saw the resignation in the almost imperceptible shrug of his shoulders and in the tightening of his mouth. His voice, when he spoke, was even, almost impersonal. "I'll see you tomorrow, then."

"Yes." Desiree's chest felt tight from the effort of holding herself together.

Finally he walked out the open door, his gaze capturing hers for one instant as he brushed past.

Desiree shut the door. And then she burst into tears.

D1393026

Dear Reader:

Romance readers have been enthusiastic about the Silhouette Special Editions for years. And that's not by accident: Special Editions were the first of their kind and continue to feature realistic stories with heightened romantic tension.

The longer stories, sophisticated style, greater sensual detail and variety that made Special Editions popular are the same elements that will make you want to read book after book.

We hope that you enjoy this Special Edition today, and will enjoy many more.

Please write to us:

Jane Nicholls
Silhouette Books
PO Box 236
Thornton Road
Croydon
Surrey
CR9 3RU

TRISHA ALEXANDER
When Somebody Needs You

Silhouette Special Edition

**Originally Published by Silhouette Books
a division of
Harlequin Enterprises Ltd.**

First published in Great Britain in 1993 by Silhouette Books, Eton House, 18-24 Paradise Road, Richmond, Surrey TW9 1SR

© Patricia A. Kay 1992

Silhouette, Silhouette Special Edition and Colophon are Trade Marks of Harlequin Enterprises B.V.

ISBN 0 373 58779 1

23-9304

Made and printed in Great Britain

This book is dedicated to Susan Brown, my Louisiana "connection," who so generously shared her heritage; and Julie Kistler, a charter member of the Society of Fabulous Megababes, for her invaluable advice and unflagging support.
Special thanks to my buddies: Elaine Kimberley, my computer guru; Heather MacAllister and Alaina Richardson, sharpies with the red pen; Betty Gyenes, who allowed me to share the navy night; and Mary Clare Kersten, who encouraged me to keep writing about the Cantrelles.

TRISHA ALEXANDER

was encouraged from childhood to believe she could do whatever she set out to do, and this perennial injection of confidence became the mainstay of her life. Professionally, she has held many positions, from secretary to ad saleswoman. After years of considering the prospect, Trisha began writing seriously. She found that she liked everything about it: reading, research, talking about writing, the act of writing itself, writers' conferences, critiquing, revising, editing—you name it, she loves it.

Another Silhouette Book by Trisha Alexander

Silhouette Special Edition

Cinderella Girl
When Somebody Loves You

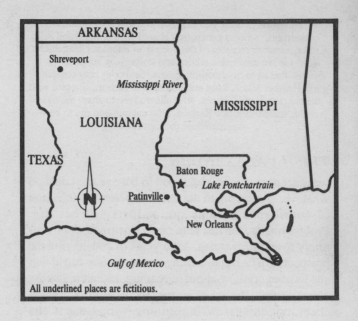

ARKANSAS

Shreveport

Mississippi River

MISSISSIPPI

LOUISIANA

TEXAS

Baton Rouge

Lake Pontchartrain

N

Patinville

New Orleans

Gulf of Mexico

All underlined places are fictitious.

Chapter One

That man was watching her.

Desiree Cantrelle hated it when men stared at her, and usually she just ignored them. But something about the way this man watched her gave her a creepy feeling, and she couldn't dismiss him so easily.

He stood sheltered from the heavy rain in the recessed doorway of one of the many pricey antique shops on Royal Street. He was tall and broad-shouldered and wore some kind of army green all-weather jacket. On his head was a camouflage hat, and the front brim was pulled down over his face.

She knew his eyes followed her as she walked past him; she could feel them even when she could no longer see them. Because it was early morning, and there were dozens of other people walking the streets of the French Quarter—most on their way to work as she was—she wasn't really nervous.

Still . . . she frowned, clutched her big totebag more securely against her body, and walked faster through the deluge. For three days New Orleans had been subjected to a steady downpour, and the early-morning sky looked leaden.

A half-block past the antique shop, Desiree's spine prickled. *He was following her.* She stopped so abruptly that a woman walking behind her plowed right into her.

"Oh, I'm sorry," the woman said.

Desiree looked back at the shop, but she didn't see the man. She searched the faces of the people on the street. He wasn't among them. What had happened to him? Shivering, she continued on her way.

When she reached St. Peter's, she turned left. She couldn't rid herself of that peculiar sensation of being followed. Her heart pumped erratically, and she whipped around. An older man with a cane shuffled slowly about six feet behind her. There was no one else on the street.

"You're getting paranoid," she muttered aloud. "Maybe he was just admiring your legs."

Pulling the hood of her yellow slicker closer to her head, she sprinted the last block and a half to her office, careful to avoid the puddles. She was wearing new boots, and she didn't want to ruin them.

She didn't look back again.

"Desiree, have you finished the Menard brief?"

Desiree tapped the Save button on her keyboard, then turned to face her boss, Julie Belizaire. "It's printing now."

"Good." Julie, a petite brunette with hazel eyes that blazed with intelligence, stood at Desiree's desk and sorted through the mail Desiree hadn't yet distributed. "Oh, swell," she muttered, tearing open an envelope. "Another letter from Dr. Puckett. Wouldn't you think the guy would get tired of his own hyperbole?'' Still muttering to herself, she stalked off.

Desiree smothered a smile. She liked being Julie's secretary. Julie always amused her, even when she was angry. Although Desiree at thirty was four years younger than her boss, she often felt motherly toward the only female lawyer in the old French Quarter law firm.

For the next hour Desiree worked diligently. When one of the other secretaries stopped by her desk to chat, Desiree waved her off. "I can't talk. Julie's letting me leave at lunchtime today, so I'm trying to get everything done this morning."

"Where are you going?"

"Home for the weekend."

"Well, have a good one."

Desiree bent back to her work. At eleven forty-five she backed up her files, printed the morning's work and turned off her computer. She cleaned up her desk, then picked up the stack of letters that were ready for Julie's signature. When a glance into Julie's office showed it was unoccupied, Desiree headed down the hall to look for her boss.

She searched the other offices. Still no Julie. Deciding she was probably in the big conference room, Desiree headed in that direction. Just before reaching the reception area, she bumped into Guy D'Amato.

His gray eyes lit up when he saw her, and he smiled. "Hi. I was on my way to your office to see if I could take you to lunch." Guy was a partner in the firm, and she'd been dating him off and on for a few months.

Desiree suppressed the twinge of guilt she felt at his obvious pleasure in seeing her. She suspected Guy was in love with her, that if she encouraged him at all, he'd propose. The sensible part of her knew he was perfect husband material: hardworking, ambitious, considerate, dependable, solvent—all those qualities any mother wants for her daughter.

But there was no excitement, no *sizzle* between them. And the romantic, adventurous part of Desiree wanted that, even though it had gotten her into trouble before.

She'd tried to convince herself that sizzle was the least important element in marriage. She'd told herself that by its very nature, sizzle didn't last. She'd reminded herself that she was a grown-up woman with a three-year-old daughter, and Guy could give them a wonderful and secure future.

But she *still* wanted sizzle.

"I'm sorry, Guy. I can't go to lunch with you today. I'm heading out to Patinville for the weekend, and Julie's letting me go at noon."

He couldn't hide his disappointment, and once more, guilt nudged at her. Guy D'Amato was very nice. She was very stupid.

"When are you coming back? Sunday?"

She nodded.

"Early?"

"I don't know."

"Maybe I could take you and Aimee to dinner Sunday night."

"I don't think so, Guy. Aimee is usually worn out after a weekend with her doting grandparents, and I'll probably be tired, too. Maybe next weekend, okay?"

"All right." He pushed his horn-rimmed glasses up on his nose. "Be careful driving."

"I will." She hurried off toward the reception area. Just as she entered the small room, she caught a glimpse of army green as a man went out the front door. Her heart leaped up into a throat suddenly dry. She gasped.

Was that the man from the antique shop?

Kathy, the receptionist, turned. "Oh, hi, Dee." She frowned. "What's wrong?"

"Kathy, who was that man?"

Kathy's frown deepened. "Why? Do you know him?"

"No. Who *was* he, Kathy? What did he want?"

Kathy flinched. "Uh, well, that's the funny thing. He was asking about someone I thought was you."

Fear jacknifed through her. "What did he say?"

Kathy's puzzled gaze met hers. "When he came in he was very polite, said he was looking for someone he'd been told worked here. He described her, and I thought he meant you, but then he said the woman's name was Elise Arnold, so I told him we didn't have anyone by that name working here."

"That's all he said?"

"Well . . . uh . . . no."

Desiree gritted her teeth. Kathy was new and young and she looked as if she were rattled by Desiree's questions. Desiree took a deep breath and told herself to calm down. "Kathy, that man was following me this morning. I'm sure of it. Try to remember everything he said, okay?"

Kathy's big eyes got even bigger. "Okay, uh, after I told him there wasn't anyone by that name here, he said he was sure the woman he wanted worked here, because he'd seen her come into our office earlier today."

Desiree could feel goose-bumps pop out on her arms. She hadn't been imagining things. He *had* been following her!

"Anyway," Kathy continued, wetting her lips nervously, "I said I was sorry, but he must have been wrong, and then he said it was very important that he talk to the woman because someone was trying to reach her." She gave Desiree an apologetic half smile. "I'm sorry, Dee. He . . . he said it was an emergency and I—"

"You what?"

"I told him your name!"

"You told him my *name? Why?" Good God. He knew her name!*

"It . . . I don't know . . . it just happened. You know how sometimes you say something and the minute it's out of your mouth you know it's a mistake?"

Desiree wanted to shake Kathy, but she forced herself to be calm and speak quietly. "What exactly did he say to cause you to tell him my name?"

"He said it was vitally important—an emergency situation—that he reach this Elise Arnold." Kathy winced. "And I . . . I said, well, I really wished I could help him, but the only woman answering his description was one of our secretaries—Desiree Cantrelle—so I couldn't help him."

Oh, God. Was that the reason he'd come into the office? To try to find out her name? Was his story about this woman just a clever ploy to obtain his *real* objective? But why was he stalking her?

"Dee, I'm so sorry. I really am. But he seemed so *nice,* and . . . oh, dear, I hope I didn't do something terrible."

"Well," Desiree said, trying vainly to push her fear away, "I can't say I'm happy about this, but what's done is done. I just hope—"

"Please don't tell Mr. Villac," Kathy said, naming her boss, the office administrator.

"I wouldn't do that, but Kathy, don't *ever* give out information like that again. To anyone. I don't care what they tell you."

"I won't. I promise. Oh, Dee, I'm sorry. Do . . . do you think you should call the police?"

"And say what? I don't even know who this guy is, and I hardly think his coming in here asking questions constitutes a crime." She made herself talk in a normal voice. "No, let's just forget it. Maybe now he'll realize he has the wrong person, and I'll never see him again. Well," she continued briskly, "have you seen Julie? I need her to sign these letters before I take off."

"She's in the conference room."

Fifteen minutes later, Desiree was on her way out the door. She'd tried to put thoughts of the man out of her mind, but she was still on edge. She walked down the stairs to the first floor and let herself out into the courtyard. Rain dripped from the branches of a shiny-leafed magnolia tree.

She opened the wrought-iron gate and quickly scanned the street. She hadn't realized she'd been holding her breath until she let it out, relief washing over her. She'd been half afraid she'd see him on the sidewalk, but he was gone.

Walking rapidly over to Royal Street, she turned right. When she reached Canal Street, she crossed and walked to the corner of St. Charles Avenue and Common Street, where she would catch the streetcar. The rain had stopped, but the sky still looked like somebody had taken huge balls of cotton and dipped them in dirty dishwater.

Desiree surreptitiously studied the faces of the people around her. None of the men wore army green jackets or camouflage hats. She breathed more easily. Yes, she was sure she had nothing more to worry about. Whoever the man was, he surely realized she was not the woman he wanted. She'd definitely seen the last of him. She even laughed at herself for getting so upset over nothing.

The streetcar rumbled into view, and Desiree counted out her eighty cents. She glanced at her watch. Already twelve-thirty. She'd hoped to be home by now, but looking for Julie, then the episode in the reception area had slowed her down. She hoped Margaret had already given Aimee her lunch. If she had, they could be on their way by one o'clock because Desiree had packed before leaving for work this morning.

Desiree smiled. She was looking forward to visiting her family in Patinville this weekend. Although she loved New Orleans and loved being independent, out from under the watchful eyes of her two brothers, who had a tendency to treat her as if she were still a child, she missed her family. She wondered if other families were as close-knit as Cajuns were. Somehow she doubted it. Her family was wonderful—supportive, loving and understanding. Well, at least most of the time.

Aimee loved going to Patinville, too. She loved her Grandma and Grandpa Cantrelle and all her cousins, especially her cousin Celeste, the daughter of Desiree's brother Neil and his wife Laura. Celeste was only eight months older than Aimee, and the two little girls were as close as sisters.

Still smiling as she thought about her family, Desiree absentmindedly climbed onto the streetcar and found a seat about halfway back. She slid over the slatted wooden seat to the window, which was partially opened for ventilation, and watched as the last stragglers climbed on. Just as the streetcar was ready to leave, a man hopped on and strode down the aisle toward her.

Her eyes took in the army green jacket and the camouflage hat.

Her heart stopped.

She stared at him, but he didn't meet her gaze. He walked on past her and when she turned, she saw him take a seat a couple of rows behind her on the opposite side.

By now her heart was going like a trip-hammer. *Bam. Bam. Bam.* She almost bolted from her seat, but with a lurch and a creak of metal on metal, the streetcar started up.

Calm down. What can happen to you here among all these people, in the middle of the day?

She had to force herself not to turn around again. But she could feel him back there. Watching her. She knew he was following her. He *had* to be following her. It was too coincidental that they both just happened to get on the same streetcar.

What should she do? Should she tell the driver? Should she stay on the streetcar?

She fingered her big totebag. There was a can of Mace in the bag, along with about fifty other things she never left home without. Julie constantly teased her about carrying so much junk around in her bag.

Wait'll I tell her.

All too soon Desiree had to make a decision. First Street was coming up, and it was her stop. She waited until the last minute, then clambered to her feet, her totebag slung over her left shoulder and clutched securely in her left hand. The streetcar driver gave her a curious look as she sped past him and practically threw herself off the car in her haste to exit.

She dashed across St. Charles Avenue, recklessly cutting in front of an oncoming car whose driver hit the horn in an angry blast. Water splashed around her feet, but she was no longer worried about her new boots.

Her breath came in short spurts, and her heart thudded against her chest as she ran. She was afraid to look behind her.

Only two blocks to go before she reached Coliseum Street and home. Two blocks. Two blocks. Two blocks.

Should she turn around? Had he gotten off the streetcar, too? The sound of rapid footsteps behind her made up her mind for her. Still half running, half walking, she pulled her totebag around to the front of her. She yanked the zipper open and shoved her right hand inside the enormous handbag until she found the slick, round shape of her can of Mace.

Simultaneously, she pulled the can out of her bag and whirled around to confront her pursuer.

"What do you want with me?" she demanded, all caution forgotten. She lifted the can of Mace and held it in front of her, ready to spray it at the least sign of aggression.

"Hey, whoa, quit waving that thing around!" He lifted his hands in a placating gesture. "I'm not going to hurt you. I just want to talk."

"You have an odd way of showing it," she said, her breath still coming fast. "You've been following me! Asking questions about me!" She kept her finger on the spray button. "Don't come another step closer!"

He stopped about four feet away from her, still holding his hands up, palms facing her. She narrowed her eyes and stared at him, her gaze daring him to move one inch closer.

"I'm sorry I frightened you," he said, his voice strong and low-timbred.

Now that she could see what he looked like, Desiree realized he didn't look very scary. What was visible of his hair under the cap looked thick and either light brown or dark blond. It was a bit too long, and curled over the collar of his jacket. He had a square face with a deep tan—as if he spent a lot of time outdoors—and a slightly off-center nose. He also had the bluest eyes she'd ever seen.

"You've got exactly two minutes," she said through clenched teeth. "And your explanation had better be good!"

"Will you please lower that can of Mace?" her would-be assailant asked.

Although her instincts told her she had nothing to fear from him, Desiree held on to the can even as she abandoned her threatening stance.

"Thanks." He lowered his hands, too, and pulled something from the left breast pocket of his jacket. He held it out to her.

Desiree could see that it was a small packet of papers. "What are those?"

"My identification. My name is Jack Forrester, and I'm an investigative journalist with World Press, based in Houston. These papers will verify that what I'm telling you is the truth."

Desiree reached out and took the papers. There was a World Press I.D. card encased in plastic with a full-face mug-shot type picture of Jack Forrester. Under the picture in bold letters was printed: JACKSON ALAN FORRESTER. She carefully read the information on the card, noting that his height was listed as six feet, his weight a hundred and seventy-eight pounds. Blue eyes. Dark blond hair. Thirty-three years old.

She quickly shuffled through the rest of the papers. Texas driver's license. Passport. Social security card. Voter's registration. She raised her eyes, meeting his steady gaze squarely.

She felt a strange tug of allure, an almost instant rapport. His eyes reminded her of the sea. Deep and bottomless, they were eyes a woman could get lost in. She almost forgot she'd been afraid of him. If she'd met him at Michaul's, her favorite Friday-night haunt, she'd probably have flirted with him.

But this wasn't Michaul's, she reminded herself, and she wasn't looking for a dancing partner. This was First Street, and this man, attractive or not, bedroom-blue eyes or not, had been dogging her since early this morning.

Mentally shaking herself, she handed him back his papers. He took them and put them into his jacket pocket. "Okay, so you're Jack Forrester. Why have you been following me?"

"I'm looking for someone—a woman named Elise Arnold."

"I know that. But by now you should also know I'm not the woman you want."

He nodded slowly. "Yes, I can see you're not. But I wasn't sure until now."

Partially mollified by his reluctant admission, Desiree said, "Who *is* this woman anyway, and why did you think I was her?"

"Elise is a friend of my sister's, and she disappeared from Houston four weeks ago. My sister asked me to try to find her. My search led me to you." He must have seen the skepticism Desiree felt, for he smiled—a warm, engaging smile—and something went *zing* in Desiree's stomach. "You don't know whether to believe me or not, do you?"

Desiree wanted to believe him. How could a man with such a charming smile and such beautiful eyes be dangerous? *Remember the last man you thought had a great smile and nice eyes.* The thought was sobering. Her earlier lack of judgment had had very serious consequences. She didn't exactly have a great track record when it came to men.

Besides, hadn't she read somewhere that the most successful serial killers were all charming, attractive men? Men who women instinctively trusted?

She sighed. "Maybe I'll be sorry later, but I do believe you. However, as I've said before, I'm not the woman you're looking for. My name is Desiree Cantrelle. It's never been Elise or Arnold, and I've never lived in Houston. I've lived in Louisiana all my life—for the last two-and-a-half years here in New Orleans. So I'll ask you again—what made you think I was her?"

His eyes studied hers for a long moment, and Desiree's heart gave an odd little thump when something flickered in their rich depths. Lordy, those eyes were lethal! When he finally spoke his voice was thoughtful. "The two of you could be twins you look so much alike." He withdrew a small, black notebook from his inside jacket pocket, opened it, removed a photograph. He held it out to her.

Desiree stared at the picture. The snapshot showed a woman in her late twenties or early thirties with thick, curly dark hair that skimmed her shoulders, and wide, dark eyes. Her full lips tilted up in a shy smile as she faced the camera. She was dressed in white shorts and a red tank top, and she was sitting on top of a redwood picnic table. Desiree could have been looking at a picture of herself.

Although she was shaken by the photograph, she was sure the similarity between her and this unknown Arnold woman *had* to be coincidence. "I'll admit this woman looks very much like me," she said slowly. "But they say everyone has a double somewhere in the world."

"That's not all...."

A gust of wind rattled the branches of a large sycamore tree, shaking raindrops over them. Desiree hugged her arms, suddenly conscious of how chilly it was and how long they'd been standing there.

"Elise told my sister her father's name was Cantrelle."

Desiree tried not to show how that little piece of information had startled her. "In Louisiana," she said carefully, "the name Cantrelle is very common. Perhaps we're third or fourth cousins or something." She handed the picture back to him. "There're many branches of the Cantrelle family around."

"Are you *sure* you've never heard of her?" He tucked the picture back into his pocket.

"Yes, I'm positive." She ignored the uneasiness pulsing through her.

"It's hard to believe two people could look so strikingly alike and not be closely related," he persisted.

"Now look, I don't care if you believe me or not. I've told you all I know. And I don't have time to stand out here in the cold and talk anymore. I'm late as it is." She pointedly looked at her watch. It was now one o'clock. "I've got to get home. Sorry I couldn't help you, Mr. Forrester."

"Where do you live?"

Desiree took a deep breath, as irritation with his persistence finally got the better of her. "It's none of your business. Now goodbye, Mr. Forrester." She turned and began to walk away.

He matched his stride to hers, coming up and walking next to her on the street side.

"Go away, Mr. Forrester." What did he *want* from her, anyway?

"How about inviting me in? Maybe we could talk some more. Maybe you'd remember something that might help me."

She stopped abruptly. "I'm not going to invite you in. I have nothing more to say to you. Besides, I'm in a hurry. I'm going away for the weekend, and I should have already been on my way."

She refused to meet his eyes. She didn't want to be swayed by eyes that reminded her of the ocean on a dazzling summer's day. By eyes that made her good sense fly out the window.

Instead she stalked off. A few minutes later when she looked back, he was still standing where she'd left him, in the middle of the sidewalk with his hands shoved in his pockets. She shrugged aside the tiny spark of regret she felt when she realized he'd finally taken the hint and she wouldn't be seeing him again.

Jack watched her go, admiring the way her legs looked in the snug-fitting black boots. What a sexy little spitfire! He liked women who didn't let anyone push them around.

From the minute she'd whirled around and waved that can of Mace at him, he'd known she wasn't Elise.

Although Jack hadn't known Elise all that well—he didn't spend enough time in Houston to really know any of his sister Jenny's friends—he'd seen enough of Elise to know she was quiet and shy. Desiree Cantrelle might look like Elise Arnold on the outside, but no one spending any time at all with Desiree would mistake her for Elise. Unlike Elise, there was nothing shy or timid about Desiree. Those dark eyes of hers had flashed at him in angry defiance, and her entire body had seemed to pulsate with energy and life. He couldn't imagine the reserved Elise standing up to him the way Desiree had.

But still . . . disregarding their personalities, it was uncanny how much Desiree Cantrelle and Elise Arnold looked like each other. No matter what Desiree said, no matter what she actually believed, Jack was sure there was a connection between the two women. And he was just the man to uncover it.

And the first step was to find out more about Desiree. So when she turned right onto Coliseum, he followed at a slower pace. When he got to the corner, he peered cautiously down the street. He saw one bright flash of yellow as she disappeared into a driveway a few doors down on the right. Jack stood there for a moment, then decided to cross the street. If he could find a place to wait where he wouldn't be noticed, he could watch to see if she really was going somewhere.

The house on the property she'd entered was a double-galleried home set back from the street in a lush garden setting and surrounded by an ornate iron fence with still-blooming plumbago peeking through the grillwork. Jack admired the well-tended grounds. Someday, if he ever had a home of his own, he wanted a garden and lots of flowers and trees. The house was shaded by two mammoth live oaks that dripped from the morning's rain and probably kept the big house cool and comfortable in warm weather. He could see another building farther back on the property, and he wondered if Desiree lived in the big house or in the smaller structure.

A half hour later, Jack's feet were numb. He wished he had his car. At least then he could turn on the heater instead of standing outside freezing his butt off. Maybe this was a dumb idea. Maybe Desiree had lied to him, and she wasn't going anywhere. He could stand out here until doomsday, and she'd probably be inside laughing at him.

Just as these black thoughts crossed his mind, he saw her. She emerged from the back of the property and opened one side of the big garage. Minutes later, Desiree and a little girl, who looked to be about two or three, had loaded a couple of suitcases into the trunk of a small red Geo and were backing out of the driveway. He wondered if the little girl was Desiree's. He was certain she hadn't been wearing a wedding ring.

Jack, with all the finely honed instincts of a veteran reporter, wrote down the numbers on her license plate as Desiree drove away. He took one last look at the house, then, whistling, he walked rapidly toward the streetcar stop.

Whether Desiree Cantrelle knew it or not, she hadn't seen the last of him.

Chapter Two

"Mommy, when are we going to get there?"

Desiree grinned. She'd lost count of the number of times Aimee had asked this same question. She patted her daughter's leg. "Soon, *chère.*"

"That's what you said the last time."

The grin erupted into a chuckle. Aimee was nobody's fool, and she wouldn't be put off with vague answers. *The apple doesn't fall far from the tree,* Desiree's mother was fond of saying, and in their lack of patience, Desiree knew she and Aimee were very much alike.

"We'll be there in ten minutes. Do you know how long ten minutes is?"

"Ummm..."

Desiree slanted a glance at her daughter. Aimee's dark eyes were narrowed in thought, and her silky blond hair, which she'd inherited from her father, fell forward in defiance of Desiree's every effort to keep it neat. Once again

Desiree marveled at Aimee's beauty. The combination of golden hair, creamy skin and eyes the color of dark chocolate was striking. How a child so lovely and bright could result from one of the worst mistakes in Desiree's life was a continuous source of mystery... and joy.

"Look at your watch," Desiree instructed.

Aimee held her wrist up and seriously studied the face of the Mickey Mouse watch both she and Celeste had gotten as Christmas presents last year from Desiree's brother Norman and his wife, Alice.

"See how the little hand is on the three?"

Aimee nodded.

"And the big hand is on the one?"

"Uh-huh."

"Well, watch the big hand. When it moves around so that it's on top of the little hand, then we'll be there."

For the next ten minutes, Aimee was quiet, and Desiree was free to let her mind wander as she drove the last few miles to Patinville, the town just west of Baton Rouge where she was born and raised.

Jack Forrester.

She hadn't been able to forget him. Ever since her conversation with him a couple of hours earlier, he'd hovered at the edge of her mind. While she'd been saying her goodbyes to Margaret and Caldwell Reed-Douglas—her landlords and friends as well as Aimee's baby-sitters—and the whole time she'd gotten Aimee dressed for the trip, she'd been thinking about Jack and what he'd had to say.

Now, as she exited Interstate 10 and turned south onto Route 77, which would take them straight into Patinville, she remembered how keenly his blue eyes had studied her and how she'd felt when she'd gazed into their depths.

Quit thinking about his eyes.

She bit back a giggle. What on earth was wrong with her? A perfect stranger spies on her, follows her, accosts her on the street, gives her some cockeyed story about a missing woman who looks like her, and she's thinking about his eyes!

You've been without a man far too long, Desiree, my girl.

Desiree sighed.

"The big hand's on the three!" Aimee said, her childish voice squeaking in triumph. She started to bounce on the seat, struggling against the restraining seat belt on her booster seat. "Where's Grandma's house?"

"You'll see it in a minute," Desiree said as she turned onto Lafayette Lane, the dead-end street where her parents lived.

"Grandma! Grandpa!" Aimee struggled to release her seat belt as Desiree spied her parents. They must have been keeping watch at the big bay window, because they were already on the front porch.

Desiree pulled in behind her mother's decrepit Plymouth station wagon—a vehicle she refused to give up, no matter how many times her husband and sons lectured her—and turned off the ignition. Then she turned to Aimee, pushed the release on the seat belt and waved to her parents.

René was already opening Aimee's door. "My darlin' grandbaby," he crooned as he scooped Aimee up into his strong arms. "How your grandpapa's missed you!" Aimee giggled as he covered her face with kisses.

Desiree got out of the car and walked around the other side, gravel crunching under her feet. She took a deep breath of the pine-scented air. Her parents' home sat just at the edge of a small wooded area, and she'd always loved its tranquil setting. She and her brothers and sister had spent many happy days playing in the woods, pretending they were explorers and hiding out from their long-suffering mother.

Arlette Cantrelle now had Aimee in her arms, and René enfolded Desiree in a bear hug. "It's so good to see you, *ma chère*," he whispered, his voice husky with emotion. Desiree hugged him back. She knew her father missed her. With the exception of her older brother, Neil, she was the only Cantrelle who had ever left Patinville. And now even Neil was back, once more working in the family's roofing and home improvement business along with Norman, her other brother.

"Hello, Papa."

René finally released her, but his dark eyes carefully studied her face, then her body.

"Don't worry, I'm still all in one piece. Those nasty big-city people haven't done anything to me," Desiree teased.

Her mother grinned, and Desiree grinned back. The two of them leaned toward each other and kissed.

"Hi, Mama. It's good to see you."

"We've been watchin' and waitin'," her mother said. "Your papa and I, we thought you'd never get here."

"Your mama exaggerates," René said, but he winked, and Desiree knew they'd probably been doing just that: watching and waiting impatiently for that first glimpse of their baby and *her* baby.

An hour later, with Aimee happily eating her way through a dish of ice cream, Desiree and her parents got caught up on one another's news.

"Everyone is comin' for supper tonight," Arlette said, her dark eyes sparkling with happiness.

Desiree sniffed. "Is that gumbo I smell?"

"What else?" her mother said. "But that's not all, of course. I've got a ham in the oven, and your papa's gonna make some sausage on the grill, and there's jambalaya and cornbread and—"

"Stop! My stomach hurts just thinking about all that food!" But Desiree's admonishment was more teasing than serious, and she knew her mother knew it. Actually, one of the highlights of coming home was eating Arlette's wonderful cooking.

"When is Celeste gonna be here?" Aimee asked.

"Uncle Neil said they'd get here early," René answered.

"Laura's pregnant again, did she tell you?" Arlette said.

"No! *Is* she? That's wonderful!" Desiree was thrilled. Laura and Neil had gotten off to a rocky start, so Desiree was doubly happy for them. She knew they'd wanted another child ever since Celeste was born. Neil had laughingly told Desiree he didn't want to be the oldest father at the PTA.

Arlette smiled her secret smile as she nodded. "An' that's not all..."

"Come on, Mama, tell me everything. You know you're dying to."

"Alice is pregnant, too!" Arlette said triumphantly.

"Oh..." Desiree felt her eyes mist at the news. Although she loved Laura, Alice was her favorite sister-in-law. She had been a young widow with two small children when she and Norman married, and she had once confided to Desiree how much she wanted to give Norman a child of his own.

"He loves Lisa and James, and he treats them as if they're his natural children, but I so want to have his baby." Alice's gray eyes had shone with intense longing.

"Both babies are due about the same time," Arlette continued, joy creasing her round face. "Around the middle of May."

For the next hour or so, they gossiped and chatted, and Desiree thought about mentioning Jack Forrester, then decided against it. Maybe later. Instead she related a couple of amusing stories about Julie and the office. Although Arlette and René resisted most of Desiree's efforts to get them to New Orleans, they had visited twice in the past year, and both times Julie had insisted on taking all of them out to dinner. Desiree knew that part of the reason for Julie's generosity was that she was a naturally warmhearted person, but the other part stemmed from the fact that Julie's own family was so different. Desiree knew her boss envied Desiree's close relationship with her own family.

"And what about boyfriends? Are you dating anyone?" her mother asked.

Desiree shrugged. "Just Guy."

"You could do worse," Arlette said.

"Leave her alone, Mama," René chided, but his tone was mild. "She'll marry when the time is right." He reached over the top of the big round kitchen table and squeezed Desiree's hand. "When she meets Mr. Right."

For some reason, Jack Forrester's good-looking face popped into her mind. Desiree caught her lower lip between her teeth.

"What's the matter, *chère?*" her astute father asked.

"Nothing."

"You don't sound too sure."

Desiree shook her head to clear it of Jack's image. "No, really, it's nothing." Again she wondered if she should tell her parents about Jack and his mission. She still wasn't sure. She didn't want to worry them, and she knew they *would* worry if they thought strange men were following her around.

Besides, she would probably never see Jack Forrester again, so she'd worry her parents needlessly if she brought up his name.

Jack had stayed at the Marriott Hotel on Canal Street the first couple of days he was in New Orleans. But since he traveled so often, and had to stay in hotels so much, he always tried to make his surroundings away from home as home-like as possible. So he'd rented a furnished apartment near the Superdome for a month, and after he returned to it that afternoon, he changed into warmer, drier clothes and fixed himself a hefty scotch and water and a fat baloney-and-cheese sandwich. He didn't like to cook, and he'd stocked the refrigerator with a few simple things for emergencies. The rest of the time he preferred to eat out.

As he ate his sandwich and sipped his drink, he thought about Desiree. He was intrigued by the idea that whether she was aware of it or not, she might know something that could help him find Elise Arnold.

Hell. Why not be honest with himself? He was intrigued by Desiree, period. For whatever reason, the moment she'd looked at him with those blazing black eyes, he'd been tantalized and *intrigued*.

The woman practically oozed sex appeal. From the tip of her shiny dark hair to the toes of her pointed black boots, she was one enticing number, full of a crackling energy and vitality that nothing could hide.

He wished he could have seen her smile. He wondered what those full, red lips would look like when she was happy. Somehow he knew Desiree Cantrelle was usually happy.

Full of the joy of living. He had read a lot about Cajuns, had long had a fascination with the culture, and he knew they were a people with a zest for life. His interest in them had started when he'd met Charles Petitjean, a fellow journalist who had covered the Persian Gulf War with him. Charles and Jack had spent many long nights in Saudi Arabia, talking while waiting for the bombs from Iraq to fall.

Charles was a font of information about his ancestry, and to pass the tense hours, he'd told Jack stories.

"Cajuns are people exiled from the old French Acadia— better known as Nova Scotia," Charles explained. In the 1700s more than five thousand of them settled in Louisiana." His voice had grown soft. "They're a wonderful people—warm, fun-loving, unfailingly cheerful. There's an old saying in Cajun families," Charles added. "*'Love life, and life will love you back.'* That's pretty much my philosophy." He grinned. "I don't spend a lot of time worryin'. Whatever happens, happens. Generally speakin', if you expect good things in life, that's what you'll get."

Jack had thought about those words many times since Charles had spoken them. He had tried to hang on to that philosophy even when he'd received the news that Charles was dead, killed by stray sniper fire when he'd been interviewing the front-line troops in Kuwait.

"Desiree, I've missed you," Alice said as they hugged.

Desiree closed her eyes. Yes, she'd missed this, too. If only she could have her independence as well as be with her family. But one canceled out the other, and always would, she knew.

"Let me look at you," Desiree said.

Alice grinned, her pretty face flushed and happy.

"You look wonderful. You're not even showing yet."

Alice darted a look at Norman, then at Arlette. "You told her!"

Arlette blushed, and they all laughed.

"Well, it's only been three months. Isn't it wonderful?" Alice said.

"C'mere, big brother. Give me a hug, too," Desiree said, and was soon caught in Norman's strong arms. "I'm happy for you," she murmured as he kissed her cheek. She was particularly happy for Norman because he'd overcome so much in the past few years. As he released her and walked over to the stove to lift the pot lids and enjoy the wonderful smells, Desiree noted that there was no limp at all—nothing to give away the fact that Norman's right leg was an artificial one.

Just then the back door opened and Celeste burst through, followed by Neil and Laura.

Laura was still as slender as a model, and Desiree noted the contentment in her face and the serenity in her blue eyes. Laura and Neil had been crazy about each other since day one. Desiree knew their relationship was loaded with sizzle.

She hugged the newcomers, then said, "I hear there's going to be an addition to the family."

Laura colored becomingly, and Neil, sliding an arm around his wife's waist, said, "In less than six months, Celeste is going to have a baby brother."

"Did you have an ultrasound?" Alice asked.

Laura laughed. "No. Neil is just sure we're having a boy this time, that's all."

"We are!" he stated emphatically. "And that's that." He walked to the stove and nudged Norman in the back. "Quit eating that. Save some for me." He picked up a wooden spoon and ladled some gumbo onto it. "God! That's hot!" He dropped the spoon, and they all laughed.

"That's what you get!" Arlette said.

I love my family, Desiree thought.

Throughout dinner, the thought kept coming back, again and again. She was the luckiest woman in the world. She had a beautiful little daughter and a wonderful, wonderful family. What more could any woman want? she thought, as she gazed around the dining-room table and studied each beloved face.

As her gaze flicked to Neil, who sat next to Laura, she saw him lean over and nuzzle his wife's neck, and she also saw Laura's quick intake of breath. The moment was gone in an instant, but something very like pain clutched Desiree's chest.

That's what I want. That. That feeling.

Completely unbidden and unexpected, Jack Forrester's ocean-blue eyes filled her mind, and she wondered what he was doing right at that moment.

What Jack was doing right then was talking to his twin sister, Jenny. He sat with his feet propped up on a beat-up ottoman, the phone cradled against his left ear. In the background a fuzzy replay of Sunday's Steelers/Saints game went largely ignored.

"Do you believe her when she says she doesn't know anything about Elise?" Jenny was asking.

"I believe she *thinks* she doesn't, but there's got to be some connection. Jenny, if you could see her. She looks exactly like Elise."

"Oh, Jack, when you told me about this woman, I was so hopeful! And now..." Her voice trailed off. "I feel so helpless. I wish I knew more about Elise's family. I wish I'd probed more, but she was always so reticent, so reluctant to talk about herself."

"You know, you're not responsible for what happened."

"But in a way I am! I told Elise so many times that she should leave Derek, that no woman had to put up with an abusive husband. I told her all she had to do was call me, and I'd help her. She was so afraid, Jack. So afraid. And it wasn't just that she was afraid of Derek and what he might do to her. She was afraid of being alone. I knew that. I knew that her feelings were all tied up with the fact that her mother and father had never been married, that her mother had died when she was so young. She felt utterly alone. And then when she *did* call me, when she finally got up the courage to do something, I wasn't there for her.''

"Jenny..." His voice was soft. "You were in Spain with Kevin. You couldn't know that Elise would pick that exact week to finally make her move. I mean, didn't you tell me you'd been encouraging her to leave for at least a year, with no success?''

"Yes, but—"

"But nothing. Quit being so hard on yourself! You're not the one who abused Elise.''

"Oh, Jack! If you could have heard the messages she left on the machine! Oh, God, she sounded so desperate. If only I knew she was okay. If only I was sure Derek didn't come home that night and do something to her.... Maybe he killed her! Maybe he killed her and hid the body! Maybe all of this is an act, and she really is dead, and..." Her voice broke, and Jack knew she was crying.

"Now come on. There's not a shred of evidence that he killed her. You know that." He hesitated, then added, "Jenny, from my conversation with the director of one of the shelters in Houston, men like Derek don't usually kill their wives. She explained to me that they really don't want to kill them—they want to control them.''

"All right, maybe she's still alive. But where did she go? Derek said she didn't take any money. He laughed. He said Elise wouldn't get very far without money, that he'd find her. He said he'd hired a private investigator. He said that she shouldn't think she was going to get away with this. That he'd find her, and when he did, he'd teach her a few lessons she wouldn't soon forget. That's what really scares me, Jack. If she really *is* in hiding somewhere, as you think, you've got to find her before he does, or before she gives up and goes back to him. I've just got to talk to her.''

"I'll find her," he promised. But he knew there were no guarantees. They had so little information to work with. "From everything you've told me about Elise, I think she would feel a strong compulsion to come back to Louisiana. And since you say Derek never knew anything about Elise's father, that she never told him the things she told you, I think that's the right angle from which to approach the situation."

"So you think we're on the right track—trying to find her through her father?"

"Yes. I think Elise has been looking for a father for a long time—if we find him, we'll eventually find her."

"What if Derek discovers she once used the name Cantrelle?"

"But you said he knew nothing about her work in the theater group."

"I know she kept it hidden from him. But what if he finds out about it, Jack? He's bound to wonder why she'd go by the name Cantrelle, isn't he? Wouldn't he put two and two together and start looking for her through the Cantrelle name, just as you are?

Jack sighed. "Jenny, don't borrow trouble. Let's go on the assumption he won't find this out." He didn't add what he was thinking—that they really had no other choice.

"So what's your next move going to be?"

"I'm not sure. I need to think about it."

"What all have you tried so far?"

"Well, since she didn't take her car, I checked all the usual modes of transport—the air, bus and train lines—but I didn't turn up anything. I didn't really think I would. You don't have to present I.D. to buy a ticket, not if you use cash."

"But if she didn't have any money—"

"We don't know she didn't have any money. All we know is that Derek said she didn't take any of *his* money." He chuckled, trying to lighten the atmosphere. "Do you want to hear the rest of this or not? You keep interrupting me."

"I'm sorry. Go ahead."

"Well, I started to call travel agencies, but there were so many of them, I gave up on that. Besides, she could have used any name. My only hope in all of this is that someone would remember her, and that was always a slim hope."

"What about car rental agencies? She might have rented a car, and wouldn't she have to show a driver's license or something?"

"I tried the car rental agencies. She didn't rent a car."

"Oh, Jack. Why wasn't I here when she called?"

"Jenny, you're going to make yourself sick if you keep worrying like this. Now try to relax. Leave this to me. This is the kind of thing I do best. I'll turn something up sooner or later."

"How can you be so sure?"

"Because if you ask enough questions of enough people, something eventually breaks. All I need is one good lead."

"I hope you're right. The longer we go with no word, the more scared I am that something terrible has happened to her."

"I know."

After they hung up, Jack went back to watching the football game, but he couldn't concentrate, so he just sat there and thought. A long time later he finally decided what to do next.

Saturday dawned bright and clear, and Desiree was glad to see the sun again. She and Laura and Alice and Denise, her older sister, had planned to go shopping that afternoon. Arlette had volunteered to watch all the children, although at fifteen and ten, Denise's two were too old for baby-sitters.

The four women spent a satisfying afternoon trying on clothes, eating lunch and doing a lot of talking and laughing.

"It's always so much fun when you come home," Alice said, her arm companionably tucked into Desiree's as they sat on a bench in Cortana, Desiree's favorite Baton Rouge mall. Denise and Laura had stopped in an earring shop, and Alice and Desiree were waiting for them to emerge. "I wish you lived here."

"You know why I don't."

"I know, but Norman's too busy taking care of me, the kids, and the business to spend too much time trying to run your life," Alice said, her gray eyes twinkling.

"It's not just Norman. Neil and Papa are just as bad. And everyone knows about me . . . and Mark."

"Honey, who cares? You've got nothing to be ashamed of. There are a lot of women having babies on their own."

Desiree shrugged. "Maybe in New Orleans, or even in Baton Rouge. But not in Patinville."

Alice's eyes were understanding. "Desiree, you have to stop beating up on yourself. So you made one mistake. Big deal."

Desiree knew what Alice said was true, but she couldn't help how she felt. She really believed a woman should be married before she had children, and she couldn't suppress the feeling of embarrassment when she ran into some old biddy who gave her a knowing look. Worse, she didn't want Aimee to feel different, and in impersonal New Orleans, Aimee didn't have problems. In Patinville, where everyone knew Desiree and her family, Aimee's origins were common knowledge.

"Alice, I know you love me, and I know you really believe what you're saying, but the truth is, I was reckless and stupid. Norman warned me, over and over again, but I thought he was being overprotective and interfering, and I didn't listen to him. I just went on my merry way, doing whatever I felt like doing, and I didn't give a thought to the consequences. And because I was naive and trusted Mark and believed him, I let myself get pregnant . . . by a married man. And I have to live with that."

"Desiree, you couldn't have known Mark was married. I mean, he out and out lied to you. And as far as getting pregnant . . . so you made a mistake. Lots of people make mistakes."

"I know, but other people's mistakes don't affect innocent people. I just don't want Aimee to grow up around people who are snickering behind her back."

It hurt every time Desiree thought about how Mark had deceived her—how foolish and gullible she'd been almost four years ago. She'd really thought he loved her, that he was going to ask her to marry him. And then Norman, who'd had Mark investigated, told her that Mark was already married. That he had two small children and a pregnant wife in Fort Worth. That he was a liar and a cheat. And that Desiree had been stupid.

Aimee was the result of this episode, so Desiree couldn't regret the past too much, for she loved Aimee with an intensity that sometimes astounded her; she wouldn't trade her for all the respectability and wedding bands in the world, but still, she had been irresponsible, and she didn't want Aimee to pay the price.

"So how are things going with you and Guy?" Alice said, and Desiree was grateful for the change in subject.

"Pretty much the same." She chuckled. "Boring. No excitement."

Alice rolled her eyes, but she laughed, too. "Here come Laura and Denise."

For the rest of the day, Desiree kept thinking about her conversation with Alice. She really didn't regret the past, but she hoped she'd learned from it. Her only regret was that she and Aimee didn't have a husband and father in their lives.

Be honest. If all you wanted was a husband and father, Guy would do very well.

Desiree smiled to herself. She wanted it all. A man she could believe in. A man who would always put her first, who would never lie to her. She wanted marriage, more children, a man who would be a good husband and father. And she also wanted...sizzle. As the thoughts formed, she didn't even try to fight them, for she knew what was coming next. And sure enough, Jack Forrester's strong, pleasing face and blue, blue eyes filled her mind.

Later that evening, after her sister and brothers and their families had gone home, and Aimee and Arlette were in bed, Desiree and her father sat at the kitchen table drinking coffee. "Papa," Desiree said, "there's something I've been wanting to ask you about."

René's dark eyes met hers. "I knew there was somethin' botherin' you, *chère*. Tell your papa about it."

So she told him about Jack. She told him everything. "Papa, do you know anyone in our family named Elise?"

"No, *chère*, I don'."

"What about second cousins or third cousins?"

"I know everyone in our fam'ly. All the cousins—second, third, fourth—you name 'em, I know 'em. And there ain't no one who looks jus' like you, I guarantee. You much prettier than the other girls, you know."

Desiree smiled.

"I hope this man doesn't bother you, *chère*. I don' like the idea of someone followin' you like that." René's forehead creased in a frown.

"I'll be fine, Papa. Really. I'm sure Mr. Forrester won't bother me again. He's probably forgotten all about me by now." *I just wish I could forget about him.*

The next day, Desiree decided to get an early start home, so after Mass—which her entire family attended together—and an enormous brunch, she and Aimee kissed and hugged everyone and promised they'd be back again soon. Then they were on their way.

They reached home a little before three, and Desiree was glad to see the Reed-Douglas's Lincoln in the garage. It always gave her a feeling of safety to know Margaret and Caldwell were home and if she needed them for anything, they'd respond immediately. She still had to pinch herself now and then to remind herself how lucky she was to have found the cottage she rented from them. The cottage used to be slave quarters and had been renovated and modernized by Margaret and Caldwell into a pleasant two-bedroom dwelling that Desiree loved.

As she unloaded their bags from the trunk of her car, the back door opened and Caldwell walked outside onto the back porch. "Hi, there," he called. "Glad to see you two made it back safely."

"Hi, Caldwell."

Aimee dashed toward the older man. "Hi, Uncle Caldwell," she called. "Look what Grandma gave me." She held up a Raggedy Ann doll.

"Your grandparents certainly love you," Caldwell said. He turned to Desiree, who had walked up more slowly. "Margaret's made some peanut butter cookies and a pot of tea. Would you like to come in?"

The Reed-Douglases had lived in England for a number of years and had happily adopted the English custom of tea in the afternoon. Although Desiree really wanted nothing more than to go into her own snug home, she knew the older couple was lonely. Their only daughter, Emily, lived in Australia with her husband and two children, and Margaret and Caldwell didn't get to see them very often. Although they were retired and had plenty of money and could spend as much time with Emily as they wanted to, Margaret had once told Desiree that she believed it was best for young people to live independently.

So Caldwell, a retired museum curator, spent his days in his beloved garden, and Margaret, a retired symphony violinist, spent her days watching over Aimee and baking cookies.

And Desiree tried to spend as much time with them as she could.

Soon Aimee was contentedly eating peanut butter cookies—her favorite—and Desiree was sipping the strong Earl Grey tea Margaret favored. Margaret, as usual, had put the ornate silver tea service and accompanying dishes on the small gateleg mahogany table that sat in front of the fireplace in the formal living room.

"So how was your trip?" Margaret asked in her cool, reserved way—a manner that masked a loving, generous heart.

Desiree smiled at her. "Great. I always enjoy going home."

"I know you do." There was a wistful expression in Margaret's green eyes.

"What did you do with your weekend?" Desiree asked. Out of the corner of her eye she saw Aimee reach for another cookie. "Young lady, you've already had three cookies. That's to be the last one, or you won't have any appetite for supper.''

"Okay." Aimee pretended to feed the cookie to her doll, then snuck the last half of it into her mouth.

"Nothing much. Caldwell took me out to dinner last night. It was our forty-fifth wedding anniversary."

"Oh, dear, I forgot!" How could she have forgotten? "Where did he take you?" Desiree asked, mentally making a note to get a belated present for them.

"My favorite restaurant—Commander's Palace."

"And you had the turtle soup and crab cakes, I know...."

They both laughed because Margaret was a creature of habit, and Desiree was always admonishing her to be more adventurous.

"And the crème brulée," Margaret said sheepishly.

"Margaret, what are we going to do with you?"

Caldwell, who had been a silent listener, said, "Meg, darling, tell Desiree about that nice young friend of hers."

Margaret clasped her hand over her mouth. "Talk about forgetful! A friend of yours was here yesterday, Desiree. A really charming young man. I so enjoyed talking with him."

"A friend?" Desiree said blankly.

"Yes, that handsome Mr. Forrester—"

Chapter Three

"Mr. Forrester!"

Margaret, who had been poised to say something else, stopped. She looked at Caldwell, whose tall, lanky body had stiffened. Then they both looked at Desiree.

Margaret frowned. "I hope it was all right to talk to him . . ." Her voice trailed off uncertainly.

"Desiree, my dear, is something wrong?" Caldwell asked.

Desiree's mind whirled. Jack Forrester! He had been there while she was in Patinville.

"Desiree—"

Belatedly, she realized Caldwell was speaking to her, alarm evident in his tone. Ashamed of herself for frightening the older couple, Desiree forced herself to answer lightly. "No, of course nothing's wrong, Caldwell. *Really,*" she added when his blue eyes still held a flicker of doubt. "I was just surprised, that's all." She hated lying to them, but what choice had Jack Forrester left her? If she told Margaret and Caldwell the truth, they'd worry themselves sick.

As she reassured Caldwell and Margaret, cold fury filled her. How dare Jack Forrester take advantage of these two wonderful people?

Calling on all her acting ability to keep the indignation and wrath out of her voice, Desiree smiled and said, "I'm sorry I missed him. Did he say how long he'd be in town or where he was staying?"

Margaret relaxed against her chair, the cloudy concern in her green eyes slowly fading. She smiled back. "No, he didn't. But he *did* say to tell you he'd be in touch."

Desiree gritted her teeth. So he'd be in touch, would he? Well, she could hardly wait. The next time she saw Jack Forrester, she'd tell him a thing or two! Just because he was so good-looking and had such great eyes didn't mean he could do anything he wanted to do. It certainly didn't mean he had a right to invade her home. To pretend to be her friend. To dupe two of the nicest people she'd ever known.

She pushed her irate thoughts away as she saw Margaret's forehead knitting again. Although Desiree wanted nothing more than to march over to her own home and rehearse all the cutting things she intended to say the very next time Jack Forrester showed his handsome face, she knew she'd have to put off this self-indulgence a while longer. "So," she said brightly, "how long did Jack stay, and what did he have to say? I suppose he's just gotten back from some country with an unpronounceable name."

Margaret's forehead smoothed out. She reached for the teapot and refilled both her cup and Desiree's. Then she lifted the delicate Sevres cup and cradled it in her slender hands. "We visited for over an hour, didn't we, Caldwell?"

Desiree looked at Caldwell. He nodded. "Yes. Mr. Forrester is an interesting and intelligent young man."

"You sound as if you liked him." Caldwell was a shrewd judge of character; he wasn't often fooled by surface charm.

"Yes, I liked him very much. He was telling us about the Middle East and some of the volatile situations he's covered." Caldwell studied her over the rim of his cup. "How did you happen to meet him?"

Desiree thought fast. She was getting in deeper and deeper. What should she do? "Uh, well…it was just one of those things." She avoided Caldwell's wise eyes. Darn it. She was such a lousy liar.

"Have you known Mr. Forrester a long time?" Margaret asked.

"No, uh, not long." Oh, God. Surely they could see right through her. Desiree was sure she had a big *L* plastered across her face.

"Are you…" Margaret hesitated, then smiled her lovely smile. "Are you interested in him, Desiree?"

Perhaps because she'd spent so much time over the weekend thinking about Jack, Desiree's denial was more vehement than it would ordinarily have been. "Interested in him?" She laughed. "Absolutely not!"

Margaret glanced at Caldwell. Amusement brightened her eyes. "I see."

"In fact," Desiree continued, ignoring the look her friends exchanged, "he'd be the *last* man I'd ever be interested in!"

A couple of hours later, Desiree repeated the same words, muttering them as she stirred a pot of minestrone soup. She said them yet again as she buttered four slices of wheat bread, then placed two of them butter-side down in a hot skillet. She unwrapped two slices of American cheese, placed them on the bread, then slapped the other two slices on top, butter-side up. The buttered bread hissed and popped as it fried. Kind of like her temper, which was still hissing and popping from Margaret's revelation about Jack's sneaky visit.

When their light supper was ready, Desiree called Aimee. Seconds later Aimee raced into the kitchen, her new doll clutched securely in her right hand.

"Supper's ready, honey." Desiree pulled out Aimee's chair—her high chair minus the tray—and lifted her up.

While Aimee, who had definitely eaten too many peanut butter cookies, played with her food and talked to her doll, Desiree ate and thought about Jack.

Damn him! She was still furious with him for going to Margaret and Caldwell's house. He must have been watching her as she walked home on Friday. He must have seen which driveway she entered. Maybe he'd even waited and seen her leave for Patinville. How else would he have known who to talk to?

The question was, why had he done it? Did he still believe she knew this Elise Arnold? What was she going to have to do to convince him she didn't? Hit him over the head?

A slow smile slid across her face. Yes. Maybe that's exactly what she'd do. Jack Forrester would soon find out he'd gotten much more than he'd bargained for when he'd messed with her!

Jack wasn't sure what time Desiree left for work, but based upon the time she got off the streetcar in the morning, he figured she'd leave by seven-thirty. Just to be sure he didn't miss her, he parked at the corner of her street at about seven-fifteen on Monday morning. He turned off the ignition and settled in to wait. The rising sun had streaked the eastern sky with pink and gold. It promised to be a beautiful day—clear and mild. The front that had brought the cold and rain had passed through the lower Louisiana coast and was on its way to the Eastern Seaboard. Jack was glad to see the last of it. He hated rain.

He fiddled with the radio until he found a station playing zydeco music. The driving beat was contagious, and he rapped his knuckles against his steering wheel in time to the music. When the song was finished, the announcer, voice rich with the upper-class New Orleans French accent, began to give the traffic report. The first time Jack visited New Orleans, he hadn't realized there were two distinct accents: the first a seaport accent commonly referred to as a Channel accent, the second this cultured soft drawl of the announcer.

Just as another song began to play, Jack, whose eyes were trained on the driveway of the Reed-Douglas home, saw Desiree emerge from the shadow of the live oaks lining their property and turn onto the sidewalk. For the few seconds it took her to walk the distance from the house to his parked car, Jack studied her, a pleasant tingle of anticipation skidding through him.

He loved the way she walked, with a lilt to her step. He'd be willing to bet she was a great dancer. She looked great, too, he thought. He was sure she brightened up that staid old law firm she worked for.

Today she wore a kelly green suit with a skirt that stopped a good four or five inches above her knees, showing a long expanse of shapely leg. Slung over her left shoulder was the huge paisley tote bag she never seemed to be without.

When she reached the front end of his car, she stopped. Jack opened the door and got out. He met her gaze and immediately saw the smoldering anger. Uh-oh. Trouble. She knew he'd talked to her landlords. Well, his old boxing coach subscribed to the same theory Jack's father had always espoused in his business dealings: the best defense is a good offense.

Jack agreed.

So he smiled at her.

He certainly had a lot of nerve, Desiree thought. Look at him standing there grinning as if he hadn't done a thing wrong.

She tried to ignore how the blue of his eyes matched the blue of his jaunty Miata.

She tried not to notice how sexy his smile was.

She tried not to see how his jeans hugged his legs and how wide his shoulders looked under the white sweater he wore.

"Good morning," he said cheerfully.

She felt like slapping him.

"Beautiful morning, isn't it?" he added.

She stared at him. What audacity!

"I thought I'd come by and give you a ride to work." His smile broadened. "Save you eighty cents."

"I have no intention of riding anywhere with you. Now or ever." *Oh, great. Now he knows he's managed to get under your skin. You were supposed to play it cool.* She'd promised herself last night, when she couldn't sleep for thinking about what he'd done, that she wouldn't lose her temper when she finally saw him. She'd decided that instead, she'd be very calm, very cool, and she'd tell him off in such scathing tones he'd slink away with his tail between his legs, just like René's old hunting dog used to do when he got caught digging around in the trash.

His smile faded, to be replaced by a look of contrition. "You're angry. I guess I deserve that."

"You're darned right you deserve that. What does it take to get through to you, Mr. Forrester? I told you on Friday that I'm not the person you want, and that I don't know anything about her. What does it take to convince you?''

''I can explain—''

''If you persist in bothering me,'' Desiree interrupted, her anger finally spilling over, ''or if you come to my home or my office again, I fully intend to call the police!'' She stuck her chin up in the air and stalked off.

She heard him coming after her, but she just walked faster. He grasped her arm from behind.

''Desiree—''

She whirled around. ''Damn you!'' she said through gritted teeth. ''What gives you the right to spy on me? That was a despicable thing to do—pump Margaret and Caldwell for information! They're decent, honest people, and they *liked* you. They believed you when you said you were my friend. How could you lie to them? Which then forced *me* to lie to them, too!''

He winced. ''I'm really sorry. I never thought of it in those terms, but of course, you're right. I shouldn't have gone there.''

''You're damned right you shouldn't have. Now, if you don't mind, I'd like you to let go of my arm. I'm going to be late for work.''

''Look, Desiree, I know you're angry. But I can explain.''

''Maybe you can, but I'm not interested.''

''Look, I know what I did wasn't very nice, but I was desperate. You're the only lead I have.''

Something about his voice stopped her from making another quick retort. She studied his face. Oh, God, she was a fool. She could feel herself weakening.

Jack sighed. ''My sister is making herself sick worrying about Elise. I...I had to do something. I couldn't just pack it in and go back to Houston without trying one more time.''

"But why latch onto me? I told you. I don't know anything."

"All I'm asking is that you hear me out. And I *do* believe you don't consciously know Elise Arnold. I just think you probably know things that would be helpful to me, and if you'd only let me tell you the whole story, that might trigger something in your memory."

"No." She wished he'd quit looking at her in just that way. It was hard to sustain her anger under the force of his compelling gaze.

When he spoke his voice was husky. "Please, Desiree. I'm not going to hurt you. Just let me give you a ride to work, that's all. If you still don't want to talk to me after that, I'll go away. I promise."

She knew she shouldn't. "Well..."

"Please?"

Sighing, she shook free of his arm and walked to his car. He opened the passenger door, and she got in. The vehicle had a new-car smell. Jack shut the door and walked around to the driver's side. Within moments they were on their way.

"So talk," she said. She looked at him. Now she tried to ignore how the sunlight slanting through the windows had turned his hair to burnished gold. Jack Forrester was altogether too appealing. Even the bump in his nose added to his rugged strength. She reminded herself that she was angry with him.

"Promise you'll listen with an open mind, okay?"

She sighed. "Okay."

He reached over and squeezed her hand. Desiree's traitorous heart leaped at his touch. No doubt about it. Too appealing. Too sexy.

"My sister and I are twins. We're close, even though we don't see each other for long stretches of time. We have a special understanding. When we were kids, even if we weren't together, if she hurt herself or I hurt myself, the other one would always know.''

Desiree couldn't help it. She just couldn't stay angry. How could anyone stay angry at a man whose tone of voice revealed how much he loved his sister? "Go on," she encouraged.

"Jenny met Elise through the work they both did with one of the community theater groups in Houston." His voice softened. "Jenny always did love to dress up and playact." He chuckled. "I can remember when she'd try to make me put on a dress and my mother's old high heels because whatever fantasy she was playing out needed another female." He laughed softly. "It didn't work, of course, but it's a wonder I grew up to be a normal man with Jenny around."

As if you could call six feet tall, broad shoulders, golden brown hair, and eyes-to-die-for normal, Desiree thought.

"Elise worked backstage designing scenery," he added. "She and Jenny met, and the two of them became friends."

"How long ago was this?" Desiree asked, interested in spite of herself.

"About two years ago. Anyway, because my work takes me all over the world for long periods of time, I didn't meet Elise until Jenny had known her for about a year."

By now Jack had eased the Miata onto St. Charles Avenue and they were creeping along with all the other slow-moving morning traffic.

"Jenny said she knew from the very beginning that there was something terribly wrong with Elise's life. Gradually, as Jenny spent more time with her, she figured out that Elise was in an abusive marriage."

Desiree heard how Jack's voice had hardened. "Physically abusive, you mean?"

"Yes, although there was a lot of emotional abuse, too. Jenny says that it wasn't long before she began noticing bruises that Elise tried to cover up. It took a long time, but eventually Elise admitted to Jenny that her husband—his name is Derek—beat her."

Desiree shuddered. She couldn't imagine living with that kind of man. She thought about her father—how kind and loving he was—and her brothers, and how much they adored their wives. Even Mark, who'd turned out to be a real loser, had never physically mistreated her. If anything, he'd treated her as if she were somebody special. That had been one of the reasons she'd been so crazy about him. Of course, she'd had no idea their whole relationship was a lie.

Jerking her thoughts back to the present, Desiree forced herself to speak. "That's awful, but if it's true, why is your sister so worried? I'd think she'd be glad her friend finally left that...jerk."

"It's complicated. Jenny feels guilty because she encouraged Elise to leave her husband. She knew Elise was afraid of being alone. She said she told Elise that if she ever felt she could leave, all she had to do was call, and Jenny would help her. And then, Elise did call. She called several times, leaving frantic messages on Jenny's answering machine. Jenny thinks something really terrible happened, and Elise simply couldn't stand it anymore."

"I'm not sure I understand—"

"Jenny was out of the country when Elise called. When she finally got the messages, Elise was gone."

"I still don't understand why your sister—Jenny—is so worried. I mean, there are lots of places Elise could have gone. She could be in a women's shelter somewhere."

"Jenny and I have checked all the shelters."

"Then she's probably with her family. When you find the right Cantrelle family, you'll probably find her."

"I've called every Cantrelle in the New Orleans phone book."

"No one here has heard of her?"

"No one."

Desiree frowned. "But she said she was from New Orleans?"

"Yes. She told Jenny she grew up in New Orleans."

"Have you tried some of the outlying towns? A lot of people refer to themselves as 'being from New Orleans' when they're really from Kenner or Metairie or Gretna."

"I've tried all the towns around."

"Maybe you should think about going a little farther out. Maybe Elise said she was from New Orleans because that's the last place she lived. Maybe she's from Slidell or Morgan City or Shreveport." Her voice grew thoughtful. "Actually, she could be from anywhere." Desiree bit her bottom lip. She loved puzzles and games, and Jack's quest for the missing Elise was very like a puzzle. Now that she'd decided to listen to him, she found herself caught up in it. "Did she tell your sister anything at all about her family?"

"Well, we know her mother died when Elise was nineteen, and that she'd never known her father."

"She'd never known her father. What do you mean by that?"

"She said her mother and father weren't married."

"But she said Cantrelle was her father's name?"

"According to Jenny."

"Did she go by the name Cantrelle before she was married?"

"No. She used her mother's name—Sonnier."

"Have you tried to locate any of her mother's family?"

"I wouldn't even know where to start. Besides, she told Jenny she *had* no family."

"And that was all she ever said about her parents?"

"Well, one other thing. She thought her father had been a lawyer."

"A lawyer!" Desiree wasn't sure why that piece of information startled her. Why shouldn't he be a lawyer? She could think of three lawyers in her own family—two cousins and her Uncle Justin. "What did Elise do in Houston?"

"She had no job at the time, but when Jenny met her she said she'd been a legal secretary in the past."

Desiree felt goosebumps break out on her arms. "Like me," she said softly.

"Yes. Like you."

"Is that how you found me?"

"Yes, I checked all the law firms in New Orleans."

"How did you do that?"

Jack slanted a glance her way. A half smile hovered around his lips. "I just called the firm, asked to speak to Miss Cantrelle and waited to see if someone answered."

Desiree shivered. She was no longer afraid of Jack, but it scared her to think how easily information could be obtained.

They were now close to the downtown business district, and Desiree glanced at her oversized watch. Ten minutes past eight. She had plenty of time. Her office didn't open until eight-thirty.

"Jack, there's something I'm still confused about. What makes you think Elise is using the name Cantrelle?"

"At the theater, she was known as Elise Cantrelle. It was a long time before Jenny knew her real name."

"Why would she pretend to have another name?"

"Well, from what she told Jenny, Derek Arnold was insanely jealous. The reason Elise didn't work is because he didn't want her around other men. He didn't want her to do anything except tend to his needs. The work with the theater group was done behind his back."

"So you think, because she used the name Cantrelle once, she'd use it again."

"Yes. Both Jenny and I feel the use of her father's name was symbolic to her. A way of saying she had an identity, that she belonged to someone."

"Oh, how sad all this is." Desiree thought about all the people who loved her. How, if anything bad happened to her, they'd all close ranks and protect her. She couldn't imagine what it must be like to have no one. "So tell me just how she disappeared."

"Derek was out of town on business. He's a manufacturer's representative. He'd been gone three days. From what Jenny says, he always called home at the same time every night, and Elise had to be there to accept the call. If not, I guess there'd be hell to pay when he got home. Well, on the last night of his trip, when he called home, there was no answer. When he kept calling and still got no answer, he called the telephone company, and they checked the line. They told him there was something wrong with it."

"And was there?"

"No. The outside phone line was cut, and Derek says Elise must have cut it to make it seem as if there was trouble so he wouldn't be suspicious."

"Do you believe that?"

Jack shrugged. "I'm not sure."

"So when he got home he found her gone?"

"Yes."

Desiree sighed. "This is a very sad story, Jack, and I sympathize with how your sister feels, but honestly, I can't help you."

"Won't you at least ask around? Talk to some of your family? See if maybe someone knows something?"

"I already did," Desiree admitted. "I talked to my father over the weekend. He didn't know anything."

They had now entered the French Quarter, and Jack turned his attention to his driving. It always amazed Desiree that anyone would even attempt to navigate the narrow, cobbled streets. "Why don't you just let me out here?" she suggested. "It's not far to the office."

"That's okay. I've come this far. I might as well take you all the way."

Soon he had pulled up in front of the wrought-iron gates in front of her building. Desiree reached for the door handle.

"Wait. Don't go in just yet." His gaze rested on her face.

"I've got to, Jack."

"I'd really like to see you again." His voice had taken on a husky edge. "And not just because I want you to help me."

"I don't think so," she said regretfully. She'd made up her mind, during that long nine months while she waited for Aimee's birth, that she would never again become involved with a man unless he was looking for commitment and a lasting relationship. Jack Forrester was just looking for Elise Arnold. Being around him would be like inviting trouble into her life.

Because she was too attracted to him.

He started to say something else, then stopped. He nodded. "Okay." He held out his hand. "Thanks for listening. And good luck to you."

She took his hand, feeling its solid warmth and strength. "Good luck to you, too. I hope you find Elise."

"Can I at least give you one of my cards? Just in case you should think of something?"

How could she refuse to take his card? When he handed it to her, she accepted it.

And then she opened the door and got out. She didn't look back.

All day long Desiree found her thoughts wandering back to the morning's ride. To Elise Arnold and the mystery surrounding her disappearance.

And to Jack.

More specifically, to the strong attraction she felt for him. It was a shame that the first man to really get her engine going had to be someone like Jack—a wanderer who would probably never lead a normal life.

All day long she worked automatically.

All day long she told herself she'd done the right thing by telling him she didn't want to see him again.

Late in the afternoon, Julie emerged from her office and perched on the corner of Desiree's desk. "You seem preoccupied today," she commented. "Something wrong?"

Desiree was tempted to tell Julie about Jack because her boss was astute when it came to assessing a situation and giving good advice. "Nothing's wrong. I just... oh, never mind."

"Are you sure?"

Because Desiree really did want to talk about Jack, she found herself telling Julie all about the events of the past few days, from the moment she'd realized he was following her until he dropped her off at the office that morning.

"Why don't these kinds of things ever happen to me?" Julie said. "I never meet anyone interesting or sexy."

Desiree laughed. "That's because you hang out with lawyers all day long."

Julie raised her eyebrows. "I think it probably has more to do with the way you look as opposed to the way I look."

"There's not a thing wrong with the way you look," Desiree said. There wasn't. Julie was perky and pretty. Her only problem was she was far brighter and more successful than most of the men she met. Desiree thought Julie probably intimidated them. Besides, she didn't suffer fools gladly, so she had never perfected the art of flattery. And in Desiree's experience, most men liked to be flattered, even if it was only by a woman listening to what they had to say...and not contradicting them. Or maybe the problem was that Julie just hadn't met anyone strong enough to meet her on equal terms.

"I have a feeling you're regretting sending this hunk on his way," Julie said.

Desiree grimaced. "Maybe a little, but there's no future in it, so why start anything with him?"

"Why indeed?" Julie picked at her thumbnail. "Unless, of course, a woman just wanted to have some fun. Just wanted to take her pleasure and run."

"I can't do that." Even if she wanted to do something like that, Desiree had Aimee to think of.

"I know. I was only teasing you."

"So you think I made the right decision."

Julie hopped off the desk. "I know you made the right decision." She grinned. "But you *could* introduce him to me! I wouldn't mind having some fun."

Desiree threw a paper clip at Julie as she made a face at her and disappeared into her office once more. Julie was right. Desiree had made the right decision. Jack Forrester didn't belong in her life. She would put him out of her mind, once and for all. And since she'd never see him again, that should be fairly easy.

At five o'clock, she began clearing off her desk. By five-fifteen, she was on her way downstairs. A few seconds later, she opened the gates and stepped out onto the sidewalk.

Sitting there at the curb was a royal blue Miata.

And standing next to it was Jack Forrester, blue eyes gleaming in the dusky light.

Chapter Four

"What are you doing here?"

His mouth tipped in an apologetic half smile. "I know what we agreed. But I changed my mind." He opened the passenger door.

Desiree looked at him for a long moment, mesmerized by the expression in his eyes. She could feel her heart beating, its rhythm relentless: don't go, don't go, don't go....

She wanted to look away, but his gaze held her spellbound. A dead leaf skittered across the sidewalk, lifted by a gust of wind, and the spell was finally broken.

She climbed into the car.

She was grateful when he didn't try to talk to her as he navigated the heavy traffic in the Quarter. Desiree used the respite to study him. She liked the way his hands looked against the steering wheel, against the gearshift. They were tanned and square, with long fingers, and they moved swiftly and competently, with no wasted motions.

She liked watching his strong, muscular legs work the clutch and gas pedal. Each time he changed from one to the other, his thighs strained against his jeans.

She liked the clean, solid look of his profile and the tangy scent of his cologne. She liked—

Oh, please. Is there anything you don't like about Jack Forrester?

Desiree smothered a giggle.

Jack slanted a look at her. "What's so funny?"

"Nothing." But she smiled.

He braked for a red light and turned to really look at her. "Nothing has certainly put a sparkle in your eyes." He returned her smile. "You're very beautiful when you smile."

Desiree's smile faded. "Jack, why did you come back?"

The light changed, and he didn't answer for a few seconds. But once they'd crossed Canal Street, he said, "I just couldn't leave New Orleans without seeing you again."

Desiree's heart skittered just as the dead leaf had earlier. She knew her reaction was crazy. Jack could have meant anything by his answer. He could have meant he hadn't given up on the idea that she could help him find Elise Arnold. But some primal instinct told her that wasn't all there was between them. Desiree knew he was attracted to her, just as she was to him. And that's what was crazy, because they could never have any kind or relationship. Jack's presence in her life would be fleeting at best. And Desiree wasn't interested in fleeting. She was interested in permanent.

"Are you sorry I came?" he asked softly. He reached over and touched her hand, rubbing his thumb over the back of it.

Something stirred deep in her belly. She swallowed. "No, I'm not sorry you came."

He smiled. After a moment, Desiree smiled, too.

* * *

Jack had told her the truth. He wasn't sure what he wanted from Desiree; he only knew he couldn't walk away from her. He hadn't been able to get her out of his mind. He'd spent the entire day, after he'd dropped her off at work in the morning, trying to decide what to do next. Finally he'd sat down at the little table in the kitchen of his apartment, got out his notebook and reviewed all his notes.

Every lead had been followed. Every lead had turned up a dead end. There was no reason to stay on in New Orleans.

Yet he couldn't bring himself to leave.

How could he leave when the only concrete clue he had was Desiree's uncanny resemblance to Elise Arnold?

He made a list of other angles he might try. The list was short: the Louisiana Bar Association, the public library for the phone books of other cities in Louisiana. He couldn't think of anything else.

Desiree's lively face kept interrupting his thoughts. Her dark eyes, filled with fire and intelligence kept interfering with his concentration. Her sassy walk, the enticing curve of her cheekbones, the tangle of glossy curls that covered her head—all these images recurred so often he finally tossed down his notebook in disgust.

He would try one more time. There *had* to be some kind of connection between Desiree and Elise. He *had* to persuade Desiree to help him.

The next thing he knew he was on his way to her office. But now that he had her in his car, he wasn't sure what to do next. If he pushed her too hard, she might decide she wouldn't talk to him anymore. But if he didn't try to get her to help him, then he was just wasting time.

And he didn't have that much time to waste. Gerald Crampton, his boss and the news director of World Press, had been reluctant to grant Jack open-ended leave.

"All you've got coming to you is four weeks," he'd said, punctuating his words with an unlit cigar that seemed to be a permanent fixture between his right index and middle fingers.

"I may need more time, sir," Jack had answered.

Crampton narrowed his eyes.

Jack smothered the temptation to smile. He and Crampton both knew Jack only called the older man "sir" when he wanted something.

"You're pushin' it, Forrester."

Jack shrugged. "I may clear this up in a week. Or it may take the full four weeks. Or I may need longer."

Crampton clamped the cigar in his mouth. When he spoke, he spoke around it, and the cigar bobbed with each word. "What if I tell you your job hinges on you bein' back in four weeks?"

"Then I'd say I'm sorry you feel that way, but—" Jack left the sentence unfinished, and met Crampton's dark-eyed gaze levelly. Jack knew Crampton was bluffing. It was an old game they played. Because they both knew Jack could write his own ticket anywhere. He was one of only a handful of investigative journalists so well respected in the industry that he constantly fended off other job offers. Tempting job offers.

But Jack didn't want to leave World Press. He liked the organization, he agreed with their policies, and he especially liked working for Gerald Crampton.

Finally Crampton spoke. "If I were you, I'd get going while the going's still good."

"Thank you, sir," Jack said and extended his right hand. When he walked away, he was smiling.

That conversation had taken place twelve days earlier. So two of Jack's four weeks were already used up. He didn't have a whole lot of time left.

Remembering this, he looked at Desiree again. She was turned away from him, staring out the window. Her full bottom lip was caught between her teeth as if she were concentrating very hard. What was she thinking? He wished she'd smile at him again. She had a wonderful smile, a ten in anyone's book. "Have you thought about what I told you this morning?" he finally asked.

She turned her head. "Yes. I didn't want to, but I couldn't seem to help myself."

He grinned. "So I've got your curiosity stirred up, have I?"

Now she smiled, and Jack felt as if someone had just given him a gift. In the dusky interior of the car, he could see the gleam in her dark eyes. "You could say that," she said softly.

Jack had a sudden, almost overwhelming desire to kiss her. And if he hadn't been driving, he might have given in to the urge. So it was probably a very good thing he was driving, he told himself. Damn. It was hard to keep his mind on business when he was around Desiree. She had the kind of effect on him that he hadn't experienced since he was a teenager with hormones gone wild.

Now, think, he lectured himself. Figure out a way to enlist her help. Because in a few minutes, it'll be too late. You're almost at her house.

When Jack turned on to Desiree's street he still hadn't decided just how he was going to get her to cooperate. He wasn't even sure how to prolong their time together. But when he pulled into the driveway of the Reed-Douglas property, Desiree solved the first part of his problem for him.

"Would you like to come in and stay for supper?" she said as he turned off the ignition.

Jack couldn't believe his good fortune. "Are you sure?"

"I wouldn't ask you if I wasn't."

"I'd love to, then."

"You might be sorry. I'm not a very good cook."

"Anything's better than baloney-and-cheese sandwiches, which is about the extent of my cooking."

"Well, okay. Come on."

She didn't wait for him to come around and open her door. She got out and walked around the back of the car. She pointed to the cottage at the back of the property. "That's my place over there."

He already knew that, but he didn't remind her of it. He didn't want her getting mad at him all over again. Not now when it looked as if she'd finally decided to be friendly.

"First I've got to collect my daughter from Margaret," Desiree continued. "She baby-sits for me."

So that little girl *had* been her daughter. Jack wondered where the father was, because Desiree definitely wasn't wearing a wedding ring. He leaned back against his car. "I'll wait for you here."

"Okay." Desiree walked over to the back steps of the Reed-Douglas house. The back porch light was on, and before she even had a chance to knock, Margaret Reed-Douglas opened the back door.

"Hi, Margaret. Is Aimee ready?" Desiree said.

"Hello, Desiree. Yes, she is." Margaret looked over Desiree's shoulder. "Oh, I see you and Mr. Forrester found each other." She smiled and waved to Jack. "Hello, Mr. Forrester."

Jack walked over to the porch. "Hello, Mrs. Reed-Douglas. It's good to see you again."

"Oh, please call me Margaret. Mrs. Reed-Douglas sounds so dreadfully stuffy."

"Only if you'll call me Jack," he said. He walked up the steps and stood just behind Desiree.

The older woman smiled at him, and Jack thought how nice she was. Just the sort of woman you instinctively trusted. Desiree was lucky to have someone like Margaret to sit with her daughter.

"How would you both like to come in for a few minutes? Perhaps have a cocktail with me and Caldwell?"

"Thank you, Margaret, but Jack and I have a lot of catching up to do, so I think we'll pass." Desiree turned to look back at him. There was an unspoken plea in her dark eyes. "Don't we, Jack?"

Jack echoed her excuse. He had no wish to have this nice woman and her equally nice husband discover that he hadn't been quite honest with them when he'd met them over the weekend. And he had a feeling Desiree was through covering for him.

Margaret said, "Well, at least come in until I get Aimee."

Jack saw no graceful way to refuse, so he followed Desiree into the large kitchen.

A few seconds later a beautiful little girl with silky blond hair and heart-melting Bambi eyes raced into the kitchen, Margaret not far behind. "Wait, Aimee. Here's your jacket."

"She doesn't really need it," Desiree said. She grinned and enfolded her daughter in her arms. "Hello, there, sweet-cheeks." She nuzzled her daughter's neck. "I smell peanut butter. Have you been eating peanut butter cookies again?"

Margaret gave Desiree and Jack an apologetic look. "She loves them so."

"Mommy, not so hard..." Aimee wriggled from Desiree's grasp. She looked up at Jack and immediately put her right thumb into her mouth.

Desiree gently removed the thumb, and Aimee tried to hide behind Desiree's back. "Aimee, *chère,* don't be that way. Say hello to Mommy's friend, Mr. Forrester."

"Jack. My name is Jack," he said, kneeling to Aimee's height. "I'm very glad to meet you. So you're Aimee."

The thumb went back into her mouth, but she nodded. "And who's this?" Jack touched the rag doll she clutched tightly in one arm.

Aimee mumbled something that sounded like *rabbity-ran.*

"Now come on, sugar. Take your thumb out of your mouth, and say it right," Desiree said.

The thumb came out slowly. "Raggedy Ann."

"Oh! Raggedy Ann!" said Jack. "That's a great name."

Aimee studied him gravely for a few seconds, then apparently deciding he was all right, gave him a dazzling smile.

Jack's heart turned over. If he'd thought Desiree's smile was a ten, then Aimee's would have to be a twelve. The smile had made the most enchanting dimple form in her right cheek. Jack had always liked children, but he'd never had the opportunity to spend much time with them. For years he'd hoped Jenny and her husband, Kevin, would have children, because Jack figured with his life-style he'd probably never have any himself. But Jenny and Kevin were still childless after eight years of marriage, so he'd about given up hope. "I like your name, too," he said to Aimee.

"My big name is Aimee Arlette Cantrelle," Aimee said proudly. "After my grandma."

The thought passed through Jack's mind that Aimee wasn't using her father's name. He wondered why.

Desiree smoothed Aimee's hair, her hand lingering on the child's head. "My mother's name is Arlette," she explained.

Jack saw the love and pride in her possessive gesture. He knew that Aimee had a mother who loved her very much.

"Well, come on, let's go," Desiree said. She looked at Margaret. "Thank you, Margaret. I'll see you in the morning."

"Good night, Desiree. And good night, Jack. I hope you two have a wonderful visit." She smiled down at Aimee. "Good night, Aimee."

"'Night, Aunt Mar'gret," Aimee said.

"See you tomorrow," Margaret said.

"'Morrow," Aimee echoed, blowing Margaret a kiss.

Desiree took Aimee's hand, and Jack followed them outside and down the path toward their cottage. Within minutes they were inside, and Desiree switched on several lamps. They were standing in a nice-sized living room that stretched across the front of the cottage.

"Take your things to your room," Desiree told Aimee, and Aimee, with another bewitching smile directed at Jack, left the room.

"She likes you," Desiree said.

"I like her, too." He looked around. "This is a nice place."

"It is, isn't it? I love it. I'm really lucky to have found it." She grimaced. "I pay much less than it's worth, but when I tried to talk to Margaret and Caldwell about it once, they wouldn't listen. They said they were particular about who they rented to. They said money isn't everything."

Jack studied the room: the polished wood floors; the faded Oriental carpet with its muted tones of rose and blue; the comfortable love seats on either side of the fireplace; the French provincial writing desk placed so whoever sat there could look out the big front window; the small mahogany drop-leaf table at the far end of the room with ladder-back chairs at either end.

He also saw the toys scattered about, the magazines on the floor, the overflowing knitting basket, the discarded plastic wrap from some kind of snack food that lay on the coffee table, and the brown leaves of the neglected Scheffelera plant that graced one corner of the room.

"I'm afraid I'm not the world's best housekeeper," Desiree said. She walked over to the coffee table and picked up the plastic wrap. "From my granola bar this morning," she said, an apology in her voice.

"I hate houses that look as if no one had ever lived in them," Jack said. "My mother's house was so perfect I was always afraid to touch anything. I always vowed if I ever had a place of my own, I'd enjoy it."

"Come on back to the kitchen," Desiree said.

He followed her through the door at the far end of the room, which led directly into a large kitchen, a cheerful mix of yellow walls, yellow ruffled curtains, white countertops, dark wood cabinets, and a bright red tile floor. Jack smiled to himself. Desiree colors, he thought.

"If you'll look in that cabinet—" she pointed to one of the kitchen cabinets. "—you'll find a bottle of scotch and a bottle of vodka—I'm afraid that's all I've got—and glasses are over there. There's ice in the freezer. Fix yourself a drink and make yourself comfortable in the living room. I'm going to go change clothes."

Jack found everything easily. After pouring himself a drink, he walked back to the living room. He gazed around again, wishing it were cool enough for a fire, but the evening was mild. He walked over to the mantel. There were several framed photographs gracing its polished wood. He walked over to study them. One of them was a large family-type formal portrait. He picked it up. There were a lot of people in it, and there was Desiree, in a red dress. She was holding a child who must be Aimee, although in the portrait she was only a baby.

He studied Desiree's smiling face for a long moment, then put the picture down and wandered over to the front window. He sure wished he could meet the rest of the Cantrelles. He couldn't rid himself of the feeling that one of them had to know something about Elise Arnold.

After Desiree left Jack in the kitchen, she poked her head into Aimee's room. "What'cha doin', sugar?"

"Gettin' my shoes off."

Desiree grinned. Aimee hated to wear shoes, and the first thing she did when she came home was take them off. "Why don't you leave your shoes on tonight, since we have company?"

Aimee frowned.

"Oh, all right. Here, let me help you." Desiree untied the laces on Aimee's high tops. When Aimee's feet were finally free of the shoes, she wiggled her toes happily. "Come to my room while I change clothes, okay?" Desiree said. "Then we'll go out and see Jack."

Aimee hopped off the bed and followed her. "Jack, Jack, Jack," she chanted. "Is Jack a wabbit?" Obviously thrilled with her witticism, she started to giggle.

Desiree laughed. "You're silly. Of course Jack's not a rabbit. He's a man. You know that." Is he ever, she thought.

Aimee climbed up on Desiree's unmade bed and continued to chant, "Jack Wabbit, Jack Wabbit," while Desiree changed clothes.

Desiree gave her daughter a mock frown. "If you're going to call him by that silly name, at least say your *R*." It's *r*abbit, not *w*abbit."

"Rabbit," Aimee said, falling on her back and dissolving into a fresh spate of giggles.

Desiree shook her head, then changed quickly, putting on jeans and a favorite plaid shirt. She tucked the tails of the shirt in, then pulled on socks and slipped her feet into worn leather loafers. "Come on, sugar, let's go."

Holding Aimee's hand, Desiree entered the living room. Jack stood, drink in hand, staring out the front window. He turned at their approach. He smiled, his eyes filled with undisguised approval as he took in Desiree's appearance. Then his gaze dropped to Aimee.

"Jack Rabbit," Aimee said.

Desiree rolled her eyes. "I'm sorry. She decided you're a rabbit. I can't talk her out of it."

Jack grinned. "Don't try. I've been called lots worse." His blue eyes twinkled. "I've been looking at all your pictures." He pointed to the mantel. "Who *are* all these people, anyway?"

Desiree walked over to the mantel, and he followed. Aimee sat on the floor and pulled a picture book from under the stack of magazines lying by the coffee table.

Desiree picked up a small framed photograph. "This is my brother Norman and his wife, Alice. It was taken at their wedding."

"Who are the kids?" Jack asked.

"The children are hers, from her first marriage." At his interested look, she explained. "Alice's first husband was a cop. He was killed, shot by a big-time drug dealer." She sighed, remembering that terrible time. "Jimmy—her first husband—was my brother Neil's partner. It was awful. Just awful."

She picked up the second photo. "And this is my brother Neil, his wife, Laura, and their daughter, Celeste."

She caressed the surface of the next framed photo. "This is Aimee on her first birthday."

"I thought so."

Then she picked up the family photograph they'd had taken two Christmases ago. "And here we all are. This is Mama...and Papa. And here's Neil again...and Laura...and Celeste. And that's Norman again, and Alice, and her two children. And this is Denise, my sister, and her husband, Jett, and their two children, Jeannine and Justin."

"Wow, that's quite a group," Jack said.

"Soon to be more."

He raised his eyebrows.

"Both my sisters-in-law are expecting babies."

He nodded. "It must be nice to have such a big family."

"It is, but sometimes it has its drawbacks."

"Such as?"

Desiree sighed. "Well, since I'm the youngest, my family has a tendency to hover just a bit too much to suit me. That's one of the reasons I moved to New Orleans."

"What were the other reasons?"

"Come out to the kitchen with me while I fix supper, and I'll tell you. Aimee, *chère,* do you want to watch the rest of *Dumbo* while Mommy cooks supper?"

"Dumbo! Dumbo!" Aimee clapped her hands and threw down her book. She grinned happily.

"I guess that means yes," Desiree said and turned on the television set, then the VCR. After a few seconds, Walt Disney's *Dumbo,* already in progress, appeared on the screen. Desiree motioned to Jack to follow her, and they left Aimee happily engrossed in the movie.

"Sit," Desiree said, and Jack sat on a kitchen chair. She opened the pantry door and rummaged on the shelves, pulling out a large jar of prepared spaghetti sauce, a couple of cans of plain tomato sauce, a jar of olive oil and a package of spaghetti. "Remember, I'm not all that great a cook."

"So tell me what the other reasons were for your moving to New Orleans. Where do the rest of your family live, anyway?" Jack leaned back, balancing the chair on its two rear legs.

"In Patinville, just west of Baton Rouge." She opened the refrigerator and extracted a large onion. Then she took a package of ground meat from the freezer and shoved it into the microwave to thaw. "It's a small town. You've probably never heard of it."

"You're right. I haven't."

Desiree pulled a large pot out of the cupboard and set it on the stove. She poured a bit of olive oil in the pot and turned the heat on under it. Then she opened the cupboard where she kept her spices and started pulling things off the shelf.

"You still haven't answered my question," Jack reminded her. "Say, do you need help?"

"No. I'm doing fine." She took a deep breath. "If you must know, I came to New Orleans because everyone in Patinville knew about Aimee and the circumstances of her birth. I didn't want her to feel as if she were different. I didn't want people talking about her or making her feel bad." She put her chin in the air and turned to face him. "You see, I wasn't married to Aimee's father."

There was no censure in his expression as he absorbed her statement. Only a quiet acceptance.

In that moment, Desiree decided Jack Forrester could become very important to her. Probably too important.

Chapter Five

What did she think he was going to do? Sneer and call her names? Obviously, this was a subject that Desiree was sensitive about. Jack chose his words carefully. "I'd hate to think people are so narrow-minded they'd be cruel to Aimee over something like that. Single mothers are not exactly uncommon, you know."

"Maybe not, but they're completely nonexistent in my family," she said. She peeled the onion and began chopping it.

"Do you want to tell me about it?"

Her shoulders stiffened. "No."

Jack wished he knew her well enough to get up and rub the tenseness out of her shoulders. He wished he had the right to comfort her. He wondered who the guy was who had hurt her so badly. Because it was obvious to Jack that Desiree was hurting. Jack decided whoever the guy was, he had to be a first-class jerk to let Desiree get away.

Desiree finished chopping the onions and scraped them into the pot. They hissed as they hit the hot olive oil. Immediately the kitchen filled with the aroma of frying onions. Jack watched her, enjoying the way her jeans clung to her nicely rounded rear as she moved about. Even though he'd never had any desire to settle down, he could see that some aspects of being married might be nice.

The microwave dinged, and she took the meat out. "What?" she said when she saw how he was looking at her.

He grinned. "I was just thinking how nice it is to sit here and watch you do all the work."

"Chauvinist!" she said, but she grinned.

"So tell me about Patinville," Jack said. He was genuinely curious about Desiree, but he also hoped something she might say would help him in his search for information about Elise.

"Oh, it's a typical small town. One main street, one bank—no, that's wrong—two banks, one pharmacy, one big grocery store, one high school." She grinned at him over her shoulder as she worked at the stove. "The only thing it's got a lot of are churches."

"What do your brothers and father do?"

She stirred the frying onions with a wooden spoon, then lowered the heat and dumped in the various sauces. "They both work in the family business." She added several spices to the mixture in the pot.

"Which is?"

"A roofing and home improvement company. My father started it years ago, and now Norman—he's the younger of my brothers—runs the place and does all the administrative work, and Neil—he's the older brother—is in charge of the crews."

"Sounds like it's successful."

"It is." She bent down, pulled another pot from a bottom cupboard and walked over to the sink, where she began filling it with water.

"What did you do when you lived in Patinville?"

"After I graduated from high school, I went to work for a local real estate agency as a receptionist. Then, for about six months, I worked at our company as the bookkeeper." She turned off the water and carried the filled pot to the stove. She set it on a back burner and turned on the heat under it. "But when I realized I was pregnant with Aimee, my father arranged for me to go to Lafayette and stay with my Uncle Justin and Aunt Lisette until I had the baby."

She extracted an iron frying pan from the cupboard. Within minutes, the ground meat was cooking.

Jack sniffed. She might not be a great cook, but her concoctions were beginning to smell good. His stomach rumbled. He hadn't eaten lunch.

"Do you like mushrooms?" she asked.

"I like anything that likes me."

"Good." Soon a couple of cans of sliced mushrooms had been added to the sauce.

Her voice turned softer. "Uncle Justin and Aunt Lisette are both such sweeties. They were wonderful to me." She opened the refrigerator and knelt, then began pulling things out of the vegetable keeper. "They don't have any children of their own, so they've always been very good to me and my sister and brothers."

Yes. When Charles had told him so many stories about the Cajun people, one recurring theme was the closeness of their family life. Jack could see it was true. Cajun families were definitely tight. They took care of their own, and loyalties ran deep.

Desiree took all the vegetables to the sink, where she began washing them. As she cleaned them, she half turned so she could see Jack. "That's enough about me. Tell me about your family. You have a twin sister—"

"Yes. Jenny. Jennifer Harriett Forrester Wharton. My mother's name is Harriett. The former Daughters of the Confederacy debutante, Harriett Cornelia Jackson." He grimaced. "My father's name is Alan, so they named me Jackson Alan. My family's big on family names."

"What're your parents like?"

Jack thought for a minute. "Well, mother's president of the Women's Forum. She's a past president of the afore-mentioned Daughters of the Confederacy, and she's a member of the board of directors of St. Phillip's Hospital in Houston. She's also a mover and a shaker with the arts council and the opera guild. She likes stuff like that." She had always liked stuff like that, Jack thought. Much more than homemaking. And a whole lot more than children. Jack pushed the thought away. It was no longer important to him. He'd quickly learned to depend on himself and no one else. Except for Jenny, he had no real ties with his family.

"And your father?"

"Like your father, he owns his own business." Jack saw no need to mention that Alan Forrester, Inc. was the largest accounting firm in Houston, handling accounts that totaled in the hundreds of millions.

"Doing what?"

"He's an accountant."

Desiree smiled. "Somehow you don't seem like the son of an accountant."

"And what are sons of accountants like?"

"Oh, I don't know. Thin and pale with thick glasses on their noses?"

Jack laughed. "Come on, Desiree. That's a stereotype."

"I'm just teasing you." She began to break up the lettuce she'd washed and put the pieces in a salad bowl.

"I think your water's boiling," Jack pointed out.

"Oops. I forgot it." She opened the package of spaghetti and added it slowly to the boiling water. Then she stirred it, adjusted the heat and left it to cook. She went back to preparing the salad.

"Do you want me to do that while you do something else?" Jack offered.

"No. You're company. Just sit there."

Jack decided now was the time to reintroduce the subject of Elise—while Desiree was mellow and busy with her cooking. "Have you thought of anything that might be useful to me in tracking down Elise Arnold?"

Desiree, who had been cutting up a tomato and adding it to the salad bowl, stopped and turned to face him. Her dark eyes studied him. "You still think there's a connection between her and me, don't you?"

Jack heard the disappointment in her voice. He sighed. "I'm sorry, Desiree. I can't help it. I believe you when you say you don't know anything, but all my instincts tell me Elise belongs to your family. Somewhere there's a link. I mean, come on, you've got a huge family. Surely there might be branches of it you don't know anything about. Someone has got to know something."

He met her gaze squarely. The kitchen seemed very quiet all of a sudden. From the living room, Jack could hear the muted noise of the movie Aimee was watching, and from the stove the soft bubbling sound of the boiling water, and from the wall the ticking of the kitchen clock.

He waited.

With a small shrug of defeat, Desiree said, "Okay. What can I do to help?"

* * *

"That was a wonderful meal," Jack said, sighing and patting his stomach.

"Thanks." It was amazing, she thought, that she felt so comfortable with him. Well, maybe not entirely comfortable. He was too attractive, and she was too conscious of the awareness simmering between them, to be completely relaxed.

But she liked him.

She enjoyed his company.

And she sure liked looking at him. Surely there was no danger in looking.

She looked at him now as he leaned back in his chair. She wondered if she'd be sorry she'd agreed to help him. She knew she shouldn't have. She knew she should have given Jack Forrester his walking papers this morning. In fact, she should never have let him talk her into getting into his car at all. That would have been the sane, sensible, safe way to act.

But Desiree had never been a person to play things safe. Despite the mistakes she'd made, despite her vow that she'd never again be taken in by charm or good looks or sex appeal, despite her pledge to find a man who would give her and Aimee security and a settled home, Desiree had a streak of daring in her.

She loved adventure.

She loved excitement.

And she loved taking chances.

Aimee yawned. Desiree glanced at the clock. "I can't believe it! It's already after seven." She stood, walked around to Aimee's chair. "Come on, sugar. It's time for your bath."

Jack stood, too.

"No, just sit there. Relax. Let me get her settled in the tub, then I'll be back."

But when she'd filled the tub with a few inches of water and tossed Aimee's bubble bath in, she could hear him rattling dishes and pots in the kitchen. She finished undressing Aimee, put her in the tub and dumped in her rubber toys, then said, "Now you play for a few minutes, okay, sugar? I'll leave the door open, so I can see you."

"Where you goin', Mommy?"

"I'm going out to help Jack."

Aimee giggled. "Jack Rabbit!" She had a bubble on the end of her nose.

Desiree stooped and kissed Aimee's forehead. "I love you."

Aimee giggled again.

Desiree walked out to the kitchen. Sure enough, Jack had already cleared the table and was filling the dishwasher. He turned at her approach and grinned. He'd found her apron and tied it around himself. There was something awfully sexy about a gorgeous guy wearing an apron, Desiree thought.

"You didn't have to do that," she said.

"I wasn't sure what you wanted to do with the leftovers, so I left that for you."

As she put the leftover food into plastic containers, Jack finished cleaning up the rest of the kitchen. Within minutes, everything was neat.

"You do good work," she said. "I wouldn't mind having you around every night." The minute the words were out of her mouth, she realized her mistake.

"And I wouldn't mind being around every night."

Desiree could feel her cheeks warming.

Jack untied the apron and laid it over the back of a kitchen chair. He walked to where she stood, stopping only inches away. She refused to meet his gaze.

"Desiree," he said softly. "Look at me." He touched her chin, lifting it.

Desiree's heart pounded wildly as she looked into his eyes.

"You're so beautiful," he murmured. "I didn't know any woman ever blushed anymore."

"I—" Oh, God. She felt like a fool. Hadn't she learned anything?

He rubbed her chin with the pad of his thumb. Her pulse went haywire. And her stomach felt as if a bunch of mice were running around inside it.

Jack's eyes darkened, and she recognized the desire she saw there. The same desire echoed deep within her. She swallowed. The kitchen was very quiet.

He bent his head. Desiree closed her eyes.

Just as his lips touched hers, Aimee called, "Mommy! When are you coming in?"

Heart pounding, Desiree jerked away from him. "I...I must go to her." She left him standing there and rushed to the bathroom.

By the time she finished bathing Aimee and putting the child into pajamas, Desiree had gotten her wildly careening emotions under control. When she and Aimee emerged from the bathroom, Jack was no longer in the kitchen. She heard the sound of the TV coming from the living room and decided he'd gone in there.

Sighing with relief—she still wasn't ready to face him—she took Aimee into her room and put her to bed. The bedtime ritual took about fifteen more minutes, and the cowardly part of Desiree hoped Jack might get tired of waiting and be gone by the time she was ready to join him.

"Good night, *chère*." She kissed Aimee's soft cheek, inhaling the smell of sweet soap and sweet child.

"'Night, Mommy." Aimee reached up and put her arms around Desiree's neck.

"I love you," Desiree whispered.

"I love you," Aimee whispered back.

"It's you and me..."

"'Gainst the world." Aimee finished their private mantra.

Desiree kissed Aimee one last time, then gently pulled free. She tucked the covers around the little girl, stalling, thinking about Jack out there in the living room. Remembering how she felt when she'd known he was going to kiss her. Wondering if he'd try to kiss her again.

"Where's Raggedy?" Aimee said.

"Here she is." Desiree reached for the doll, handed it to Aimee. "Good night," she said again. She snapped off Aimee's bedside lamp.

She walked out to the hall, pulled Aimee's door halfway shut. She stood there for a moment. Smoothed down her hair. Retucked her blouse into the waistband of her jeans. Wet her lips.

Okay, don't you think you've stalled long enough?

Taking a deep breath, Desiree walked slowly down the hall to the living room.

Jack sat on one of the love seats, his back against the armrest and his legs up. They were too long for the length of the love seat, so he'd propped them up on the other armrest. He had found her photo album and was looking at it.

He looked completely at home.

Trying to speak nonchalantly, Desiree said, "Well, you look comfortable!"

He looked up, gave her a teasing smile. "I figured I deserved a rest after all my hard work in the kitchen."

Those eyes of his would be her undoing.

Desiree sat on the other love seat. Jack swung his legs down, turned to face her. The smile still lingered in his eyes.

Desiree squirmed. If he kept looking at her like that, she would never be able to maintain her composure.

"Well," she said brightly, too brightly. "Have you decided what your strategy's going to be in your investigation?"

His eyes twinkled. *Oh, so that's the way it's going to be,* they seemed to say.

Desiree wanted to look away, but she knew if she did she'd lose whatever advantage she had. And she had to stay in control. On guard. At all times. Because it would be all too easy to forget that Jack Forrester was a transient in her life. That one day soon he'd pack up and go home. That if she wasn't very, very careful, he'd take a big chunk of her heart with him when he went.

"I thought I'd spend tomorrow at the library. I decided to go with your idea and check all the phone books for other cities in Louisiana."

"You're going to check out *every* Cantrelle? That'll be an enormous job!"

He shrugged. "I don't see what other options I have."

"Have you tried the social security office?"

"I tried them first."

"And?"

"Nothing useful. The first social security number assigned to Elise Sonnier Arnold was issued nine years ago— in Houston."

"Jack, how old is Elise?"

"Twenty-eight."

Only a couple of years younger than Desiree herself. "So at nineteen, she got her first social security number..."

"Yes."

"Didn't you tell me her mother died when she was nineteen?"

"Yes." Jack, who had still been holding the photo album, shut it and placed it on the coffee table. He leaned forward, arms resting on his knees.

"Did you check the death records in Houston? To see if her mother died there?"

"I thought of that, but I turned up nothing."

"What about the New Orleans records?"

"Again, nothing."

Desiree sighed. "Frustrating, isn't it?"

He grinned. "Now you know exactly how I feel."

"I can see why you were so persistent once you found me."

"I might have been persistent anyway."

Desiree decided to ignore his innuendo. "Back to my earlier question. What do you want me to do while you're laboring at the library?"

"Could you possibly check the rolls of the Louisiana Bar Association for me?"

"Sure. For what?"

"Well, for starters, just get me a list of all lawyers named Cantrelle." He frowned in thought. "I don't suppose the names of the people who work for the law firms might be listed, too?"

Desiree shook her head. "That'd be impossible. Staff changes take place daily."

He nodded. "What time tomorrow do you think you'll have the information?"

"Hard to tell. It depends how busy I am."

"How about if I just pick you up after work again?"

Desiree started to shake her head. It wouldn't do to get in the habit of depending on him.

"Aw, come on. I don't want to bother you by calling you at work . . ."

The trouble with doing sensible things was they were usually the least interesting of the available options.

Taking her silence for acquiescence, or maybe just pressing his advantage while she was in a weakened state, he said, "I'll be waiting at the curb at five o'clock."

"Better make it five-fifteen. I hardly ever get out right on time."

"Well, now that we've settled that…" He stood. "I guess I should be going. You've probably got lots of things to do."

She stood, too. "Yes." She really didn't have anything that urgently needed doing, but she still had enough sense of self-preservation to grasp the straw he'd handed her.

"Thanks again for the meal. It was great."

She walked with him to the front door. He turned to face her. She looked up, into his eyes.

And was lost.

Again.

He moved a step closer. "Desiree…" His voice sounded husky and laden with unspoken meaning.

Desiree opened her mouth to answer, but the answer died on her lips.

In the next moment, Jack drew her into his arms, and this time, when his lips descended to meet hers, they reached their goal. The kiss started slowly—just a soft brushing of cool, firm lips—first this way, and then, angling his head, settling more firmly, with more demand.

Desiree sighed, the sound absorbed in his mouth, as his breath mingled with hers. Her whole body hummed, as if someone had reached inside and turned everything on. Her heart swelled. She forgot to breathe. She forgot to think. But she hadn't forgotten how to feel.

He deepened the kiss, tasting her, claiming her, igniting her. One hand moved up under her hair, holding her head firmly in place. The other traveled slowly down her back until it rested against her bottom, where it seemed to burn against her skin. He pulled her tight, aligning her body with his. Now she could feel all of him against her: hard, male, arousing.

Powerful sensations rocketed through her. A fire had started in her belly, a fire that would soon rage out of control. Desire—sharp, potent, reckless—raced through her.

She wound her arms around his neck and strained against him. She lost track of where the first kiss ended and the second began. She couldn't have said when he no longer had to hold her in place. She wasn't sure when his hands began to stroke her, when the tails of her blouse left her waistband, when his palms had captured her breasts, when his thumbs began their tender assault, when the pleasure-pain had escalated to a need so powerful it was all she could think of.

But when he unhooked the front of her bra, the haze that had taken over her senses suddenly evaporated, and she yanked out of his grasp. "No, no..."

"Desiree..." His voice was thick and uneven. His mouth bore traces of her lipstick. His breathing was ragged.

"No." She backed up. She could feel hot tears threatening. God, she wished she could crawl into the ground and hide forever. What had happened to her? She had been all over him. What must he think? That she fell into bed with anyone who asked? My, God, she'd only known Jack Forrester for three days! She must be crazy. She must be sex-starved, or something. Hadn't she learned *anything* from her mistakes?

She didn't know where to look. She couldn't meet his gaze.

He touched her shoulder. "Desiree, I'm sorry..."

She flinched. "Please, Jack. Don't say anything. Just go."

She turned her back on him and refastened her bra. She rebuttoned the bottom button of her blouse. She tucked it in. She stalled for time.

When she finally turned around once more, he had gotten himself under control, too. The lipstick traces were gone. "I'm sorry," he said again.

"Let's just forget it, okay?"

"Desiree." The word was a whisper. His eyes were gentle.

Please, please, she begged silently. *Don't look at me like that.* "Good night, Jack." She opened the front door.

"We can't pretend this didn't happen."

"We *will* pretend this didn't happen." She didn't say *or else.* He was smart enough to understand.

She saw the resignation in the almost imperceptible shrug of his shoulders and in the tightening of his mouth. His voice, when he spoke, was even, almost impersonal. "I'll see you tomorrow, then."

"Yes." Desiree's chest felt tight from the effort of holding herself together.

Finally he walked out the open door, his gaze capturing hers for one instant as he brushed past.

Desiree shut the door.

And then she burst into tears.

Chapter Six

Jack could have kicked himself. What had possessed him to lose control like that? He had rushed her. He knew from the things she'd said earlier in the evening that she was sensitive about her situation. That she was vulnerable. That she'd been hurt badly. He'd known she wasn't a woman who could casually enter into a love affair. She'd made that very clear.

So why hadn't he done the smart thing? Why hadn't he just said good-night and gone home? Tonight he'd forgotten his basic tenet: think before you act. He hadn't thought at all, just acted on instinct, on feelings. He was powerfully attracted to Desiree, and he'd indulged that attraction, giving no thought to the consequences.

Aside from consideration for Desiree's feelings, he wanted and needed her help. His whole reason for being in New Orleans, for taking time off from his job, was to find out what had happened to Elise Arnold.

What if he'd blown it? What if, after thinking about what had happened between them, Desiree decided she didn't need the complications he was introducing into her life, and she refused to see him again?

He was a damned fool.

All the while he lectured himself, he drove back to his apartment much too fast. But by the time he'd parked his car in the underground garage, taken the elevator up to his floor, unlocked the door of the apartment and turned on the lights, he'd calmed down enough to be philosophical. After all, what was done was done.

If Desiree decided not to cooperate with him any longer, there was probably nothing he could do to change her mind. He might as well quit worrying about it.

He opened the refrigerator, removed a can of soda, popped the top and took a long swallow. Then he walked into the living room, parted the drapes and stared out the front window.

The lights of downtown New Orleans winked below like tiny fireflies. He could see the dark ribbon of the river, the mammoth gray hulk of the Superdome, the red-and-white lights of the cars on the street below, but all were superimposed with an image of Desiree as she'd looked when she'd pushed him away: her lips swollen, her cheeks flushed, her expression stricken.

Even closing his eyes didn't banish the image.

Something had happened to him tonight. It had started in the car, when he was driving her home from work, when she'd first smiled at him—a faint stirring deep within.

It had grown when he had met Aimee and seen mother and daughter together, seen the love between them.

The feelings had gotten stronger when they'd talked in the kitchen as Desiree made supper, when she'd talked about her family, when she'd revealed so much of herself in her admission about Aimee's birth.

And then, when he'd kissed her, when his mouth first tasted the sweetness of hers, when his hands touched her firm yet pliant body, felt the softness of her skin and the fullness of her breasts, those feelings had erupted into full life.

What he'd felt, *still felt* for her was more than desire.

More than passion.

More than anything he'd ever felt for any woman before.

Even now, just remembering, his body ached, his hands trembled, and his heart thudded with slow painful beats.

Admit it, Forrester. Admit it.

Okay, goddammit, okay! I want more than information and help from her. I want more than sex from her. I admit it!

What do you want? Are you afraid to say it?

Hell, no, I'm not afraid to say it.

Then why don't you?

Jack clamped his teeth so hard his jaw ached. But that taunting inner voice wouldn't leave him alone.

Can't fool me. You're afraid.

Shut up. Shut the hell up.

You stupid jerk. Did you think you were immune?

Jack pounded his right fist into his left palm, then winced. God, he *had* thought he was immune. He'd been so smug when he'd seen buddies of his fall head over heels for some woman. He'd never been able to understand how they could just toss all their plans and dreams out the window just became they'd gotten the hots for some good-looking skirt.

He'd vowed that kind of thing would never happen to him. He wanted different things from his life than any woman would ever want. His life, his ambition, his nomadic existence, would be anathema to a woman. Women like Desiree Cantrelle wanted ruffled curtains, a picket fence, a wedding ring and kids. They wanted a husband coming home every night. They wanted security and safety and routine. They wanted ties.

Jack wanted professional challenges, life on the edge. No ties.

Unfortunately, he was also damned afraid he wanted Desiree Cantrelle.

The two desires would never mesh.

Desiree felt as if someone had beaten her up. She stretched in her secretary's chair. The small of her back ached. Her neck and shoulders ached. Her head ached.

She was one sorry mess.

She rotated her head in slow circles. Some of the tension in her neck eased. She'd been working on a long deposition for what seemed like hours. She glanced at her watch. It was nearly noon, thank God. Instead of eating lunch in the office, she decided to take her lunch and walk down to Jackson Square and sit on one of the benches on the Moonwalk overlooking the river. She needed fresh air and blue sky. She needed the serenity of the water. She needed to think, although God knows, she'd been doing little else since Jack had left her the night before.

Jack.

She no longer felt upset by what had transpired between them. She was just disgusted with herself. She'd made the decision to keep their relationship strictly casual, then at the first opportunity, she'd completely forgotten her resolution. With all her heart she wished she'd been able to resist the powerful attraction she felt for him, for now things could never be the same between them. She was afraid they'd be awkward with each other now, and since she'd agreed to help him in his quest for Elise Arnold, it would be so much easier if she'd been able to keep their relationship friendly but casual.

Unfortunately, she felt anything but casual about Jack. Each time she remembered his touch, his heated kisses, she felt exactly the way she did when she stood at a great height and looked down. As if the bottom were falling out of her stomach.

That's why she felt so lousy today. She'd lain in bed and gone over and over last night's events. She hadn't been able to fall asleep for hours. And when she finally did, her dreams were laced with erotic images. Of him. Of them. She'd awakened from one particularly vivid and explicit dream to find her heart racing and her cotton sleepshirt clammy with perspiration.

Even now, remembering the dream, Desiree could feel her cheeks warming. She leaned her head against her computer monitor and closed her eyes.

"Desiree?"

Desiree jumped.

"Is something wrong?"

Julie stood in front of the desk, her forehead furrowed.

"No, nothing's wrong. I was just resting my eyes for a minute." Desiree managed a feeble smile. "The Templeton deposition is a long one."

Julie nodded. "Awful, too, isn't it?"

"Yes." Desiree, despite a headful of thoughts of Jack had still been shaken by the contents of the deposition—a recitation of the events that had led up to the murder of Buster Templeton—told to Julie by Janet Templeton, his wife.

"Hard to believe a woman would put up with that much abuse for that long a period of time," Julie said, shaking her head.

"I know." In the deposition, Janet Templeton related how Buster, for eighteen years, had beaten, battered and abused her. How he had nearly killed her at least a half dozen times. How she had called the police again and again. How she had tried to leave Buster. How he had found her no matter where she went, and dragged her back. Threatened her to force her to come back. Even threatened the lives of her mother and sisters. And how, one day, Janet Templeton had simply had enough. So when Buster, in a black rage, had swung his meaty fist at her and she'd heard one of her teeth break and tasted bitter, coppery blood in her mouth, she had picked up the heavy mallet she'd been using to tenderize a round steak for his dinner. She'd swung it up and then down onto his head with all the pent-up rage and strength that all those years of abuse had fostered.

Janet Templeton had told her story in an unemotional, flat voice, as if all her ability to feel had been killed along with her husband.

Desiree shuddered, thinking about Janet. "The scary part is that while I was typing up everything, I didn't feel the least bit sorry for Buster. In fact, I was glad she killed him."

"I know."

"It's a miracle she didn't kill him years ago." Desiree frowned, reminded of Elise Arnold, who, according to Jack and his sister, was also an abused wife. "Wouldn't you think a woman would suspect that kind of thing about a man before she married him? I can't believe a man could completely hide these tendencies. Don't you think women like Janet would have at least had a hint before they married abusive men?"

Julie grimaced. "Well, in Janet's case, I think I'd have had my first clue when I found out his name was Buster!"

Desiree couldn't help laughing.

"I shouldn't make fun of something so serious, but honestly, sometimes if you don't laugh you'll spend your whole day crying." Julie's stomach emitted a soft growl, and she rolled her eyes. "Sorry about that. I'm starving. Do you want to go to lunch with me?"

"I brought my lunch, but I'm going to walk down to the river and sit there and eat it."

"Can I tag along?"

"Sure." Julie would probably be better company than her own thoughts.

"I'll pick up a Po' Boy or something on the way."

"Okay."

Twenty minutes later, Desiree and Julie sat on a wooden bench warmed by the sun and watched the activity on the river. Desiree munched at her tuna salad sandwich and tried to empty her mind. She sighed.

"Something's bothering you," Julie said. "But if you don't want to talk about it, that's okay." She stretched her legs out in front of her, and the sun glinted off her shiny black pumps. "If you *do* want to talk about it, though, I've got a willing ear. And I don't repeat things."

Desiree knew that. Julie's discretion, her loyalty and her kind heart were all traits Desiree valued.

She sighed again. "Maybe I should talk about it. Maybe I need an objective ear. I'm not sure I'm thinking straight right now, and I've got to come to a decision."

Julie took a bite of her oyster Po' Boy and quietly waited.

Desiree tried to keep her voice as neutral as the unlucky Janet Templeton's. "I told you about Jack Forrester, the investigative journalist who followed me home last week...."

"Oh, yeah, the hunk." Julie's hazel eyes sparkled.

"Well, yesterday he was waiting for me when I left work."

"I swear, you really *do* have all the luck!"

"And I invited him to stay for supper."

"I don't blame you. I would've, too."

"And we ended the evening with—" Desiree hesitated, then plunged ahead. "Him kissing me, and me kissing him back, and things going just a little too far before I stopped it. And now I'm embarrassed, and I don't know what I'm going to do or say when I see him again." She cut a glance at Julie.

Julie absentmindedly tore off a piece of the bread from her sandwich and threw it to an aggressive pigeon who had been watching her. The pigeon swooped on the bread, and several other squawking birds converged on the spot, their wings flapping excitedly.

"I don't even know if I *should* see him again."

"Desiree," Julie said thoughtfully, "tell me something. Answer me as honestly as you can." She tore off another small piece of bread. The pigeons dive-bombed.

"Okay."

"How do you feel about this guy? Not the physical stuff. I know you're attracted to him. I mean the man himself. Do you like him?" She took another bite of her sandwich, chewed slowly.

Desiree nodded. "Very much."

"Do you *want* to see him again?"

Desiree stared at the river's surface. Today the water looked almost blue, and it was smooth and flat as a polished stone. "Yes. God help me, but I do."

"Well, as I see it, you have two choices. You can live dangerously and see him again, or you can play it safe and forget about him." Julie's face assumed her don't-interrupt-when-I'm-analyzing-this-problem look. "If you see him again, anything can happen, which is positive. If you don't see him again, nothing will happen, which is negative. So your real choice is between positive or negative." She smiled, obviously pleased with herself.

"You think I should go for it."

"I don't know. That's your decision to make. But if you don't, you'll always wonder *what if*. I mean, there's no reason to anticipate the worst. Who knows? *You* might get tired of *him*. Or the two of you might fall in love. But at least you'd be doing something instead of waiting for something to happen." Julie frowned. "Darn! That's it! That's my problem. I keep waiting for something to happen to me instead of going out and making it happen. Waiting is negative. Doing something is positive." She popped the last of her sandwich into her mouth, shooing away the pigeons in the process. She stood and brushed the crumbs off her black skirt, then tugged down her black-and white-checked jacket.

Desiree, who still wasn't convinced she shouldn't just put Jack Forrester out of her mind forever, stood, too. She drained the last of her diet soda, then threw her trash into the nearest container. She and Julie walked down to Jackson Square, threading their way through a tour group. The pure, sweet sound of a saxophone floated through the air.

As they walked back to the office through Pirates' Alley, Julie said, "I don't know what you've decided to do about Jack Forrester, but our talk today has made me make a decision about *my* life."

"Oh?"

"I'm tired of the same old things. I'm tired of dull, predictable dates with dull, predictable lawyers. I'm sick of playing it safe. So I'm going to finally do something I've always wanted to do." Her eyes gleamed.

"Which is?"

"Promise you won't laugh."

Desiree smiled. "I won't laugh."

"I've always wanted to be an actress."

"Really?" Desiree said, delighted. Now that she thought about it, she realized one of the reasons Julie was such a successful courtroom lawyer was because of her flair for the dramatic. "How're you going to go about it?"

"I don't know. Call around. Sign up for lessons or something." Julie grinned. "I'll find a way."

"Julie, I don't understand why you haven't done this before if you've always wanted to."

Julie moved over to make room for a group of tourists who were hogging the sidewalk. "I'm not sure, either. I think I've just been scared to do it. Scared I wouldn't be any good. Scared people would make fun of me. Or think I was stupid."

Desiree constantly marveled at how low Julie's self-esteem could be. If either of them should have low self-esteem, it should be Desiree. Julie was educated. She'd graduated from Louisiana State University with honors, and she'd been third in her class at Tulane Law School. Desiree, in contrast, had only a high school education. Julie came from a well-to-do family who patronized the arts, who read extensively, who were sophisticated and well traveled. Desiree's family, although she loved them and wouldn't trade them for anyone else, were basically very ordinary people. Her oldest brother Neil, had been the only one of them to go to college, and he'd only gone for two years. And again, except for Neil, none of them were readers or travelers or interested in any kind of highbrow pursuits.

The Cantrelles were physical people. They liked to eat, to make love, to dance the spirited dances of their Acadian forefathers at the *fais-dodos*. They liked lots of children and noise and big family gatherings. The women liked to cook and gossip and take care of their men. The men liked to hunt and fish and take care of their women.

Julie had never done anything to embarrass her family.

Desiree had.

Yet, for all this, Julie seemed to envy Desiree.

Desiree couldn't figure it out.

Desiree didn't find the time to check the Louisiana Bar Association roster until late in the afternoon. Seventeen Cantrelles were listed throughout the state, but three of them were her relatives, so she only typed fourteen names on Jack's list. She smiled when she saw her Uncle Justin's name. Outside of the members of her immediate family, her Uncle Justin was her favorite.

Of course, the fact that he and her Aunt Lisette had gladly welcomed her when she was pregnant with Aimee had something to do with her feelings. But she had always felt especially close to them. They were both warm, giving people, and she enjoyed being around them.

Desiree thought it was a darned shame they'd never had any children of their own. The two of them were meant to be parents. Instead, they'd lavished their generosity on Desiree and her sister and brothers as well as on the dozens of other Cantrelle cousins.

It was also because of her uncle that she had gotten the training to land a good-paying legal secretary's position in New Orleans. Although Justin, at sixty-nine, was now retired from the practice of law, he had still been working four years ago when she had come to stay with him and her aunt, and he had put Desiree to work. She had learned so much in the year she spent with them—for they'd insisted she stay on until Aimee was six months old—that she'd had no trouble at all finding a job in New Orleans.

Remembering that peaceful hiatus and her uncle and aunt's thoughtfulness made Desiree resolve to call them over the weekend. It had been awhile since she'd driven up to Lafayette to see them. Maybe she and Aimee could go soon.

Finally the day was over. Making sure she had the list of Cantrelle attorneys to give Jack, Desiree cleared off her desk. She dawdled as she gathered her things. Butterflies had taken over her stomach as she thought about seeing Jack in just a few minutes.

When she could stall no longer, she waved goodbye to her co-workers. Three minutes later she opened the front gate, half hoping Jack wouldn't be there.

He was there.

Just like the day before, he leaned against his car, his arms folded across his chest, his right ankle crossed over his left. He wore boots, jeans and a light blue sweater. He had the rugged, outdoors look she'd always associated with Texans. The late-afternoon sun fired his hair with scarlet, and his eyes glinted ocean-blue, deep and mysterious.

Desiree felt as if someone had squeezed all the breath out of her. She hoped he wouldn't see how nervous she was.

"Hi," he said, giving her a half smile.

"Hi." She tried to smile but couldn't. She walked closer.

He straightened, reached for the door handle, but avoided her eyes.

He's as nervous as I am! This knowledge helped to calm her. If Jack was nervous, that meant he at least cared how she felt. Now she could admit what had *really* been bothering her: that he, like Mark, did not respect her, that what had happened between her and Jack the night before would have been of so little importance to him that he wouldn't care how she felt.

She lowered herself into the passenger seat of the car.

When he was seated beside her, he inserted the key in the ignition, then hesitated. Hand still on the key, he turned to look at her. "Are you angry with me?"

"No! Of course not!"

"Are you sure?" His eyes shone with concern.

"I'm sure." The last of her embarrassment melted away. Knowing that he didn't think less of her, knowing that what she thought and felt was important to him—made all the difference. She smiled. "I'm very sure."

His answering smile warmed her heart. He reached over and squeezed her hand, then started the car and they were on their way.

Everything was going to be all right, Jack thought. She wasn't angry. She wasn't going to tell him to get lost. He could feel the relief sliding through him. "Did you have a chance to check the bar association roster for me?" he asked.

"Yes. I've got the list in my purse." She patted the enormous tote bag she never seemed to be without.

"Along with about a hundred other things, I'd guess," he teased. "I've never understood why women need so many things. All I carry is I.D., money, a comb, a handkerchief and my keys."

She grinned. "We women need slightly more than that."

"Such as?"

"Oh, let's see." She began ticking items off on her fingers. "Wallet, coin purse, checkbook, tissues, unmentionables, makeup, comb, brush, hair lifter, hair spray, perfume, a notebook, a pen, a flashlight, keys, I.D., breath spray..." She opened the bag and looked inside. "My can of Mace, nail clippers, nail file, nail polish, an extra pair of panty hose in case I get a run, my lunch, a bottle of aspirin, my collapsible toothbrush, toothpaste, dental floss..." She chuckled, pulling out a bottle. "Mineral water."

"Mineral water!"

"I believe in being prepared."

He laughed. He couldn't help it. "Is that it?"

She was struggling to keep a straight face. "Nope. I also have a book in here." She lifted it out—a paperback novel with a shiny cover. "And a cup, my coupon container, my address book, a sewing kit..." As she talked she took these items out of her bag. "I've also got a screwdriver, a bottle opener, a pair of scissors, safety pins...what else? A bag of pretzels for Aimee...a half-eaten box of raisins...Aimee likes raisins...gum, one of Aimee's hair barrettes..." She frowned. "Now what's this? Oh, I know! It's part of a toy."

"Desiree, this is ridiculous! How do you ever carry all that junk?"

She gave him an indignant look. "Junk? This isn't junk. These are the necessities of life!"

They both laughed as she refilled the voluminous tote bag, and Jack fully relaxed for the first time that day. He was grateful to her for making it so easy on them both.

His relaxed state lasted until he reached Desiree's street. Then she said softly, "Jack, pull over for a minute, will you?"

He gave her a quizzical look, tried to quell his sudden uneasiness.

"I want to talk to you, and I don't want to be sitting in the driveway where Margaret and Caldwell can see us and wonder what we're doing," she said.

He pulled over to the curb and cut the engine. The early-evening stillness settled around them. He turned toward Desiree.

She ducked her head for a moment, then raised her chin and looked at him. Her dark eyes gleamed in the shadowy light of a street lamp a few feet away. "When you asked me if I was angry, and I said I wasn't, I meant it, but..."

He ignored the sudden tightness in his chest and kept his voice light. "I had a feeling there was going to be a *but*."

She sighed. "This is hard to say, because maybe I'm making an assumption that isn't true, but...well, the only way I can continue to help you is if we keep our relationship strictly business."

"*Are* you going to keep helping me?"

"I want to, but I won't be able to if...if anything like last night happens again."

Jack sighed. He knew what she was saying made sense. Hadn't he been saying the same thing to himself all day long? Why was it, then, that he didn't feel relieved that she had reached the same conclusion? Why this curious, hollow, let-down feeling? "Am I allowed to ask why you feel this way?" he said stiffly, knowing he was being unfair, knowing she was right, yet unable to help himself.

Now it was her turn to sigh. When she answered, there was only the barest trace of a tremor in her voice—the only giveaway that she was the least bit agitated. "Before I answer that question, will you answer one of mine?"

"All right."

"Do you like your job?"

"I love my job."

"What do you like best about it?"

Jack hesitated, but her honesty with him compelled him to be honest with her. "The stimulation, the challenge, the travel, the excitement and adventure."

"Jack," she said softly. "You and I are poles apart in what we want out of life, and I think you know that. There's no room in my life for a casual love affair. I don't want to get too deeply involved with someone who's going to move on to the next adventure as soon as he finishes his business in New Orleans. I don't want to get hurt again."

Jack was ashamed of himself. "You're right. I know you're right. I'm sorry."

She immediately turned toward him, touched his forearm. "No, don't blame yourself. What happened just...well, it just happened."

Jack yielded to the impulse to cover her fingers with his own. A sharp sense of loss stabbed him. "I hope we can still be friends," he said, his voice husky with regret.

"I want that, too. More than anything." She gently pulled her hand away.

His skin still tingled from her touch. He wished...he wasn't sure what he wished. He wanted to tell her how much he admired her, how much he wished things *could* be different between them, but he didn't say anything.

Because Desiree was right.

They *were* poles apart.

Anything other than friendship between them would just be asking for trouble.

And nothing would ever change that.

Chapter Seven

The weather turned cool again, and some of the leaves began to change color. But Desiree didn't have much time to enjoy the nice weather because for the rest of that week and into the following week she had to work overtime every night. Julie had a full caseload, and in addition to doing Julie's work, Desiree had been assigned a new associate attorney—Barry Sylvester. She complained to Julie, who, in turn, complained to Claude Villac, the office administrator, but he was adamant.

"We've got a hiring freeze on now, and Desiree is the only secretary, besides mine, of course, who isn't already handling more than one attorney's work. Use your paralegal more."

"I felt like telling the old geezer that there was a darned good reason why I've had you exclusively, and that's because I've got the heaviest caseload!" Julie said, voice spewing disgust, as she repeated the conversation to Desiree. "I'll make it up to you, *chère,*" Julie mimicked, in a perfect imitation of Mr. Villac's French accent—an accent he cultivated to remind everyone of his roots as a descendant of an aristocratic and influential Creole family who had helped shape New Orlean's destiny. "And they'd darned well better! When my name comes up for senior partner, they'd better remember who's bringing in the most money around here!"

Julie was the best trial lawyer in the firm. Before hiring her, Fortier, Montegut, and Villac had rarely handled any criminal cases. Now, although the old guard decried the notoriety some of Julie's cases had brought to them, all had to privately admit that the income and referrals that came as a result of her skill and hard work were welcome.

But Desiree had her doubts that Julie would ever be named a senior partner. No woman had ever made senior partner in the firm's one-hundred-and-sixty-four-year history.

"He *did* say," Julie added with a grimace, "that the situation was only temporary. That as soon as the hiring freeze is lifted, they'll get someone else to do Sylvester's secretarial work." She sighed. "And I guess I *will* have to use Francesca more." She made a face, and Desiree couldn't help laughing. Francesca Lamont, the paralegal Julie shared with another of the junior partners, was the office joke. "Perhaps you could teach her how to file," was Julie's parting shot.

Desiree laughed again, resigned to her fate. She knew that if Julie hadn't been able to budge Mr. Villac, no one could, because even though Mr. Villac might not vote for a partnership for Julie, it was obvious to everyone in the firm that he had a soft spot in his heart for her.

Besides, there was a silver lining to Desiree's overloaded schedule. Because she was so busy, she hadn't had much time to think about Jack.

She hadn't seen him in nine days—since the previous Tuesday—although they'd talked several times by phone. He had spent the previous week following up leads connected with the fourteen attorneys whose names she'd provided him, and he'd just gotten back to New Orleans the previous evening. She and Aimee had been snuggled up together on one of the love seats when Jack had called to let her know he was back and to report on his progress.

"So it was another dead end?" Desiree asked, trying to ignore the pleasure she felt at hearing his voice.

"Yeah. It turns out this guy *did* have a daughter, but the ages don't match up. If he would have only agreed to talk to me on the phone, I could've spared myself a trip to Shreveport."

Desiree could hear the weariness in his voice. "You're discouraged, aren't you?"

"It's hard not to be. The thing is, I can't spend much more time on this. My leave is technically up on Monday, although I called my boss earlier today and told him I wouldn't be back to work until after Thanksgiving."

Desiree's heart plummeted at his words. She tried to keep her dismay from showing in her voice. "So you'll be going back to Houston," she said quietly, admitting to herself for the first time since she'd said she wanted a 'strictly business' relationship, that there had always been a glimmer of hope that somehow, something would happen to allow her to explore her growing feelings for Jack.

"What...what are you planning to do tomorrow?" she said.

"I still have five attorneys to check out. I'll get back on that."

For a moment they both fell silent. Then Jack said, "Well, I guess I should let you go. You're probably busy." There was a note of wistfulness in his voice, Desiree thought, or was that just wishful thinking on her part?

"I was reading to Aimee," she admitted, reluctant to say goodbye, "but I was almost finished."

There was an awkward silence. Then he cleared his throat and said, "I've missed seeing you."

Desiree's heart contracted. *Oh, Jack, I've missed you, too.* Good resolutions forgotten, she said, "You sound like a man in need of company." Ignoring her inner voice, which was telling her she'd be sorry, she plunged on. "What are you doing tomorrow night?"

"Tomorrow? I don't know. Nothing, I guess."

"Julie—my boss—and I are planning to go to a favorite haunt of mine—a Cajun restaurant-dance hall called Michaul's. It's a great place with great food. Would you like to go with us?"

"That sounds like fun. But I don't dance."

"It doesn't matter. It's fun to watch. There're a lot of regulars who go, and they can really dance. Do you like Cajun music?"

"I love it."

Desiree smiled, glad she'd asked him. He needed to relax and have some fun and forget about everything. She was a big girl. She could handle one evening in his company. There was no harm in being kind to him. Besides, she told herself, Julie would get a kick out of meeting him.

"What time do you want me to pick you up?" he asked.

"Oh, you don't have to come out here to get me. We'll meet you there."

"It's no trouble."

Desiree gave in with no further argument. She ignored the small voice inside that said, *now, this isn't a good idea.* She refused to examine her real motives. She was just being a friend. Jack was lonely. He was discouraged. He didn't know anyone else in New Orleans. She'd do the same for anyone.

But after they'd hung up, and she'd gone back to Aimee and the Dr. Seuss book she'd been reading to her, Desiree admitted that even though all those reasons she'd given herself were true, there was another, more compelling reason she'd invited Jack to go out with them the following evening.

She couldn't stand the thought of never seeing him again.

Friday dragged.

Barry Sylvester, who was turning out to be a real pain-in-the-neck with his eager-beaver, who-can-I-impress mentality and his supreme confidence that his law degree made him at least twice as intelligent as Desiree, drove her crazy the entire morning.

He hovered over her desk, asked her five times if she'd finished the Houghton brief and made her redo a letter three times—because he changed his mind about what he wanted to say. The last time he had told her she would have to redo the letter "because I've made some corrections"—and made it sound as if *she* was the one who had made a mistake—she nearly hit him.

Finally, just before noon, Desiree marched into Julie's office, shut the door firmly and said through gritted teeth, "If someone doesn't get Barry off my back, I may kill him."

Julie pursed her lips, studied Desiree's furious expression for a few seconds, then stood. She sighed. "Okay. Tell him I want to see him."

Five minutes later, a red-faced Barry emerged from Julie's office. He sent Desiree a look filled with daggers, but she didn't care. Barry was a jerk. He had a lot of growing up to do.

Five minutes after that episode, Guy D'Amato entered Desiree's cubicle and leaned over her desk. "Hi." He smiled.

Oh, dear, she thought. *Not today.* "Hi, Guy," she said with a sigh.

"How's it going today?"

Desiree made a face. "I've had better days."

"Oh?" His gray eyes clouded with concern, and he pushed his glasses up on his nose.

Why did Guy have to be so nice? she wondered. She would have taken great pleasure in brushing off someone like Barry, but Guy was another story. She inclined her head toward Barry's alcove and muttered, "I'm having problems with the new associate."

"Oh. Well, he'll learn."

"Yeah, but will I live long enough?" She grinned. "Actually, will *he* live long enough? If he doesn't straighten out his act soon, I'll probably poison him."

Guy gave an appreciative laugh. "Not you. You're too nice."

That's exactly what I was thinking about you.

He cleared his throat. "Uh, I was hoping you'd have some time for me this weekend."

"Oh, Guy, I'm sor—"

"Don't say no again, Desiree. I've hardly seen you for two weeks."

Desiree bit her bottom lip, remembering she'd half promised him the previous Friday, when she'd pleaded exhaustion, that she'd try to clear time for him this weekend.

"First you went home for the weekend, then last weekend you were too tired because of all the overtime. . . ." His voice trailed off.

Why did he remind her of a dog who just wants someone to pat him on the head and tell him they like him? Why couldn't Guy produce tingles and shivers and butterflies and all those symptoms that made a woman *want* to go out with a man? A vivid image of Jack—suntanned face, blue, blue eyes, and irresistible grin—flashed through her mind.

She could hardly believe only two weeks had gone by since she'd met Jack. He was already more important to her than Guy could ever be. The knowledge saddened her. "Guy," she said gently. "I really am sorry, but it doesn't look good for this weekend, either. I...I have a friend in town, and I'm going to be tied up."

His face filled with disappointment.

Oh, God. She hated to hurt him. She hated to hurt anyone. "I'm sorry," she said again.

His eyes were filled with a hurt he didn't even try to disguise. He shrugged, the gesture poignant and resigned.

"I..." *Oh, shoot.* "Maybe we can get together Sunday night." The minute she made the offer, she was sorry. "I can't promise anything, but give me a call Sunday afternoon, okay?"

His hopeful expression made her feel terrible.

After he walked away, she knew she was going to have to do something about Guy... and soon. It wasn't fair to him to let him think there could ever be anything between them. At one time, she might have kidded herself into thinking she'd come to care for him. But now that she'd met Jack and realized that what she was looking for actually existed, she knew there'd never be any hope for her and Guy.

The trouble was, there wasn't any hope for her and Jack, either.

Jack had really missed Desiree more than he'd ever thought possible. He didn't know how it had happened, but she had, in a short space of time, become important to him. He knew it was probably foolish to have accepted her invitation for the evening, but he couldn't help being glad she'd invited him to tag along with her and her boss.

He didn't know what people wore to a Cajun restaurant where they played zydeco music and danced, but he didn't really have much choice. All he'd brought with him was one suit—which he darned sure knew he shouldn't wear—and casual clothes. He figured in the unlikely event he needed anything dressier, he could buy it. So far he hadn't felt the need to go shopping.

After looking through his meagre supply of clothing, Jack decided on one of his newer pairs of jeans and a royal blue crewneck sweater. He checked himself out in the mirror, decided he didn't look bad and picked up his jacket and keys.

It didn't take long at all to get to Desiree's, and he ended up being fifteen minutes early. It was only six forty-five. He parked the car in the driveway, noticed that except for the back porch light, no lights shone at the Reed-Douglas house.

He walked along the back path to Desiree's cottage. He rang the bell, a nice feeling of expectation firing his gut.

Desiree opened the door and smiled, a smile that socked him in the solar plexus. "Hi," she said brightly. "You're early. Come on in. The sitter's not here yet, but she should be any minute. She just lives up the street." She stood aside.

He walked past her, then turned. When he got his first full look at her, he thought his heart would give out.

Lord have mercy, he thought. There ought to be a law or something.

She looked incredible. Sassy. Sexy. Stunning. He couldn't think of any word that did her justice. He swallowed, his throat suddenly dry.

She was wearing a short black leather skirt that ended midthigh, paired with black tights that hugged her long, lovely legs. On her feet were patent leather shoes with tiny heels.

Clinging to her torso like a second skin was a long-sleeved, round-necked, black knit top studded with silver bangles and sequins. The delectable curves of her full breasts were outlined in breathtaking clarity.

Slowly, his gaze traveled up, past the enticing arch of her slender neck to her faintly flushed cheeks and bright eyes. Her hair tumbled around her face in wild curls, and long, sparkley silver-and-crystal earrings dusted her shoulders. She knew he was inspecting her. She probably knew exactly what reaction he was experiencing.

Their gazes met. She lifted her chin, dark eyes flashing.

Jack decided she was magnificent.

He loved her outfit.

And he knew she knew he loved it.

In a voice not quite steady, he said, "You look great."

"Thanks. These are my dancin' clothes." She grinned.

She walked ahead of him into the living room, and Jack wiped his suddenly clammy hands against his jeans.

To cover his agitation, he sat down on a love seat and crossed his legs. To his relief, Aimee came racing into the room a second or so later. She looked adorable in pink bunny-footed pajamas, her cheeks a matching shade. Her blond curls were still damp from her bath. She grinned when she saw him. "Jack Rabbit!"

"I think you're the rabbit tonight," he said, grinning at her, thinking if he could be sure he'd have a child like Aimee, he might not mind having children. He pointed at her feet.

She giggled, the sound warm and wonderful. She peeked at him through her long lashes. She was definitely going to be a charmer. Rather like her mother, he thought, giving Desiree a glance over Aimee's head.

He was disconcerted by the expression in Desiree's eyes, an expression she quickly covered by saying brightly, "Did you brush your teeth, sugar?"

"Uh-huh," Aimee said with a nod. She grinned at Jack again.

He grinned back, wondering what that expression had been. Could it have been wistful? And if so, what had it meant?

Just then there was a knock on the door, and Desiree stood and walked over to answer it. As she passed by Jack, he caught a whiff of her perfume—something that smelled like sandalwood and jasmine.

"Hi, Heather! You're right on time," Desiree said.

A pretty red-headed teenager walked into the room, and Aimee shouted, "Heather!"

"Hi, Aimee," the girl said. She gave Jack a shy look.

Desiree introduced them, then proceeded to give Heather some instructions. "Don't let her stay up past eight o'clock. She can have some ice cream, but she'll have to brush her teeth again if she does. The ice cream is in the freezer. And help yourself to soft drinks or chips or whatever you want. You know where everything is."

Heather nodded.

"And we'll be at Michaul's in case of an emergency. I wrote the number down by the phone," Desiree continued. "Oh, and the Reed-Douglases will be home by ten or so, so if you should need them—"

"I know. Don't worry."

Within minutes, they were on their way. Jack had never been as aware of anyone as he was of Desiree sitting so close to him in his two-seater car. Her scent filled his senses. She hadn't put her jacket on, and the sequins and bangles on her shirt glittered in the darkness. Jack wanted to touch her more than he'd wanted anything in a long time. She reminded him of the North Star, so radiant and so beautiful it overshadowed everything in its realm.

He couldn't remember when he'd last felt this way. The only experience at all similar was when he was a sophomore in high school and Susan Richardson, the most beautiful girl at his school, had been his date for a big dance. He'd been so excited, and so hopeful, and so scared. Jack could still recall exactly how he'd felt when he'd kissed her, how his hands had shaken, how his heart had pounded.

He felt exactly the same way now.

Only now he was a grown man, and the feelings were much more powerful.

Desiree Cantrelle was as dangerous to his equilibrium and his future as a stick of dynamite wired to go off at the first touch.

Michaul's was more and less than Jack had expected. It was not pretentious at all. The floors were bare, the tables were plain, the decor was more warehouse than restaurant. But the band, three young Cajun men and a thin woman who played the washboard, were terrific. Their music was infectious and toe-tapping, although Jack couldn't understand a word they were singing. They all sounded as if they had mouths full of marbles.

He and Desiree had arrived at the restaurant ten minutes early, so they were already seated close to the bandstand when Julie arrived.

"There's Julie," Desiree said, rising to meet her.

Jack watched curiously as she walked over to a short, dark-haired young woman. They hugged, and then, arms linked, walked toward Jack.

"Julie, I'd like you to meet Jack Forrester. Jack, this is Julie Belizaire, my boss and my friend."

Jack extended his hand. Julie's hand was small, her handshake firm.

"I've heard a lot about you," she said in a rapid, precise voice with only a trace of a Southern accent. She grinned. "All good, of course."

She had a nice smile, and a direct, honest gaze. Her round face was spattered with freckles, and her eyes looked green or hazel. He wasn't sure which. He decided he liked her.

For the next hour he enjoyed listening to the two women talk. At first he'd thought they were a study in contrasts, but now he was beginning to realize there were a lot of similarities between them. They were both lively, animated women with the gift of warmth. And he could see how much they liked each other, something that impressed him. In his experience, if a woman didn't have women friends, she was probably a woman he'd rather steer clear of.

After they'd all eaten and the table was cleared away, like an unseen signal had been given, two men walked over to the table. They nodded to Jack, then looked at Desiree and Julie.

Desiree smiled. "Hi, Don, Grady. How are y'all doin'?"

Jack smiled at Desiree's new persona. He wondered if she even realized that she'd lapsed into her native accent.

"We're doin' fine," the tallest man drawled. "We're glad to see y'all back. Y'all haven't been around for a coupla weeks." He reached out his hand, and Desiree stood. The other man went around for Julie.

Desiree slanted Jack a glance. She smiled. "You don't mind, do you, Jack?"

He shook his head. "No, of course not. Go ahead."

He turned his chair so he could watch her dance.

The band struck up a lilting number, with a catchy rhythm that Jack would have been hard-pressed to define. He noticed how almost everyone in the place got up for this dance and how different it seemed to be from the others he'd witnessed.

The dance floor was huge, a football-shaped field designed to hold a lot of people and give them room to move freely. All the dancers stood in rows, not paired. They all moved independently, but their moves all matched. They dipped and turned, and did intricate footwork.

All the waiters and waitresses were up there, too. Jack wished he had some dancing ability. He would have loved to be there with them.

Even though Jack couldn't dance himself, he recognized excellence when he saw it. And Desiree was spectacular. Her body moved fluidly and effortlessly. Her head swayed from side to side, and with each movement the glittery earrings and tank top flashed and sparkled.

He couldn't take his eyes off her.

When the dance was over she stayed on the floor, and this time the tall man who'd come to get her put his arms around her and they began an energetic, foot-stomping dance to much faster music. Desiree's hair swirled out each time her partner twirled her around, and her head was thrown back in laughter most of the dance. Jack couldn't prevent a twinge of envy as he saw how much fun she was having. His only consolation was there was nothing remotely romantic about the dance.

The next dance was different.

The next dance was slow and seductive, and Desiree's partner pulled her close, and the two of them moved as one through the steps, their bodies closely meshed.

Jack's stomach twisted into knots as he watched them. He saw how Desiree's partner had one hand resting low on her back. He gritted his teeth. An inch lower and he'd be caressing her rump. He couldn't tear his eyes away from the two of them.

"Hey, it's only a dance."

He started. Julie had sat down across from him. He hadn't even been aware she'd come back to the table. She smiled knowingly. "Don's just a dancing friend. Desiree doesn't date him. She never has. There's no reason for you to be jealous."

"I'm not jealous," Jack said quickly, too quickly.

In answer, Julie's smile broadened. Her eyes gleamed. "Sure looks like it to me."

"Well, maybe, just a little—"

She chuckled. "At least you're honest. Some guys would never admit to being jealous."

"Desiree seems to bring out all sorts of new feelings in me."

Julie's expression sobered. "Jack, I know this is none of my business, but I'm going to say it anyway. I can see how attracted to Desiree you are. I don't really blame you. She's a wonderful girl. But—"

"But what?"

Julie sighed. "She's extremely vulnerable. I know she doesn't look it. On the surface she seems bold and confident and completely sure of herself. She looks as if she knows the score, as if she can handle anything. But that's not the real Desiree. The real Desiree has a tremendous need for love and security. She needs someone she can count on, someone who can give her a lasting relationship. She especially needs someone who won't take everything she has to give, then run out on her."

"Is that what you think I'd do?" He wanted to be angry with Desiree's friend, but her words were too disturbing. They echoed his own feelings too accurately.

"Isn't it?" Julie challenged.

He shrugged. "I don't know."

"Well, Jack, I suggest you give this matter some thought, and decide whether you will or you won't. And if you decide you don't want the things Desiree wants, I strongly suggest you pack up your marbles and go home."

Chapter Eight

*P*ack up your marbles and go home.

The words reverberated in Jack's brain. Throughout the evening, each time his gaze met Julie's, he remembered the admonition. And when he and Desiree, after seeing Julie safely to her car, were on their way back to Desiree's home, he remembered them again.

The evening had been wonderful.

The evening had been terrible.

Wonderful because he'd so enjoyed being with Desiree and watching her dance.

Terrible because he knew Julie was right.

I won't touch her tonight. She's set the ground rules, and I'll follow them.

But when they walked together through the inky darkness toward her front door, Desiree only tempting inches away, her scent surrounding him in the navy night, he wondered if he'd be able to stick to his determination.

He didn't really have a choice.

When they reached Desiree's door, she promptly opened it. And Heather, the baby-sitter, was sitting right there, in the living room. She looked up as they entered. "Hi. Did you have fun?"

"Yes, lots of fun," Desiree said.

And then she asked him if he'd mind taking Heather home.

"No, I can walk," the girl protested. "It's only half a block. I'll call my dad like I usually do."

"There's no need since Jack is here."

Jack guessed he should be grateful Desiree had made things so easy for him.

While Heather gathered her things, he said, "I really enjoyed tonight. Thanks."

She smiled, causing his heart to speed up. That smile of hers was as potent as 100-proof scotch. "I'm glad you came."

"Is it okay if I give you a call tomorrow?"

"Sure." Her dark eyes held an unreadable expression.

Later that night, as he tried to go to sleep, he went over and over everything that had happened that night. How he'd felt seeing Desiree. His emotions when he watched her dancing with other men. What Julie had said. And especially those fleeting emotions he'd glimpsed in Desiree's eyes—first when he had been talking to Aimee, then when she'd said goodbye.

What would have happened between them if Heather hadn't been there? Would he have been strong enough to withstand his attraction to Desiree? Or would his good intentions have evaporated under the powerful emotions and desires she elicited?

And what would she have done if he'd gathered her into his arms and kissed her? Would she have pushed him away, reminded him of their agreement?

Or would she have succumbed to the electrical charge that sizzled between them?

Would she have let him come into her bed?

He guessed he'd never know.

Desiree decided she couldn't trust herself to see Jack again. And if he called her today, as he said he was going to, she would firmly refuse any invitation he might extend.

All Saturday morning she repeated this vow. While she cleaned the bathroom. While she did the laundry. While she dusted and ran the vacuum. While she helped Aimee pick up her toys.

She said it again while she prepared lunch. And again while she and Aimee ate their macaroni and cheese. She said it one more time as she settled Aimee in for her nap and prepared to take a long, relaxing bubble bath. This was the first day she'd had off in a while. She might as well enjoy it.

The phone rang just as she had stripped off her clothes and put one foot into the tub. She grabbed for her robe and raced to the phone, hoping its ring wouldn't wake Aimee.

"Hello," she said breathlessly.

"Hi."

Jack. Just the sound of his voice, soft and husky, caused her insides to flutter alarmingly. "Hi."

"Are you busy?"

"No. I was just getting ready to soak in the tub."

"Oh, I'm sorry. Shall I call you back?"

"No!" She softened her voice, embarrassed. So much for good intentions. "I can talk now. In fact, it's a great time. Aimee's taking her nap. What're you doing?"

"Oh, nothing much. I spent the morning going over my notes. Trying to decide what approach to take next."

There was a short silence, then he said, "Would you let me take you and Aimee to dinner tonight?"

"Oh, Jack..."

"I thought about you all night."

Her heart teetered alarmingly. She wanted to say yes. "Jack, we agreed—"

"I know what we agreed. But I don't have much time left here, and...well, Aimee'll be with us."

She had absolutely no spine. No sense. "Okay, what time do you want to pick us up?"

Desiree knew she'd always remember the evening. Everything about it was perfect. Jack showed up dressed in a dark suit that complemented his blond good looks and set her heart to racing. She knew the three of them looked nice together. She was wearing a matching lightweight wool skirt and sweater in a soft peach shade, and Aimee was dressed in a blue dress with eyelet ruffles.

Jack took them to The Court of Two Sisters. Aimee behaved like an angel. The food was fabulous. And Jack was a charming host.

Desiree knew how dangerous it was, but she pretended they were a family. She watched Jack and Aimee together. She saw how much pleasure he seemed to derive from Aimee's company and her obvious affection for him. Like mother, like daughter, Desiree thought. We know a good thing when we see him.

Later, when he brought them home and carried a sleepy Aimee to the door, Desiree's heart twisted as she saw how Aimee had curled into his embrace, how her little arms had instinctively twined around his neck. A fierce longing shot through Desiree. If only things could be different. If only

Jack wasn't Jack. If only he didn't have the kind of career he had, the kind of life-style he had. If only he wanted the same things Desiree wanted.

She swallowed over a sudden lump in her throat.

Jack even helped her get Aimee ready for bed. And after Desiree tucked her in, he bent over the bed and kissed Aimee's forehead. "Good night, honey," he murmured.

"'Night, Jack Rabbit," Aimee said. "I love you."

Desiree saw his shoulders stiffen. She couldn't see his expression. "I love you, too, sweetheart," he said, so low Desiree hardly heard the answer. She bit her bottom lip, blinked furiously to keep tears from falling. Suddenly she couldn't stand it anymore. The knowledge hit her like a bat slamming into a ball, hard, powerful, undeniable.

She was falling in love with Jack Forrester.

And she didn't know if she could let him go without ever having known what it was like to make love with him.

Desiree didn't see Jack for the next three days. On Saturday night, he'd left soon after helping her put Aimee to bed, because Desiree, shaken and afraid, had said she was tired. Then she took a sleeping pill. She didn't want to lie in bed thinking. She didn't want to examine her feelings. She didn't want to try to decide what to do. Not that night.

But all day Sunday she thought about him. And when Guy called her Sunday afternoon, she hardened her heart. She might not know what to do about her feelings for Jack, but she knew exactly what she had to do about her feelings for Guy. So she invited Guy to come for dinner, and somehow she got through the evening.

As soon as the kitchen was cleaned up and Aimee settled, Desiree said, "Guy, we've got to talk."

Then she took him into the living room, and as kindly and gently as she could, she told him she didn't think they should see each other again. When he asked why, she told him that, too.

"I just don't feel about you the way a woman contemplating a serious relationship with a man should feel. I like you. I respect you. But I'm not romantically interested in you. I'm sorry."

After Guy left, she sank down on the couch and cried.

Monday was an awful day, but then most Mondays were. Desiree didn't have much time to think, and when her thoughts did stray in Jack's direction, she pushed them away.

Monday night they talked by phone, and he was solicitous. He brought her up to date on his activities that day and told her he had now contacted all the attorneys on his list. He sighed. "I sure had hoped to come up with something. I wish there was someone else I could talk to."

Desiree thought fleetingly of her Uncle Justin in Lafayette. But he was retired now, and she knew he had no knowledge of Elise Arnold. So she didn't say anything.

"I've got a couple of other things to check out tomorrow and Wednesday, and then I guess I'll be done."

Pain squeezed Desiree's heart. Thursday was Thanksgiving. Was he going to go home Wednesday night? She was afraid to ask. She was afraid not to ask. "I . . ." She cleared her throat. "I guess you want to be home Thursday."

"Thursday?"

"You know, for Thanksgiving."

"Oh, yeah . . . Thanksgiving."

He sounded uncertain, which surprised her. "Won't you be spending Thanksgiving with your family?"

She heard him sigh. "No. My parents left Saturday for a two-week Mediterranean cruise."

"But your sister—"

"Is going to Boston with her husband. His family lives there."

"You mean you'll be all alone for Thanksgiving?"

"It's no big deal. I'm used to spending holidays by myself. I hardly ever think about it."

Desiree was appalled. She couldn't imagine spending a holiday without family around. How could he bear it? No one should be alone on a holiday. She didn't even have to think about what she should do. "Jack, I'm going home to Patinville for the four-day weekend. Would you like to come with me?"

When he didn't immediately answer, Desiree wondered if he was trying to come up with an excuse, an easy way to say no without hurting her feelings. But then he said, "I can't think of anything I'd like more," and her heartbeat escalated.

She smiled. She knew it was foolhardy to take him with her. She knew she was asking to get hurt. She knew she would probably regret this decision.

But she didn't care.

She could hardly wait until Wednesday.

Jack offered to drive to Patinville. Desiree asked him if he'd mind driving her car since his didn't have a back seat. "Your car isn't designed for children," she said.

He agreed with her suggestion, so, early Thursday morning, after moving her Geo out of the garage and putting his car in its place, they left for Patinville.

"Tell me about your family before we get there," Jack said.

"What do you want to know?"

"Oh, you know, some history. Hit the high spots. I know you have two brothers. Start with them."

Desiree got more comfortable in the passenger seat. "Why don't I start with my parents, instead?" When he didn't disagree, she said, "My father is seventy-three years old, retired from the family business but still very active physically. He's energetic and enthusiastic about life. You'll like him. My mother just turned seventy. She's a lot like my father, but she's more stubborn and bossy than he is. She's a typical Cajun mother—loves her children to distraction, tries to tell us all what to do, feeds us until we're miserable."

"You love them," he said softly.

"I adore them. They're wonderful parents."

"What about your sister and brothers?"

"Well, Denise is the oldest. She's forty-three, she's married to Jett Hebert, and they have two children, Jeannine, who is fifteen, and Justin, who is ten. Denise and Jett own a little restaurant in Patinville—I'll take you there this weekend—and they both work in it."

"What kind of restaurant?"

"Cajun. What else?"

He chuckled. "Suits me. I love the food."

"Me, too."

"Continue... After Denise comes, who... Neil?"

"Yes. You remembered. I'm impressed." She knew it was silly to derive so much pleasure from the fact that she was important enough to him that he'd remember her brother's name. Then she realized it probably wasn't just *her* that was important, but any Cantrelle. She knew Jack was still convinced there was some connection between her and Elise Arnold. That was one of the reasons she was glad she was taking him home to meet her family. Maybe he'd finally accept that there *was* no connection.

"How old is Neil?"

"He'll have his forty-first birthday in just a few weeks. Gosh, that's hard to believe."

"What's he like?"

"You and Neil will probably hit it off. He's an ex-cop, was on the Baton Rouge Police Force for twelve years. He's quieter than most of my family, more introspective, more thoughtful. He's had some hard knocks, but he's survived them. He had a disastrous first marriage, but now he's married to a wonderful woman. Her name is Laura, and they're wild about each other. They have a little girl, Celeste, who's four. She and Aimee are like this." Desiree held two fingers close together. "And Laura is expecting their second child in May."

"And after Neil..." Jack prompted.

"Comes Norman, who is thirty-seven. He's totally different from Neil. Norman's outgoing, physical, rarely takes life too seriously, thinks the best of everyone. His biggest fault is his tendency to want to take care of everybody, including me. He's an amputee, has an artificial right leg."

"Oh? How'd that happen?"

"A bad automobile accident five years ago." Desiree sighed, remembering the trauma of those days when the entire family was afraid Norman might lose his life as well as his leg. "He's bounced back, though. He's married to one of the nicest women you'll ever meet. Her name is Alice. She has two children from her first marriage—Lisa, who I think is ten, and Jimmy, who's about sixteen. And Alice is also expecting a baby about the same time as Laura."

"And then there's you."

"Yes, and then there's me."

"It's kind of intimidating—"

"What? My family?"

"The sheer size of your family."

"I haven't even mentioned all my uncles, aunts and cousins. We counted them up once, and I think there are close to one hundred Cantrelles and DesJardins—my mother was a DesJardin—and that's just counting the *first* cousins!"

Jack whistled. "Incredible. My entire family consists of my folks, my sister and her husband, and my mother's one brother who never married."

"That's it?"

"That's it."

Desiree couldn't imagine the kind of family Jack described. She loved the feeling of belonging to so many people—the roots and traditions and settled feeling it gave her. No wonder Jack had chosen his nomadic life-style. No wonder he didn't seem to mind when he spent holidays alone. No wonder he seemed to have no desire to establish a home. He'd never known anything else but what he had now.

Poor Jack, she thought. *And poor me. Just my luck to get interested in a man like him.*

She wondered what her family would think of him.

Jack's first impression of Patinville was that it was a nice little town, if you liked nice little towns.

He had always preferred cities. Exciting, noisy, invigorating cities like New York City, Hong Kong, San Francisco, Singapore, London. Of course, he was unencumbered and had always had enough money to travel first-class, stay in the nicest places and avail himself of everything these cities had to offer. He knew that made a difference.

If he were to ever settle down in one place—a very unlikely occurrence—he supposed it might be nice to live somewhere similar to Patinville.

It seemed to him they had no sooner entered Patinville than they were arriving at Desiree's parents' home. It was a modest brick ranch house set at the edge of a wooded area on a dead-end street. When he pulled Desiree's Geo into the driveway, an older couple emerged from the front door.

Amid a flurry of hugs and kisses and exclamations on the part of Desiree and her parents, he watched quietly from the sidelines. An unfamiliar feeling crept into his chest as he saw how much these people all loved one another, how obvious it was that Desiree's parents missed her terribly.

Then Desiree turned to him, and smiling, beckoned him forward. "Jack, I'd like you to meet my parents, René and Arlette Cantrelle. Mama, Papa, this is Jack Forrester, a friend of mine."

Her father, a robust-looking man with thick salt-and-pepper hair and lively dark eyes very like Desiree's, extended his hand, saying, "Hello, Jack. It's very nice to have you come to our home." His handshake was surprisingly strong for a man of his age. He smiled, and Jack thought he must have been a real lady-killer in his younger days.

"Nice to meet you, Mr. Cantrelle."

René frowned. "We're not so formal around here, no. Call me René."

Jack smiled. "René."

Now Desiree's mother, a short, plump woman with short gray hair and eyes as dark as her husband's, smiled and welcomed him. Jack noticed that she gave him a very close inspection, and he wanted to smile again. Arlette Cantrelle was definitely a protective mother hen who wondered if her chick was in safe hands around Jack. He wished he could reassure her, but lately, he wasn't sure if it *was* safe for Desiree to be around him.

He looked at her now, as she walked arm in arm with her mother up the walk toward the front door. She wore snug-fitting jeans that hugged her long legs and shapely rear end. The jeans were paired with a bright red sweater, and she'd tied a red ribbon around her head. She looked young, gorgeous and deliciously sexy. No. Her mother was right to look him over. He only hoped he'd disguised his baser tendencies.

The inside of the house matched the outside: simple, homey, welcoming. After showing Jack the room he'd be using for the duration of their stay—"This used to be our sons' room," explained Arlette—he unpacked his few things, then joined the family in the big kitchen at the back of the house.

Delicious smells surrounded him. Some he recognized; others he didn't. There were several pots simmering on the stove, and he knew there was a turkey roasting in the oven. His mouth watered. He hadn't eaten breakfast.

As if she were a mind reader, Desiree's mother said, "Are you hungry, Jack?"

He grinned. "Always."

"We're not goin' to have our dinner for a couple of hours yet, but I've got some snacks." She gave René a mock frown. "I'll bring the snacks into the livin' room. Why don't you two go watch the football games or somethin' so Desiree and I can talk?" She gave Jack a sly grin. "Woman talk, you know."

Soon Jack was comfortably settled into a big easy chair, a cold beer in one hand, and something Arlette called a sausage ball in the other, one eye on college football and the other on Aimee and her grandfather. She was sitting on René's lap, and he was whispering in her ear. She giggled, the sound causing that funny little ache right around Jack's heart. It struck him that within just a few days, he would be back in Houston, back to his sterile life, and he wouldn't see enchanting Aimee or her equally enchanting mother again.

Sterile? Why had he thought of his life in those terms? It wasn't sterile at all. It was exciting and... The thought trailed off. It was exciting, yes. It was also lonely a lot of the time.

A feeling almost like depression settled into his chest, but he didn't have long to wallow in it because a few minutes later the front door burst open and a little blonde about Aimee's size came racing through. "Aimee, Aimee," she cried, and Aimee tumbled off René's lap. The two little girls stood there grinning at each other, then Aimee said, "Celesse! Come see my new doll!" and they dashed out of the room, squealing and laughing. Jack grinned at Aimee's mangled pronunciation of her cousin's name.

He stood, turning toward the couple who had entered the living room. René said, "Neil, Laura, I want you to meet Desiree's friend, Jack Forrester."

Neil Cantrelle, sharp eyes assessing Jack, held out his right hand. "Jack," he said.

"Neil." Jack turned to Neil's wife, a lovely, delicate-looking blonde with the bluest eyes he'd ever seen. "Hello, Laura."

She smiled and reached for his hand, too.

Then Desiree and her mother were in the room, and there was more hugging and kissing. Within ten minutes, more family arrived. This time it was Desiree's older sister, Denise, her friendly faced husband and their two children. And fifteen minutes later the other brother, Norman, accompanied by his pretty little wife, Alice, and two more children came in. By now people were sitting all over the place—some on the floor, some on arms of chairs.

Never in his life had Jack seen so much hugging and kissing or heard so much talking at once.

Soon the women all drifted off to the kitchen, and Jack could hear their laughing, chattering voices accompanying the clink and rattle of pots and dishes.

The children all wandered off into the family room to play video games, and soon only René, Jett Hebert, Neil and Norman Cantrelle, and Jack were left in the living room.

Neil turned to Jack. "So how long have you known Desiree?"

The question was innocent enough, but Jack knew a protective brother when he saw one. The thing was, he didn't blame Neil. If he had a sister like Desiree, he'd be protective, too. Lord knows, looking the way she did, she could use all the protecting she could get.

If he wasn't such a nice guy, he would've already tried to get into her bed.

"We met a few weeks ago." He wondered if he should elaborate, then decided he'd wait for Desiree to bring up the subject of Elise.

Suddenly René gave him a startled look. "You're the one she told me about. The one looking for that other girl."

So René remembered.

"What girl?" Norman and Neil said in unison.

"Some girl who looks like Desiree," René explained. "Jack thought—"

Jack decided to intervene. He explained his mission in New Orleans and how he and Desiree had gotten to be friends. "Anyway, she thought this weekend might be a good opportunity for me to talk to you about this, even though she said none of you would be able to help me."

Neil's dark eyes were still; Norman's eyes were narrowed, and Jack knew both brothers were taking his measure, deciding how they felt about his following their little sister home from work, deciding if they trusted him.

For the rest of the day—all through dinner, and after dinner, and into the evening, as they ate and drank and watched television and talked—Jack knew they were still trying to make up their minds. He tried in every way he knew to show them he was no threat to Desiree.

Finally, when Neil and Norman and their wives and children were ready to leave, Neil walked up to Jack and said, "Maybe you and Desiree would like to come over tomorrow night. We'll have a chance to talk more."

"Sounds good," Jack said.

Neil smiled, and Jack knew he'd passed the test, whatever it was.

Several times during the day, Desiree wondered what Jack was thinking. She saw how he hung back, watching and listening, instead of really taking part. Her family could be intimidating, she knew, but she hoped Jack liked them. She wasn't sure why this was so important to her—after all, Jack would be gone soon, so what did it matter?—but still, she was proud of her family, she loved them, and she wanted Jack to love them, too.

Why is that? Because you think if he loves them, somehow, magically, everything will be okay? That he'll suddenly change?

Desiree refused to listen to that carping inner voice that wouldn't seem to leave her alone.

By the time evening came, Jack had loosened up. When Denise asked him to tell them about his job, he complied.

"No two stories are ever the same," he said. "I've covered all kinds of wars, from simple skirmishes to full-blown air wars, and it's always different, always exciting."

"It also sounds dangerous," Denise commented.

"Yes, many times it is."

"How did you happen to become an investigative journalist?" Alice asked.

"I kind of fell into it. After I graduated from Stanford, I figured I owed myself a vacation. I'd been in school for six straight years, first getting my bachelor's degree, then my master's. Anyway, I set out to tour Europe, and while I was in London I got caught in the middle of an IRA bombing. I wasn't injured, but I saw everything that happened, and because I've always kept a journal, I wrote it all down and sent it to a friend of mine who works for the *Houston Herald*. The *Herald* published the story, and one thing led to another. Eventually I got an offer from World Press." A wry smile tipped his lips. "Now I can't imagine doing anything else. The work is addictive."

"Yes," Neil agreed. "It's like police work, I imagine. Once you've done something like it, it's hard to go back to being a plain, simple person with an ordinary job. Danger and tension are more powerful addictions than drugs or alcohol."

Jack nodded thoughtfully. "You're right. The danger and constant tension keep your wits sharp and your body in tune with all the forces around you. There's no other feeling that quite compares to it."

Denise cut a look Desiree's way, and Desiree saw it. She knew Denise well enough to know that her sister was already worried about Desiree ending up with a broken heart.

Desiree had to admit that Jack's words had given her pause. Down deep she'd always known his work was important to him; she just hadn't realized how all-encompassing it was, what a formidable rival it was.

She also hadn't realized what a difference there was in not only their family life, but in their educational and social backgrounds. When he'd told her about his mother and her charity work, it hadn't really registered in Desiree's mind, but Jack's parents were probably wealthy. He was even farther away from her in terms of background and interests than she could possibly have imagined. And when you added the fact that Desiree had had a child without benefit of marriage, well...

She tried to put her depressing thoughts out of her mind. She decided to enjoy the rest of the time she had with him, take what little she could get and then go on with her life.

She really had no other choice.

"Desiree," Laura said as she prepared to leave. "Can we take Aimee home with us to spend the night with Celeste?"

"Oh, I don't know—"

"Please, Mommy. Please."

"Please, Aunt Desiree," Celeste piped up, blue eyes that were exactly like her mother's—wide and beseeching.

"Oh, let the girls be together," Arlette said. "Come here, my babies, give Grandmama a kiss."

Desiree relented.

Soon everyone was gone except for her parents and Jack. Jack, who had been sitting in an easy chair with his legs stretched out in front of him, said, "I have to walk some of this food off." He rubbed his stomach. "I still hurt from everything your mother stuffed into me." He stood. "Want to go for a walk with me?"

Desiree nodded.

After they'd both donned jackets, they walked outside. The clear, cool night air whispered around them as they walked up the driveway and down the road toward the edge of the woods. Desiree looked up. A full moon was clearly visible in the starry night. She sighed. "It's beautiful out tonight, isn't it?

"Beautiful," he murmured.

Something about his tone caused her to look up, and what she saw there in his face, clearly visible in the bright moonlight, was enough to set her pulses racing.

Jack reached for her hand and tugged her toward the trees on the right side of the road. When the shadows engulfed them, he turned her to face him. His hands settled on her shoulders, and Desiree, whose heart was beating faster and faster, raised her eyes to meet his gaze.

"Desiree," he said, his voice gruff. "More than anything in the world, what I want right now is to kiss you."

They stared into each other's eyes as his words settled into her brain, beating there like the wings of a bird. All around them were soft night sounds: the rustle of some nocturnal animal deeper in the woods, the chirping of crickets, the distant sound of a car.

Desiree wet her lips and said huskily, "Then what are you waiting for?"

Chapter Nine

She lifted her face, and at the first touch of Jack's lips, all Desiree's sensible resolutions vanished. She wrapped her arms around his neck, and let him pull her close.

The world spun as she lost herself in his embrace. In that moment, nothing else existed.

Only Jack.

"Desiree," he muttered as his lips trailed down to her neck. "I don't know what's happening to me. I can't even think straight for wanting you."

Her heart thundered in her ears as his mouth captured hers again, his tongue thrusting deep inside, claiming her, branding her. Deep in her belly was an answering throb.

His hands kneaded her back, then slid lower, pressing her closer. A kaleidoscope of sensations rocketed through Desiree, consuming her like tongues of fire consuming dry wood.

She wanted him.

She wanted him with an intensity and hunger that was painful. And she knew he wanted her with the same powerful, driving need. For the hunger raging through her body was echoed in the hard, hot, pulsing answer she felt through the fabric of her jeans.

But sanity returned with the sound of an approaching car.

Desiree tore her mouth from his. "Jack—"

"No, don't. Don't turn away from me—" He pulled her deeper into the woods, away from sight, and tried to capture her mouth again, but she kept her head averted. "Oh, God . . ." he moaned, releasing her suddenly. "I'm sorry. I don't know why you have this effect on me, but all I have to do is touch you, and bingo, I lose control."

Desiree's heart still hammered in her chest, her breathing was still labored, and she still ached inside. She longed to appease the ache, but she knew tonight was not the time to do it.

She wasn't sure when the right time might be. She only knew she and Jack had to return to her parents' home, they had to go to separate rooms, and they had to pretend all was calm, all was normal. They had to pretend they'd taken a casual walk. They had to act like casual friends.

It might be the hardest thing Desiree had ever had to do.

"Jack," she said, finally looking up into his eyes. "It's not your fault. I wanted you to kiss me. I—I still want you to kiss me—" She raised her hands when he would have taken her in his arms again. "No, wait, let me finish. I—" Oh, shoot, she might as well be truthful with him. He knew how she felt anyway. She'd made her feelings all too plain. "I don't think this weekend is the time to explore our feelings. When we get back to New Orleans, we'll talk about it, okay?"

He hesitated, his eyes gleaming in the darkness, then said slowly, his voice rough and uneven, "It's not going to be easy, being around you for three more days, and not touching you.''

Desiree squeezed her eyes shut. Her emotions were so ragged, so frazzled, she felt as if she might burst into tears. Oh, God. She wanted him so. Why did he make her feel this way? Why did she care so much? Why had she fallen in love with him? For she *had* fallen in love with him, and she had to face it. No more pretending she might fall in love with Jack. She was all the way, head-over-heels, mindlessly, hopelessly in love with Jack Forrester. Mr. I-don't-need-anyone Jack Forrester. A man who was as different from her as the sun was from the moon, as night was from day. A man who would, without question, break her heart into tiny pieces and never look back.

''Let's walk,'' she said, more upset than she wanted him to see. She headed back toward the road and heard the rustle of leaves and twigs as he followed her.

They didn't talk. They walked around the neighborhood until Desiree felt calm again. Then she turned toward home, with him at her side.

When they reached her parents' home once more, Jack stopped her at the door. ''Are you okay?''

''Yes.''

He touched her cheek, and Desiree leaned into the caress. ''Desiree,'' he said softly. ''I promise you I'll never do anything unless you want me to.''

She nodded. She'd always known *she* would have to make the choice.

Still holding her cheek, he leaned forward and dropped a light, tender kiss on her half-open mouth. ''Ready?'' he whispered.

''As ready as I'll ever be.''

He nodded, opened the front door and stood back to let her walk in ahead of him.

* * *

On Saturday night Desiree and Jack were invited to join her siblings and their spouses at the local Knights of Columbus annual Thanksgiving dance.

"It'll be fun," Desiree promised. Her eyes twinkled. "And this time I'm going to make you get up and try the dances!"

"Oh, joy," Jack said. If there was anything he hated, it was making a fool of himself.

Desiree laughed.

The sound of her laughter never failed to stir him. There was something infectious about its uninhibited delight. He didn't think he'd ever get tired of listening to Desiree laugh. He also didn't think he'd ever get tired of looking at her. He looked at her now as she stood over the ice cream section of the local supermarket. She had volunteered her services when her mother mentioned needing some groceries, so Jack was pressed into service, too.

Today Desiree wore faded jeans, an oversized bright green sweater, green socks and loafers. Long silver earrings in the shape of stars swung from her ears. Everything about her glowed: her hair, her eyes, her skin, her smile, even her cherry-red lipstick. Jack thought she looked like an ornament—bright, shiny and beautiful.

"What?" she said, looking up and catching him studying her. She gave him a quizzical smile. "Do I have lipstick on my teeth or something?"

He shook his head.

She dropped a carton of pralines and cream into the shopping cart, but her gaze stayed riveted to his, compelling him to answer honestly. "I was just thinking how much I like being around you."

Pink tinged her cheekbones, but she didn't avert her gaze. "I like being with you, too," she said softly.

Something around Jack's heart tightened painfully. He would miss her when he returned to Houston. He would miss her very, very much.

That night, Denise and Jett came by the house to pick up Jack and Desiree. When the four of them entered the Knights of Columbus dance hall, the band was just warming up, but the big room was already three-quarters full.

"Cajuns take their dancing seriously," Desiree said.

"Are *all* these people Cajuns?"

"No, not all. Some are Italians. Some are Irish. But the majority are Cajuns—some full-blooded French and others with a bit of Spanish blood mixed in."

Soon Neil and Laura and Norman and Alice joined their group. They commandeered a long table toward the back of the hall. Jack looked around with interest. The musicians began warming up, and there were discordant sounds of guitars, keyboard and an accordion. The drummer did a few cadences, as well.

"This is the band that played for our wedding reception," Alice offered. "They're really good. The Bayou Boys."

Jack thought of the various wedding receptions he'd attended in Houston. Elegant country club affairs. He thought this might be a lot more fun.

Once the music started, both Jett Hebert and the Cantrelle brothers led their wives to the dance floor.

"Come on, Jack," Desiree said, laughing.

Jack knew this was a no-win situation. If he refused to go out and at least try the dance, Desiree and her family would think he was a poor sport. If he went out there and made the fool of himself he knew he would, they'd feel sorry for him. Of course, there *were* compensations, he decided, once he was actually up on the floor and had Desiree in his arms. He now had a perfectly legitimate excuse for holding her.

She looked gorgeous tonight, he thought, in a red dress made of some kind of silky, floaty material. With it she wore matching red pumps and long, dangling red earrings made out of some kind of bright stones.

"Now this is a slower dance—the easiest ones to learn. Have you done any dancing at all?"

"Sure, but nothing complicated."

"This is just your basic two-step. Look, like this."

She gently but firmly led him in the dance, and after a few turns around the floor, Jack got the hang of the rhythm and relaxed a bit.

Desiree tilted her head back and gave him a dazzling smile. "That's it! You've really got it now!"

She sounded so happy, she made him feel good. He tightened his hold on her, pulling her closer. Her hair smelled sweet and fragrant, like summer roses. He could feel the softness of her breasts pressed against his chest, the firm muscles of her back where he held her, and the brush of her thighs against his as they glided across the floor.

All around them other couples swayed and swirled to the seductive, lilting music, but Jack was so lost in the sensations generated by dancing with Desiree, he was almost oblivious to anything else. When the song ended, he didn't want to let her go.

The next number was much faster, but after a couple of stumbling efforts, Jack found he was able to master the footwork. It helped that Desiree didn't try to teach him anything too fancy.

"You're a natural-born dancer, Jack," she said, eyes sparkling. "Isn't this fun?"

He had to admit it was. But it was also a kind of agony for him. Because the longer they danced, the more he wanted her. One part of him savored the delicious friction, the permitted intimacy. Another part of him knew this was just going to make things harder for him when the inevitable parting came.

This weekend had shown him something—something he hadn't known before. Desiree Cantrelle was not a woman he would easily forget. If he could forget her at all.

"So, little sister," said Denise. "Just how serious is this relationship?"

Desiree's eyes moved from Denise, to Laura, to Alice. All three women were eagerly waiting for her answer. The band was taking a break, and the men had disappeared in the direction of the bar. "It's not really a relationship," she hedged.

"Looks like a relationship to me," Denise insisted. "How about you two? What do you think?"

"I'll never believe the two of you are just friends," Laura said.

"Not the way he looks at you," Alice added.

"Not to mention the way you look at him," Denise said pointedly.

Alice chuckled. "I saw how the two of you were dancing. Why, you couldn't have fit a postage stamp between you on that last dance. And Jack looked positively blissful!"

"Actually, I think the word is besotted," Laura said, her blue eyes dancing.

"Come on, tell all," Denise said.

Desiree could feel herself blushing. "Okay, I'll admit I'm very attracted to him...."

"We already figured that out," said Alice. She sipped from her glass of soda.

"And I know he's attracted to me..."

"Yes, go on..." Denise prompted, dark eyes full of devilry.

"But you all heard what he said during Thanksgiving dinner. He loves his work. He'd never give it up to marry and settle down somewhere. So..." She drew circles in the condensation made by her glass of soda.

"There's no future in it," Denise finished. All the merriment disappeared from her eyes.

Desiree nodded. She looked at her sister, then at her sisters-in-law. There was sympathy and understanding in all three pairs of eyes.

"If what you feel for Jack is just a physical attraction, you'll get over it," Alice said.

Desiree didn't answer, because just then the men returned, but for the rest of the evening she kept thinking about Alice's words. If only this were just a physical attraction, she thought, how much simpler life would be. She almost wished she could stop time, because she knew when she and Jack returned to New Orleans, she would have to make some choices.

And she already knew that no matter what her choice was, she would end up miserable.

Sunday morning Desiree and Aimee went to Mass with Desiree's mother, but her father said he wanted to stay home and talk to Jack. All through Mass Desiree worried about what her father might say. Surely he wasn't going to ask Jack his intentions? She could hardly wait to get home.

But when she and her mother got back to the house, both René and Jack were sitting companionably in the living room, and she couldn't just blurt out something like, "Okay, what were you two talking about?"

She resigned herself to waiting until she and Jack were in the car on their way back to New Orleans.

In the meantime, she worried and grew more and more impatient to be off, but Arlette wouldn't be hurried. First she insisted on packing up leftover turkey and dressing. "Your papa and I, we cain't eat all this food, you know?"

"But Mama, with Aimee staying here until Christmas," Desiree protested, "there's only me to eat it!"

"There's Jack, too," Arlette said, a knowing twinkle in her eyes.

Desiree slanted a glance at Jack, wondering if he'd heard, but if he had, he was pretending he hadn't.

Then, with the plastic containers of turkey and dressing safely iced down at the bottom of a plastic cooler, Arlette said, "There's still room in here for some of my gumbo." She pulled out another plastic container.

"No, Mama, no. I'll never eat all this."

"Freeze it, then."

"Why don't *you* freeze it?"

"Me? I can make this anytime. You, you can't cook! You need some good food, you know?"

Desiree rolled her eyes. She knew from experience it wouldn't do any good to argue with her determined mother.

After Arlette had packed the container of gumbo, she looked at the remaining space thoughtfully. The next thing Desiree knew, there was a foil-wrapped portion of boudin sausage and a plastic bag full of cookies filling up the rest of the cooler. Good Lord. She had enough food for a dozen meals in there.

Finally the Geo was packed. And then it was time to say goodbye. Suddenly Desiree was reluctant to go. Although she'd made arrangements to leave Aimee with her parents months ago, it suddenly hit her that the four weeks until Christmas was a very long time. She and Aimee had never been separated for more than one night since Aimee's birth. If Margaret and Caldwell hadn't had plans to leave for

Australia to spend the holidays with their daughter, Desiree might have changed her mind and taken Aimee home with her.

Desiree said her goodbyes to everyone else, then held out her arms to Aimee. Aimee came willingly enough, but as Desiree held her and kissed her several times, Aimee squirmed to be free.

"'Bye, Mommy," she said cheerfully, not a tear in sight.

Ten minutes later, Desiree and Jack were finally off. Desiree knew it was silly, but she had a lump in her throat when she and Jack pulled out of the driveway. Even though a part of her was excited about the prospect of time to herself and the opportunity to be alone with Jack, she already missed Aimee.

"Feeling a little teary-eyed?" Jack said softly.

"Uh-huh." Desiree blinked. It would be ridiculous to cry.

"It's not too late to change your mind. We can turn back and get her."

Desiree gave a shaky sigh. "No. I'm okay. Besides, I *can't* change my mind. I won't have anyone to sit with Aimee after next week. Margaret and Caldwell are going to Australia for the month of December."

"The month will go quickly," Jack said.

"Oh, I know. It's just that we haven't been apart before. She hasn't *wanted* to leave me before." That was it. That's why Desiree felt so funny. Aimee had wanted to stay with her grandparents. She'd preferred staying in Patinville to being with Desiree. Desiree bit her bottom lip. Aimee was growing up.

She felt Jack's hand cover hers. She looked at him.

He smiled, his blue eyes tender.

Her heart twisted at his expression. He cared about her; she could see it in his eyes.

After a minute, he removed his hand. "While you were at church, your father asked me about Elise."

In a flurry of packing the car and saying goodbye to Aimee, Desiree had completely forgotten about wanting to know what her father and Jack had talked about.

"He said he'd been thinking about what you'd told him, and his curiosity was aroused. Anyway, I told him everything I knew."

Desiree chuckled. "I was afraid he might have been asking you your intentions toward me."

Jack smiled. "He probably wanted to."

"So are you satisfied now that Papa doesn't know anything?"

"Actually, your father said he'd make some phone calls, ask around, see if he could find out anything for me."

Desiree digested this information. "Really? That's funny, because when I talked to Papa he said he knew everyone in our family, down to third and fourth cousins, and there was no one who could have been Elise."

"That may be, but he told me he'd call if he uncovered anything."

"Call you?"

"No. I told him to call you. I said you'd know how to get in touch with me."

Desiree wanted to ask whether he'd still be in New Orleans or whether he'd be back in Houston, but she was afraid to. For the rest of the way home they listened to music or chatted about her family. They avoided the topic of their relationship. Desiree was glad. Although she'd told Jack they'd talk, she wasn't sure she was ready. Obviously, he wasn't either.

They arrived in New Orleans at four-thirty in the afternoon. By the time they'd unloaded her car and carried everything into the cottage, it was almost five o'clock and the winter dusk had settled in, casting amethyst shadows everywhere.

Desiree opened the garage door, and they switched the cars. As she climbed out of her car and closed up the garage again, Jack pulled back into the driveway. He cut the engine and the lights and climbed out of his car.

As he walked toward her, Desiree's heart began to pound. She'd been dreading this moment. She turned away, began walking toward her cottage. She didn't turn around, but she heard him following her.

Wordlessly, she opened her front door. He came in behind her.

"Desiree—"

"Jack—"

They both spoke at once. She laughed self-consciously.

"You go first," he said.

"No, you go first."

He nodded, his gaze resting on her face. He wasn't smiling. "Okay. I've been thinking."

"Yes. I have, too."

"I'm going to drive back to Houston early tomorrow morning."

Desiree's heart plummeted. She could feel the blood draining from her face. *Please, God. Help me be strong. I don't want him to see how much I care.*

"I need to talk to my boss in person. I've decided I want more time off."

Desiree held her breath. Did he mean? . . .

"I owe Jenny. She's never asked me for much, and the least I can do is follow this mystery through to the end."

He did mean it. He was planning to come back! Hope combined with happiness made her feel almost giddy.

"Besides," he said, his voice dropping to a husky whisper, "we have some unfinished business."

Desiree wasn't sure who moved first. All she knew, in the next second, was that she was in his arms, and he was kissing her, and her entire being felt as if someone were shooting off fireworks inside her.

She also knew that if Jack wanted to, she was going to let him stay the night.

Chapter Ten

But he didn't ask.

When the kiss ended, he gently pulled back, holding her lightly by her shoulders. Voice tight with emotion, he said, "While I'm gone, do some thinking, okay?"

Desiree understood without him spelling it out that what he meant was, *do some thinking about us.*

She nodded.

He squeezed her shoulders, dropped a kiss on the tip of her nose and whispered, "I'll call you when I get back. Thanks for the weekend. It was great."

That had been three days ago.

Now it was Wednesday evening, and Desiree still hadn't heard from Jack. She'd had a terrible three days. She missed him, and she missed Aimee. Terribly. She couldn't remember what she'd done with herself before she'd had Aimee. She called her parents' home so many times that her mother finally lost her temper.

"Desiree, don' you think I know how to take care of a child? I had four of my own, you know!"

"Sorry, Mama. I just miss her."

"Well, she's gonna grow up some day, you know? The trouble with you is, you need a husband and a few more children."

Desiree knew her mother was right. She knew she was being ridiculous. She also knew if Jack had stayed in town, she probably wouldn't have felt quite so abandoned. She wished he'd come back to New Orleans. The waiting was hard on her nerves.

She should have gone to aerobics tonight, but she'd been afraid Jack would call, and she wouldn't be home to get the call. So instead of going, she'd sat on the couch and stared at the phone.

She'd also ruined her manicure, she thought ruefully, staring at her chipped fingernail polish. Sighing, disgusted with herself, she looked at her watch. Nine o'clock. If he was going to call, she was sure he'd call by ten.

The phone rang.

Desiree vaulted off the couch and raced to the phone.

"Hello?" Her heart was going like a trip-hammer.

"Desiree?"

Her heart plunged. It wasn't Jack. It was her Uncle Justin. "Uncle Justin?" Even though she was disappointed, she smiled. "Uncle Justin, how are you? Oh, it's so nice to hear your voice!"

"It's always good to hear you, too, *chère.* Your Aunt Lisette and I, we miss you." His voice, rich with a pronounced French accent and more formal than her father's, rolled across the wire.

"I was thinking about you the other day, thinking I should call you," Desiree said. "What's going on? Is everything all right?"

"Yes, *chère,* everything, it is fine. I am keeping busy, as usual, doing some charity work at the agency and tending my garden. You know how I am."

"Yes." Her uncle was one of the most generous, kind-hearted men she'd ever known. "And Aunt Lisette?"

"She's busy, too, with the Ladies Guild and her volunteer work at the Center." He cleared his throat. "*Chère,* the reason I called you, your papa, he called me yesterday. He told me about this young man who followed you home one day."

Desiree frowned. "Oh?"

"Yes. He told me what this young man wanted. About the young woman he's looking for."

Uneasy about the sober note that had crept into her uncle's voice, Desiree waited quietly.

"Desiree, *chère,* I would like to talk to this young man."

"Why?" she blurted out.

There was a pause, then her uncle said, "I would rather wait until I see you in person before telling you. Do you think you could persuade Mr. Forrester to accompany you to Lafayette? Would you bring him here to see me?"

A dozen questions tumbled through Desiree's mind, but she didn't voice them. "Well, I'll certainly ask him, Uncle Justin, but I'm afraid Jack's not in New Orleans right now."

"But he's coming back, isn't he?"

"Yes. He just went home to Houston for a few days. I expect him back in New Orleans any time."

She heard her uncle sigh. Then he said, "Will you call me after you've had a chance to talk to him? Let me know what he says?"

"But Uncle Justin, what should I tell him? Do you know something about Elise Arnold?"

"Yes, it's possible I know something."

"Then I'm sure Jack will agree to make the trip to Lafayette."

"Good." He sounded relieved. "And, *chère*..."

"Yes?"

"When you call..." He hesitated. "Please, I must ask you. Don't say anything to your aunt about our conversation or your reason for calling. This matter will be just between us, okay?"

Desiree's uneasiness grew. "All right, Uncle Justin, if that's what you want, but won't she wonder why I'm coming to Lafayette?"

Silence.

"Uncle Justin?"

"I don't want her to know the real reason you're coming, *chère*. I was hoping you'd just act as if this young man was a friend you wanted us to meet. Could you do that, *chère?* When we've had a chance to talk, you'll understand why."

"Yes, Uncle Justin," she said slowly, "I suppose I could do that."

Jack called at nine forty-five, barely giving Desiree time to digest her uncle's disturbing request. When she heard his voice, her heart leaped with pleasure.

"I'm back," he said without preamble.

"I'm glad," she answered honestly.

His voice dropped a notch. "Did you miss me?"

Her pulse accelerated. "Yes."

"I missed you, too."

Desiree closed her eyes. Suddenly she wanted to see him, to touch him. To have him kiss her. To make love with him. Couldn't he feel her need through the phone wire? She took a deep, shaky breath. "So," she said lightly. "How did things go in Houston?"

"Very well. I had to do some fast talking, but my boss finally agreed to let me take extended leave. I won't be expected to report for my next assignment until the first of January."

Excitement fired Desiree's belly. Almost five weeks! Unreasoning hope cascaded through her. Maybe . . . her mind refused to think past that point.

"So how have *you* been?" he asked.

"Busy. Missing Aimee." She had no intention of telling him how much she'd missed him, how she'd been on pins and needles waiting for him to return. It was bad enough he knew as much as he did about her feelings. "And guess what? I have some news for you." She told him about her uncle's call.

"Desiree . . ." Excitement rippled through his voice. "Maybe we're finally going to have a breakthrough."

We're. He'd included her in his statement. She smiled, pleasure warming her.

"When can we go?" he asked.

"Well, I've been thinking. I have a lot of vacation time accumulated. Why don't I take Friday off, and we can drive up to Lafayette Friday morning?"

Friday morning dawned bright and clear with a little nip in the air. A perfect day, Desiree decided. She looked through her wardrobe carefully. She wanted to look her best. She wanted to dazzle Jack. She wanted him to take one look at her and decide she was the best thing that had ever happened to him. She wanted him to want her as much as she wanted him.

And she didn't want him to leave her again.

She finally settled on her black-and-white tweed skirt, a white long-sleeved blouse, black leather vest and her black boots. She added some chunky black-and-silver jewelry and studied herself in the mirror.

She looked pretty good, she thought, grinning at her reflection. She couldn't wait to see him.

But when he arrived at eight o'clock on the dot, she had a panic attack, and stood frozen for several minutes before she calmed down enough to open the door. The minute she saw him, the panic evaporated, and anticipation skidded through her.

He looked wonderful, but then, he always looked wonderful to her. He wore a yellow sweater with baggy, charcoal cotton pants, and he gave her a big grin, blue eyes shining. "Ready?"

"Yes." All her worries, all her doubts, all her fears—vanished. The only important thing was that Jack was here. They were going to be together for a couple of days. Desiree didn't know what was going to happen, either on this trip, or in the future, but right now, she didn't care. Tomorrow she might decide being with Jack, loving him, was too big a risk, and she'd opt for playing it safe once more.

But today she was going to enjoy every minute.

"Tell me about your uncle," Jack said, when they were about twenty miles outside of Lafayette.

"Well, you already know he used to practice law..."

Wednesday night when she'd told him about her uncle's call, she'd reluctantly admitted that Justin Cantrelle was a retired lawyer. Jack had immediately wanted to know why she hadn't put his name on the list she'd given him, and she'd had to explain that she'd never thought there was a chance her uncle knew anything so she'd purposely left both his name and her two cousins' names off the list.

"Tell me how he fits into the family," Jack prompted.

"He's my father's youngest brother. My father is seventy-three, so that makes Uncle Justin sixty-nine, almost seventy. As I told you before, I lived with Uncle Justin and Aunt Lisette while I was carrying Aimee."

Her voice had grown soft, and Jack slanted a glance at her. Maybe he was finally going to find out something about Aimee's father.

Voice reflective, she continued. "They were so good to me. Aunt Lisette fussed over me the whole time, and Uncle Justin—he was still working then—he gave me a part-time job in his office. That's how I got the training to be a legal secretary."

"Sounds like they really think a lot of you."

"Well, they don't have any children of their own, and I know that's always bothered them. And I'm the youngest of the nieces and nephews. Plus, Uncle Justin and my father have always been especially close. They're the only two brothers born of my grandfather's second marriage . . . Oh, it's so complicated-sounding when you don't belong to my family, but my father's father—my grandfather Cantrelle—was married twice. He had two sons from his first marriage, Claude and Andre, and they're both well into their eighties now. Then, from his second marriage, there were four children, two boys and two girls."

"So when you found out you were pregnant with Aimee, you went to live with your uncle and aunt."

"Yes."

Jack chose his words carefully. "If you don't want to talk about this, or if this is none of my business, say so. But going to live with your uncle and aunt, was this something you wanted to do or something your parents wanted you to do?"

"It was a mutual decision. I... Oh, shoot, I might as well tell you. It's no great secret, it's just that I'm ashamed of my poor judgment and lack of good sense. Aimee's father was a salesman. He worked out of Fort Worth, Texas, but he covered Louisiana. I met him because he rented the apartment over the office of my family's business, and at the time, I was working in that office. His name was Mark Hodges, and he was good-looking, sophisticated, charming—'' Suddenly she chuckled. ''Rather like you, actually.''

Jack frowned. He wasn't sure he wanted to be compared to the sorry son-of-a-gun who had run out on her.

''Anyway, he made a big play for me, and I was flattered. All I saw was the surface charm, and I liked the money he spent on me, the places he took me.'' She made a sound that was half laugh, half exhalation. ''I was extremely easy pickings.''

''Don't be so hard on yourself,'' Jack said.

She turned to look at him. ''Why not? It's the truth.'' She grimaced. ''Norman warned me. He warned me over and over again. But I didn't listen. I didn't want to hear what he had to say. Anyway—to make a long story short—Mark was married. Of course, I didn't know that at the time. I'm not the sort of woman who goes out with married men.''

''I never thought you were,'' Jack said.

She gave him a little half smile. ''Thanks. It turns out he had a wife and two little kids in Fort Worth. But I didn't find all that out until much later. In the meantime, I got pregnant and I told him. I had some rosy idea he'd be happy about the news.'' She grunted. ''I sure got a rude awakening. He cleared out the very next day. Never said a word, just disappeared. Left the rent money in an envelope in the apartment and took off. Norman's the one who told me Mark was married....'' Her voice trailed off.

Jack clenched his fists. What a bastard!

''Anyway,'' she continued after a moment, ''I was so devastated and embarrassed and I felt so rotten about letting my family down, and my parents knew how I felt, so even though they really wanted me to be with them, they suggested I go stay in Lafayette.''

Jack felt better. He'd been afraid her parents were ashamed of Desiree, too, but he could see that they'd simply wanted her to be protected and safe from censure—by anyone.

''So I went, and it was a wonderful time for me. I spent a lot of time thinking, and I grew up a lot. I was twenty-six when this all happened, but I wasn't a very mature twenty-six. I'd been pretty sheltered, and I'd always lived at home. I wasn't very experienced.''

''We all make mistakes, no matter how old we are.''

Her voice sounded rueful when she answered. ''True, but some of us make whoppers.''

''Have you ever tried to get in touch with Aimee's father?''

Her voice hardened. ''No.''

''Seems to me he should be contributing to Aimee's support.''

''I don't want anything from him. In fact, if I could pretend he never existed, that'd be fine with me.''

''What's going to happen when Aimee gets older, when she starts to ask questions about her father?''

Now she sounded uncertain. ''I . . . I don't know. I'll tell her the truth, I guess. I don't really have a choice.''

Jack nodded. The truth was always best. ''Well, I'm looking forward to meeting your uncle, since you like him so much.''

On the outskirts of Lafayette, they stopped for lunch. It was nearly one o'clock by the time Desiree called her uncle from the restaurant. Twenty minutes later they pulled into the driveway of an attractive two-story brick colonial in an older section of the city.

A slight man dressed in dark slacks and a burgundy shirt walked outside. As he came closer, Jack could see he was very tanned, and that his hair was completely white. Desiree hugged him and said, "Hello, Uncle Justin. You're looking well."

"Hello, *ma chère.*" He held her at arm's length. "And you, you look very beautiful, as usual." Then he turned his dark-eyed gaze on Jack.

Jack leaned forward and extended his right hand. "Jack Forrester, Mr. Cantrelle."

As they shook hands, Justin Cantrelle studied Jack, and Jack could see the intelligence blazing from his eyes. "Thank you for coming on such short notice, Mr. Forrester."

"Please, call me Jack."

Justin Cantrelle permitted himself a small smile and nodded. He turned back to Desiree. Now his smile broadened, and his eyes filled with warmth. "It's so good to see you again."

She kissed his cheek. "Yes, I've stayed away too long."

They followed Justin into the house, through the foyer, and off to the left into a large, sunny, living room filled with bright chintzes and glowing antiques. A large yellow Lab came bounding across the room and nearly knocked Desiree over.

"Genevieve, stop that!" Justin said sharply.

Desiree knelt, laughing as the dog lapped at her face. "Hi, Genevieve," she crooned. "You missed me, didn't you?"

When the dog was finished with Desiree, she walked over to Jack and began sniffing at his pant legs. He grinned, rubbing her on the back of the head. He liked dogs, especially Labs. That was one of the few things he really regretted about his constant traveling. There was no way he could ever have a pet.

"Where's Aunt Lisette?" Desiree asked as she sat in a large wing-back chair near the front window.

"Your aunt is at the Center this afternoon," Justin answered. He turned to Jack. "My wife, she does volunteer work three afternoons a week at the Catholic Youth Center. But she'll be home later." He rubbed his hands together. "Now, what can I bring you to drink? Coffee? Iced tea? Or perhaps you'd prefer something stronger."

"I'd love a glass of iced tea," Desiree said.

"And you, Mr. Forrester?"

"Coffee, please."

Minutes later Justin carried in a tray containing a tall glass of iced tea and two cups of coffee. After they were all served, Justin sat facing them. "My brother tells me you are looking for a young woman who looks like Desiree."

"Yes," Jack said.

"And her name is Elise Arnold?"

"Yes."

"Do you have a photograph of this young woman?"

Jack, who had anticipated this request, pulled the snapshot out of his notebook. He handed it to Justin.

For long moments, Justin Cantrelle studied the photograph. The room was very quiet, with only the ticking mantel clock and the dog's breathing breaking the silence. Then Justin sighed deeply and handed the photograph back to Jack. Jack carefully tucked it back into the inside flap of the notebook. Justin tented his hands and pursed his lips.

Jack glanced at Desiree. She was watching her uncle intently, her forehead furrowed. He turned back to Justin.

"How old is Elise Arnold?" Justin finally asked.

"Twenty-eight."

Justin nodded. In a quiet, very calm voice, he said, "I am going to tell you something that has remained a secret for a very long time." His gaze rested on Desiree for a moment, then he turned and stared into space as he spoke.

"Approximately twenty-nine years ago Lisette and I were having some serious problems. We had been married nearly ten years, and we were childless. Lisette was very unhappy, and for nearly a year we were estranged in all the important ways. I didn't know what to do. I tried in every way I could to show her our lack of success in having a child was not important enough to let it come between us, but she was so devastated and felt like such a failure, she just grew farther and farther away from me."

He sighed. His eyes were filled with sadness as he continued. "Yes, it was a terrible time for us. I, too, was miserable. The lack of intimacy was terrible, for Lisette and I had always been each other's best friend. We had shared everything, talked about everything, and we'd always laughed so much together. I . . . I hate to admit how weak I was, but I couldn't stand the loss of that closeness. I turned to my secretary, a lovely young woman whom I admired very much. I'm sorry to have to say that we became lovers."

"Oh, Uncle Justin," Desiree said.

"But I felt so guilty. I loved Lisette so much, and I knew what I was doing was wrong, so I went to my secretary and told her our love affair must stop. I told her I would give her enough money to get settled somewhere else like Shreveport and even help her find a job, if she wanted, but she would have to leave Lafayette. She agreed."

"What I didn't know was that she was pregnant with my child. She didn't tell me. Only after that child was born did she write and say she had had a little girl, my little girl, and she thought I might like to know."

After a pause, Uncle Justin went on. "I believe Elise Arnold is my daughter."

The words trembled in the air. Jack looked at Desiree, saw how still and pale she was, how wide and stricken her eyes were as she stared at her uncle. Jack's skin prickled as he turned back to Justin and saw eyes filled with pain.

"Does Aunt Lisette know any of this?" Desiree said, her voice uneven.

Justin's gaze never wavered. "She knows about the affair. I told her, and she has forgiven me. She doesn't know about the child, because I knew that would break her heart. And I'd already hurt her so much, I just couldn't hurt her anymore. Besides, what good would it have done?"

"Didn't you ever try to see the baby?" Desiree asked. "How could you just ignore the fact that you had a child?"

"I tried. The letter from my secretary was postmarked Shreveport, but when I looked for her there, she was gone. I had no idea where she'd gone. I didn't know much about her—she had only worked for me a short time. I knew she had an aunt somewhere, but I didn't remember the aunt's name. I have to be honest, *chère,* even though I know this will make you think less of me. I was relieved when I didn't find her in Shreveport. I told myself she had probably been lying to me to make me feel bad, that there wasn't a baby after all. I preferred to think these things because it made everything so much easier for me." His face twisted. "You probably think I'm a terrible person."

Desiree smiled sadly. "Uncle Justin, I could never think you're a terrible person. And believe me, I have no room to make judgments about anyone. I'm not exactly perfect myself."

Jack cleared his throat. "Mr. Cantrelle—"

"Please. If I'm to call you Jack, you must call me Justin."

"Justin, what makes you so sure Elise is your daughter?"

Justin met his gaze squarely. "My secretary's name was Michelle Sonnier."

Jack and Desiree looked at each other, and he saw the same spark of excitement reflected in her dark eyes that he knew was shining in his.

Justin spoke again, softly. "When you told my brother the name of Elise's mother, he knew it sounded familiar. Finally he realized where he'd heard it. That was when he called me."

"You know, Jack, I've been thinking," Desiree said. They were in his car, driving back to New Orleans. It was Friday night. They had decided not to stay overnight in Lafayette. "You've been spending an awful lot of time looking for Elise without really knowing whether she's dead or alive."

He expelled a gust of breath. "Yeah, I know. But I don't see how we can ever know unless I find her . . . or someone finds her body."

"Don't you think it might be better to try to establish, for sure, that she's still alive?"

"Yeah, that'd be great, but I don't know how I can do that. Short of shooting Derek Arnold with truth serum and demanding to know whether he killed his wife, I'm fresh out of ideas."

Desiree hesitated, suddenly wondering if what she was about to propose was wise. She took a deep breath. "I have a suggestion."

"Oh?"

"Why don't you use me?"

In the light cast from an oncoming car, Desiree could see Jack's frown. "Use you? How?"

"As a decoy."

"In what way?"

"Well, what I thought you could do is somehow—I'm not sure how, that would be something you'd have to figure out—let Derek Arnold know about me. Maybe you could get the information to him that you had found a woman you thought was Elise Arnold, and that she lived in New Orleans. You could even say the woman says her name is Desiree Cantrelle, but you don't believe it. You could let him know where I live, then just wait and see what he does."

"But if he killed Elise, why would he do anything?"

"That's just it. If he doesn't take the bait, you'll know he probably *did* kill her, and you can go on from there. But if he *does* come to Louisiana, it'll prove she really did run away from him."

Jack pulled out into the passing lane and passed an eighteen-wheeler, then pulled back into the right lane of the highway. "I don't know, Desiree. It sounds pretty far-fetched to me."

"It'd work, Jack, I know it'd work," Desiree said eagerly. "It's at least worth a try."

"Now, I'm not saying I agree with you," Jack said thoughtfully. "But for the sake of argument, let's say we did it. And let's say Derek came to New Orleans. That still wouldn't prove conclusively that he didn't kill Elise, you know?"

"Why do you say that?"

"Because even if he did kill her, he would want to divert suspicion. He'd probably figure out that if he didn't at least check you out, it would look highly suspicious. After all, he's playing the role of the concerned husband right now— at least to everyone except Jenny."

"I say let's cross that bridge when we come to it. I think he'd be bound to say *something* that would give him away, don't you think?"

"What I think is that this is a crazy idea. A dangerous idea. Listen, Desiree, a guy like Derek Arnold might do anything. I don't want you in danger."

Desiree felt a surge of happiness at the concern in Jack's voice. "But Jack, I don't think he'd do anything to me. After all, I'm *not* his wife, and I can prove it. I'm no real threat to him."

"No. There are too many variables. Too much danger."

"Oh, come on, Jack. I want to do this. I . . . after listening to my uncle's story, I don't know . . . I just feel so close to Elise. I want to know what happened to her. And if she's alive, I want to find her." She turned in her seat so she could look at Jack. "She's my cousin. She's family."

Jack was silent for so long, Desiree almost said something else. Finally he spoke. "I have to admit that the investigative journalist part of me likes your idea, but the other part of me—the man—is scared to death something might happen to you."

Desiree hugged herself. He cared. He really did care.

"The only way I'll consider letting you do this is if I can be with you at all times."

"But, Jack—"

"At all times," he repeated.

"Jack," she said patiently, "I have a job. You can't come to work with me every day."

"I'm not really worried about the time you're at work. If we don't tell him where you work, he won't be able to go to your office. I'm worried about the time you'd be alone."

"So what are you suggesting?"

"I'm suggesting that I move in with you."

Chapter Eleven

Desiree's heart thudded up into her throat. "Move in with me?"

Jack's lower jaw jutted out stubbornly. "That's what I said. If I can't be with you when you're not at work, I won't let you do this. I won't put you in that kind of danger."

"I don't know, Jack." Oh, it was so tempting. Not only because she wanted to do this for her unknown cousin, but because the thought of being with Jack, having him in her home, caused her insides to jump around like Mexican jumping beans.

She looked out the window. In the distance she could see the lights of New Orleans. Soon they would be home.

"If the idea of my moving in with you bothers you so much, we'll just forget the whole thing," Jack said, breaking into her thoughts.

She glanced at him. He gave her a thoughtful look before turning his gaze back to the road. She bit her bottom lip. She knew that if she allowed Jack to move into her cottage, she would never be able to withstand her feelings for him. And she was fairly certain he felt the same way.

So if she said yes, she'd agree with his condition, she'd be saying yes to more than just trying to trap Derek Arnold.

She'd be saying yes to a physical relationship with Jack.

She'd be saying yes to possible unbearable heartache.

She'd be saying yes to the biggest risk she'd ever taken.

She said yes.

They decided to wait a week before putting their plan into action. Desiree explained to Jack that Margaret and Caldwell wouldn't leave for their trip to Australia until the following weekend.

They were sitting in her living room. They'd been home for about an hour. Desiree met Jack's gaze squarely. "I don't want them to know I've let you move in here. By the time they return from their trip, you should be—" she forced herself to say it "—gone." She ignored the pain that grabbed at her heart. "So they'll never have to know you were here." His eyes, so still, so clear, pierced her with their unwavering intensity.

He nodded slowly.

She tried to ignore the pain. He hadn't denied what she'd said. *It's not too late to change your mind.* She wished he'd say something, anything.

"Desiree . . ."

Why were his eyes so beautiful? Why did she feel this way about him?

"You don't have to do this, you know."

She swallowed, perilously close to tears. "I know I don't." She couldn't let him go without at least trying. She just couldn't. She knew all the odds were against her. She knew Jack was not likely to change. She knew she would probably end up getting hurt very badly. Again. And it would be infinitely worse this time, because what she had felt for Mark didn't come close to what she felt for Jack.

But she had to take a chance.

Because she loved him.

And she simply couldn't bear having him leave her with nothing. Even if all she ended up with were memories, at least she would know what it was like to be loved by him.

She took a deep breath. The urge to cry disappeared. She felt strong and sure of herself. She had never been the type of person to run away from anything. She had always taken risks. She had always fought for what she wanted.

She would fight for Jack.

With all the weapons she had.

She smiled. "I want to do this."

He studied her for a moment, then nodded. He stood. "It's late. I'd better be going."

She stood, too. They walked to the front door together. He put his right hand on the doorknob, hesitated, then turned to face her.

She lifted her face.

He touched her shoulders lightly, bent his head and brushed his lips across hers. "I want you to be sure," he whispered, his warm breath faintly reminiscent of the coffee they'd drunk earlier.

"I'm very sure," she said.

He didn't kiss her again. She understood that he was the one who wasn't sure.

"I'll call you tomorrow," he said before he opened the door. "Sleep on this. If you change your mind, I'll understand."

Desiree met his gaze. "I won't change my mind."

The next week seemed to last forever. Jack alternated between thinking it would never end and worrying about what would happen when he moved in with Desiree.

He had never wanted a woman as much as he wanted her.

He had never been as afraid of his emotions as he was now.

He had never, ever, believed he'd be in this position.

In love.

He admitted it, finally.

In love.

In love with a woman who wanted exactly the opposite out of life than he did.

In love with a woman who, when he was with her, had the ability to make him forget everything but how much he wanted her.

In love with a woman who, when he was away from her, occupied his thoughts every waking moment.

And some sleeping moments.

During that week he called her every day, but he purposely stayed away from her, thinking maybe his desire for her, his love for her, would magically diminish. At times he prayed it would go away completely.

But he had no luck putting Desiree out of his mind.

What he accomplished by his self-imposed exile from her was to want to see her so badly he began to lose sleep. By the end of the week, he was a mess.

On Saturday morning, Desiree called him. A rush of happiness flooded him at the sound of her velvety voice.

"The Reed-Douglases are leaving on a one o'clock flight," she said. "They'll be gone by eleven."

"I'll be there at noon."

After they hung up, he called his sister. He brought Jenny up to date on his progress, including a report of Justin Cantrelle's disclosure. Then he carefully gave her instructions, after outlining his and Desiree's plan. "I want you to call Derek Arnold and tell him that you asked me to look into Elise's disappearance. Tell him I called you and said I thought I had located Elise, that she's living in New Orleans at—" Jack gave her Desiree's address. "—And going under the name of Desiree Cantrelle. Tell him I'm not positive it's Elise, but I think it is."

"Isn't this dangerous to Desiree?" Jenny asked.

"I plan to protect her."

"How can you protect her twenty-four hours a day, Jack?"

"I'm going to move into her place."

"Oh." He heard a lot in that "oh." "I guess you know what you're doing," she said doubtfully.

He wished she hadn't managed to revive his own grave reservations about the wisdom of what he was doing. "We'll be careful," he assured her. "But I'll need to know the minute you talk to Arnold. I plan to put someone on his tail, but I don't want them to watch him if there's no reason to."

"I will," Jenny promised. "Do you want me to call him now?"

"No, wait until this afternoon. I'll be at Desiree's by noon. You can call me there." He gave her the number.

After talking to Jenny, Jack called a friend of his in Houston—a private investigator named Paul O'Malley. He briefly explained the situation. "Paul, I want you to watch Derek Arnold. The minute he makes a move toward New Orleans, I want you to let me know. I'm not sure if Jenny will get in touch with him this afternoon, but I'll call you as soon as she does."

"You've got my beeper number, haven't you?" Paul asked.

"Yes."

"Well, if I don't answer at home, beep me."

Jack gave Desiree's name, address and phone number to Paul. They said goodbye, then Jack finished packing up his things. Before he left the apartment, he opened the refrigerator and cleaned out the few foods he thought might spoil. Then he turned out the lights, picked up his one suitcase, slung his hanging bag over his shoulder and walked out.

Desiree had been a basket case all morning. Even her call to Aimee didn't succeed in settling her down for very long. By the time Margaret and Caldwell had kissed her goodbye and given her all their last-minute instructions concerning the house, she was so nervous and so excited she thought she might burst. As soon as their Lincoln pulled out of the driveway, she dashed into her cottage, stripped off her clothes and took a fast shower. She'd spent the morning cleaning, so the inside of the cottage sparkled. She'd even picked some of Margaret's fall roses, and they now sat, spreading their fragrance, in a crystal vase on her coffee table.

After her shower, she stared at the clothes hanging in her closet. She wanted something special, but she didn't want to look as if she'd spent time trying to make herself look nice. She shoved one garment after another to the end of the rack. Then spied her gold corduroy jumpsuit.

Perfect, she thought, once she'd zipped up the oversized front zipper and stood barefoot, looking at her reflection in her full-length mirror. She blow-dried her hair, spritzed herself with perfume. She dug out her black flats, and had just finished putting on big gold earrings when she heard the doorbell.

Her heart gave a little flip.

Jack.

When she opened the door, she hoped her face didn't betray how excited she was. Even though she'd decided to go for broke, to fight for him, to try to make him love her, she had to retain some measure of pride.

Because if she lost this gamble, her pride would be all she'd have left.

"Hi," he said, pleasure lighting his eyes. Dressed in white jeans, an olive T-shirt, and dark green linen jacket, he looked so sexy and so handsome, he nearly took her breath away.

She led him to Aimee's room, where she'd cleared out some space in the closet for his clothes. "Here's two drawers for you, too," she said, pointing to a white chest in the corner.

She avoided looking at Aimee's youth bed, which was obviously much too small for a man of Jack's size. She wasn't sure what she'd say if he asked where he was going to sleep.

He didn't.

She left him then, and walked out to the kitchen, wiping her clammy hands against her thighs. Her heart pounded. Lordy, she was nervous.

"Desiree..."

She jumped, putting her hand over her heart. When she turned around, she saw Jack leaning against the doorway of the kitchen. He had removed his jacket, and his T-shirt molded against his chest in a way that emphasized his well-developed muscles. He gave her an apologetic smile. "I didn't mean to scare you."

"I just didn't hear you, that's all." She managed a shaky laugh. "If you're going to be staying here, you're going to have to make some noise—otherwise, you'll give me a heart attack."

He nodded, his smile fading.

Why was he looking at her like that? "Uh, are you hungry?" she said, her gaze sliding away from his. She had to calm down. Tension was a killer.

"No. I ate a huge breakfast." He straightened, walked into the room, pulled a kitchen chair out and straddled it, leaning his arms on the back of it. The noonday sun streaming through the kitchen windows lit the hair on his forearms, turning it to burnished gold. "Don't you want to know what Jenny said when I called her?"

"Yes," Desiree said gratefully, tearing her gaze from the appealing sight of those bronzed arms, those clean, strong hands. She walked to the refrigerator, took out a can of diet soda. "Want some? Or a beer?"

"A soda is fine."

She pulled a can from the refrigerator, and as she handed it to him, their fingers brushed. He popped the top and took a long swallow while she seated herself across the table from him and opened her drink.

He began to tell her about his phone call to his sister. For the next hour they talked, and gradually Desiree relaxed. When they had exhausted the subject of Elise, Jack said, "I don't want to interrupt your normal schedule. You go ahead and do whatever it is you usually do, and I'll try to stay out of your way." He stood. "Do you mind if I watch the LSU game?"

"No. I have to go to the supermarket, anyway." She stood, too. "What would you like for dinner? Want me to get a couple of steaks?"

"I thought I'd take you out for dinner." His warm gaze held hers.

She felt breathless and as excited as a girl going on her first date. "That sounds nice."

He took her to Antoine's. Desiree had only been to the fabled restaurant once. This time was much more memorable. They were put in a little private alcove upstairs, and everything about the evening was magical.

Jack looked breathtakingly handsome in his dark suit paired with a striped shirt. Everything about him seemed bigger than life, she thought. His eyes seemed bluer, his smile seemed sexier, his voice seemed more seductive. All he had to do was look at her, and shivers raced down her spine. Every time she thought about going home, closing the door, and having him there—in her home—for the entire night, and for many more nights to come—she could hardly breathe.

Desiree knew they made a handsome couple. She was wearing a short clingy black crepe dress with a draped bodice and a deep V in the back. She'd pulled one side of her hair back from her face, securing it with a rhinestone comb, and long rhinestone waterfall earrings glittered from her ears. With the outfit she wore sheer black stockings and black satin evening shoes with very high heels.

She wondered what Jack was thinking. All through dinner he was attentive and charming, but he was holding something back. Several times she caught him looking at her with a peculiar expression in his eyes.

"What?" she finally said. "That's the third time you've given me that look. What's wrong?"

"Nothing's wrong." His blue eyes glittered in the subdued lighting of the restaurant. "I was just thinking, that's all."

"Tell me what you're thinking," she insisted.

His mouth twisted. "I was thinking that you are completely irresistible."

Desiree swallowed. Her gaze locked with his.

"You look sensational tonight. Every man in the place is jealous of me," Jack said softly.

Desiree could feel her cheeks warming. But she didn't drop her gaze. For long moments, they looked into each other's eyes. Finally, in a low, rough voice, he said, "Eat your dinner. It's getting cold."

The meal was superb, but Desiree was so keyed up it was hard for her to do it justice. She kept thinking about the expression in Jack's eyes.

During dessert, Jack said, "I hope Jenny's able to contact Derek Arnold tomorrow." Before they'd left for dinner, he had talked to his sister again, and she'd told him she hadn't been able to get in touch with Derek. "I don't want this situation to drag on too long. I don't want anything to happen to you."

After dinner, when they left the restaurant, Jack took her hand. The simple act caused more flutters in Desiree's stomach, and she wondered how much tension a person's system could stand.

"Would you like to walk awhile, or maybe take a carriage ride?" He squeezed her hand. "Or do you just want to go home?"

"Let's just go home."

Jack put the top down on the Miata, and Desiree nestled into her velvet jacket and enjoyed the cool night air as they cruised through the New Orleans streets. He found a radio station playing adult contemporary music and when the hauntingly beautiful strains of "The Music of the Night" from *Phantom of the Opera* played, he turned up the volume so that the music swelled around them.

Desiree was so full of anticipation and the thrilling newness of her love for Jack that she wasn't sure she could stand it. In no time at all, it seemed, they were home. Desiree got out and waited while Jack pulled the Miata into the Reed-Douglases' side of the garage, then they walked together up the path to her cottage.

Soon. Soon. Soon.

Her heart pounded in time with her thoughts. A fine tingling trembled through her body, and she shivered.

"Cold?" He put his arm around her, drawing her close.

Desiree closed her eyes. Oh, God. She wanted this. She wanted this so much. He kissed her cheek, and her heart leaped into her throat.

They reached her door, and she extracted her keys from her purse. She had forgotten to leave any lights on, so she fumbled with the lock, her fingers clumsy from nervous tension.

"Here, let me," he said softly, taking the keys from her hand, but he kept his arm around her. She could smell his cologne, something clean and tart, reminding her of a crisp autumn day. The door swung wide, and together they walked into the house.

Moonlight streamed through the big front window. She could hear the mantel clock ticking, and the chirping of crickets outside the door, and the distant hum of the refrigerator.

"Desiree..."

She swallowed, turning slowly into his arms.

Shyness, and fear, and uncertainty, paralyzed her.

His voice was a whisper, a caress. "Desiree, look at me." With his right hand, he lifted her chin. His left hand moved unerringly to her back, and his fingers slowly stroked her bare skin, sending delicious shivers throughout her body. "I've wanted to do that all night," he said huskily.

Her heart felt as if it might jump right out of her body as his right hand trailed down her neck, back up to her ear, then settled under her hair. With gentle pressure, he nudged her toward him.

"I've also wanted to kiss you all day," he said against her parted lips, their breath mingling for a tantalizing moment before his mouth settled onto hers.

The shyness vanished.

The fear vanished.

The uncertainty vanished.

Jack, her body cried. *Jack,* her heart cried. *Jack, I love you,* she thought as her evening purse slid to the floor and she lifted her arms and wrapped them around him.

She breathed him in, absorbed him, tasted him. Sensations pummeled her, exploded within her, transported her. She felt as if she were in the middle of a whirlwind, and the only thing holding her rooted to the earth was Jack.

She wasn't sure where one kiss ended and another began. There was only Jack and the steady pounding of her heart. Only Jack and the heated demand of his mouth. Only Jack and the insistent driving force of their mutual desire.

The room was very quiet. Only the sounds of their ragged breathing and Desiree's soft moans interrupted the silken silence.

After a long time, Jack tore his mouth from hers, put his hands at the sides of her face and muttered, "Desiree, are you sure?"

"Yes," she whispered, and she was. This might be all she'd ever have, but it would be enough. She'd rather have this than nothing.

Wordlessly, he lifted her in his arms and walked unerringly back to her bedroom. He kicked the door open with his foot, then set her on her feet. The shades in the room were down, so very little light penetrated. "We need some light," he whispered. He moved toward the bedside lamp.

"Wait," Desiree said. Earlier, hoping, shamelessly planning, she'd prepared. For this and for every other contingency. She wanted this. She wanted to make love with Jack. But she didn't want another pregnancy. Not unless she had a husband to go along with another baby.

She walked to her chest of drawers, fumbled for a moment, then found what she was looking for. Lifting the pack of matches, she struck one, and lit the three candles in their crystal holders sitting on top of the chest. Then she opened the top drawer and removed a foil packet.

The candlelight danced over the room with delicate sorcery. Desiree slowly walked back to Jack. A little hesitantly, she held out the packet.

"It's okay," he murmured. "I've already got one. Don't you know I'd never jeopardize your well-being?"

Their gazes met, and she smiled. Slowly, she reached for his tie, but her fingers fumbled as she tried to undo it. His eyes were like two brilliant gemstones in the candlelight. "Let me help you," he murmured, covering her hands with his and guiding them.

Desiree could feel the blood rushing through her veins, pumping through her heart, fueling her body with life. She knew she would remember this night forever.

They undressed each other slowly. First his tie. Then her shoes. Then his jacket. Then her dress. Then his shirt. Then her slip. Then his belt and pants. Then her stockings.

When all that was left to remove were Desiree's filmy bra and panties and Jack's cotton briefs, Jack drew her into his arms once more. His hands whispered over her body, caressing her arms gliding over her back, trailing slowly around to gently brush her breasts.

Desiree's insides turned to liquid as her breasts tightened under the tender assault. A pulse beat deep within her, settling into her core.

While he touched her, his lips grazed hers, then dropped to the hollow in her neck. When his moist mouth dropped lower, trailing teasing kisses across the swell of her bosom, Desiree gripped his upper arms, feeling the hard muscle flex under her palms.

Very slowly, very gently, he backed her up toward the bed. When they were lying side by side, he propped himself up with one arm, and smiled down at her.

"You are the most beautiful woman I've ever seen," he whispered, fingers tiptoeing over her skin.

"I'm not beautiful." She touched his chest, ran her fingertips through the crisp hair, felt its texture, its resiliency. His palm closed over one breast, and its heat undulated through her body in slow waves. Deep within, a steady pulse throbbed, and an ache spread from the center of her being to encompass her entire body. Catlike, she stretched, pushing toward him. His hand tightened, moved, touched, stroked, teased, caressed.

Against her own palm she could feel the heavy beat of his heart. Her gaze remained locked with his as they absorbed the new sensations.

She liked the way he felt. She liked the hardness of his chest, the swell of his muscles, the wiry mat of hair on his chest. Boldly, she explored him, letting her hand move slowly down his body, past his trim waist, then tentatively, almost shyly, to the place she knew was throbbing with the same need building in her own body.

When her palm closed around him, he gave a sharp gasp and pulled her hand away. "Not yet," he moaned. Then suddenly, he shook with laughter. "Not unless you want me to explode."

Desiree laughed softly, delighted with him, delighted that he could joke, delighted that he didn't take himself too seriously.

He bent down, let the tip of his tongue wet her lips, slid it inside her mouth, then out. His breathing sounded ragged in the still room.

His mouth slid lower. He undid the front fastening of her bra, gently parted it. His tongue lapped at her breasts, then gently suckled.

Desiree arched. Fiery darts of pleasure-pain zoomed through her as he turned his attention from one aching breast to another. "Jack," she whimpered as his hand glided down her torso, over her waist, then slowly, oh, so slowly, crept under the elastic band of her panties, stopped for an agonizing moment while Desiree's heart went boom, boom, boom, then finally, when Desiree's hands gripped his shoulders in mute appeal, slid unerringly into her center, finding the exact spot that cried for his touch.

Desiree hadn't known one person could stand such agony. Such ecstasy. Such pain. Such pure, unadulterated pleasure. "Oh, God, Jack," she moaned.

He moved his head up until his mouth found hers. Before capturing it in a deep, drugging, demanding kiss, he said, "Is that a plea for mercy? Do you want me to stop?"

She could see the gleam in his eyes, the smile tugging at his mouth. "Only if you have a death wish," she muttered.

He shouted with laughter. "Desiree, you're wonderful," he said. And then his mouth covered hers, and Desiree was lost in a sea of sensations so wonderful she hoped she'd never surface again.

Chapter Twelve

Desiree thought she knew what making love was all about. Jack taught her she didn't have a clue.

What he taught her had little to do with the physical sensations he evoked with his kisses and his touches. It had everything to do with the inner Desiree.

Until she made love with Jack, Desiree hadn't known that there was a part of her that was completely isolated, completely insulated, completely hidden from view.

This hidden part of her was like a diamond enclosed in a box, buried deep within, swathed with layers of cotton, cocooned and protected, closed off in the warm darkness where its brilliance couldn't be seen.

But as she made love with Jack, Desiree could feel the box opening. She could feel each layer of cotton as it was removed. And when she was finally exposed, when she lay in full view of the light and the sun and the beauty of the world around her, she shimmered and glittered with dazzling clarity.

She trembled with this knowledge. Part of her was afraid, part of her still wanted the safety of that closed box. And as he stroked her, as he felt her body respond, as the physical pressure built, she said, "No, no." She tried to push his hand away.

"Yes," he whispered. "Yes."

"No, I—"

"Yes."

She quit fighting. She let him remove her panties. She let him sink his fingers inside her pulsing warmth. She let him set up a rhythm that beat like a drum throughout her body. She let him bring her up, up, up.

"Jack, Jack." She said his name again and again.

"Let it happen." His breathing was as labored as hers.

Up. Up. She pushed against him. He increased the pressure.

Up.

And then she was there. Oh, God. She was there. Her body arched, and he held her tight against him. And as the radiance spread through her in wave after wave, she felt as if she were melting, as if the hard diamond was now a molten liquid blazing its way to each part of her.

"Now," Jack whispered when her body finally stilled. "Now you can touch me." He helped her slide his briefs down, and in the candlelight she could see how beautiful he was. The tempo of her heartbeat increased as she let her fingertips glide over him.

She heard him catch his breath, and she smiled, feeling powerful and strong. She would make him feel the same way he'd made her feel.

She took her time. She explored his body with her fingers, then kissed him, breathing in his scent. He quivered under her touches, and moaned her name. Once he tried to push her away, but she smiled and wouldn't let him.

"You're torturing me," he said.

"Good."

But when her hand finally closed around him, she could feel the leashed power straining to be set free. With a sound that was half growl, half groan, he shoved her hand away, and rolled on top of her.

She opened herself to him: her body, her heart, her soul. And when she felt his heat, his strength, his passion, she responded in kind. She drew him in, her body adapting to his, closing around him, making him a part of her as they started a slow climb toward fulfillment.

Jack, with one last, mighty plunge, shuddered, and Desiree could feel him coming apart inside her, his heat coursing through her, and she wrapped her legs more tightly around him and held him close, and within moments, she felt the radiance once more, but this time it kept coming, over and over again.

Finally their bodies calmed, but they stayed fused, and Desiree loved the feeling. She closed her eyes, kept her arms and legs wrapped around him. Kept him deep inside her.

He kissed her then, his tongue going deep, and she could feel his heart beating against hers.

She loved him.

Oh, God, she loved him.

Could he feel how much she loved him?

"Jack," she whispered, when he finally broke the kiss.

"What?" he whispered back, kissing the corner of her mouth, then letting his mouth slide across her cheek to settle against her ear.

She shivered as he nipped at her ear, then nuzzled against her neck. "Just Jack. I like saying your name."

"I like everything about you," he said, gently rolling them both so that they were lying on their sides. He started to withdraw from her.

"No, don't. Stay there. I like feeling you there."

"Oh, Desiree," he murmured. "You're wonderful."

He kissed her again, driving his tongue deep, rolling fully onto his back and bringing her on top of him. She could feel him hardening inside her, but he didn't move, and she didn't, either, except to settle more firmly.

Oh, that felt good. She wished they could stay like this forever. She adjusted herself, and he moaned. "You're going to kill me," he said.

She lifted her head, gazed into his eyes. The candlelight cast flickering shadows across his face.

He touched her hair, ran his fingertips over her face, her eyes, her nose, her mouth. All the while they looked at each other. Then his gaze dropped to her breasts. He reached for them, held one in each hand, his thumbs teasing the tips into hard nubs again. His chest heaved, his breathing became labored once more, and inside her, she felt him. She couldn't believe how he made her feel. She wanted him again.

This time, it was hard, hot, and fast. This time, when the spasms finally receded, they lay gasping for breath.

"Enough, already," he said, giving a weak laugh. "I'm exhausted." He lifted her off him, laid her on the bed, then pulled the comforter up and over them. Then he gathered her into his arms, tucked her head under his chin and said, "Sleep. We need sleep." He chuckled. "So we'll have enough strength to do this again."

Completely contented, Desiree snuggled into him. Within moments, she was asleep.

They soon settled into a routine. If you could call bliss a routine. Desiree went to work during the day and Jack stayed at the apartment, making phone calls and talking to Jenny. Derek Arnold was away, Jenny reported. He didn't answer his phone. She thought he might be back by the end of the week.

In the evenings Desiree and Jack cooked dinner together, and mixed in with the cooking was a lot of touching and kissing. Sometimes they forgot the food and retired to the bedroom where they made slow, delicious love.

Then they'd usually take a bath together. Desiree would fill the big, old-fashioned, claw-footed tub with bubble bath, and giggling, they'd lower themselves into the hot, scented water. Jack would sit with his back against the back of the tub, and Desiree would sit between the V of his legs, and he'd soap her, sliding his hands in all her secret places. The combination of the hot water, and the soap, and his erotic caresses would drive her wild. They'd end up making such a mess in the bathroom that it would take them an hour to clean everything up.

By that time they'd be starving, and they'd finish dinner and eat, feeding each other and doing a lot more touching and kissing.

Then it would be time to cuddle on the couch and watch rented movies.

Then, of course, it would be time for bed again.

Desiree was living in a haze of sensual awareness, in a blissful, I'm-so-in-love-I-can't-see-straight state of mind. In a glorious, heated, thoroughly aroused condition that she was sure everyone could see and recognize.

All Jack had to do was give her a certain look to set her off, to get all the juices flowing, to turn her into a quivering mass of flesh he could do anything to and with.

She was astounded that this was so. She'd always known she liked men. She'd also known she liked sex. But she'd had no idea she could be so wanton, so shameless, so completely obsessed by another human being.

All she cared about was Jack.

All she thought about was Jack.

From the moment she left him in the morning, when they kissed lingeringly, several times, until the moment she stepped into the Miata at night, she counted the minutes until they'd be together.

One night, they were so impatient for each other, and so keyed up, that Jack, when they were halfway home, reached over and slid his hand up her thigh.

Her startled gaze met his, and she could feel heat spiraling through her. She swallowed. "Jack," she said weakly.

"Touch me, too," he said, his voice rough and urgent.

"But—"

"It's dark," he whispered. "No one can see."

Heart pounding, Desiree did as she was told. The rest of the ride home was by turns agony and ecstasy. By the time they reached the house, they were in such a frenzy, they'd barely gotten the door shut before they tore at each other's clothes and made love standing up in the middle of the foyer.

It was incredible.

Afterward, thinking about it—and she thought about it a lot—Desiree could feel herself getting hot all over again.

Another time, they were laughing and teasing each other when the phone rang. It was Alice who of course didn't know Jack was staying with Desiree. Desiree was standing in the hallway, talking to her, when Jack came up behind her. He slid his hands around her and pulled her up against him. Then he tormented her. He cupped her breasts, teasing them while he nuzzled her ear from behind. When he slid his tongue into her ear, Desiree gasped.

"What's the matter?" Alice said.

Desiree could hardly speak. "Oh, nothing, I...something startled me. It's nothing, really."

"Nothing, huh?" Jack whispered. "I'll get you for that."

She elbowed him, slapped his hands away, but he kept it up, laughing evilly as he kept up the steady assault, and Desiree could feel herself dissolving, coming apart at the seams. Oh, God, she thought. I'm so weak. I need him the same way I need air.

When she finally made up some excuse, and hung up the phone, she was giddy, and aching for him. They barely made it to the bedroom before he was thrusting inside her and she was clutching at him, moaning, and calling his name.

They were insatiable.

They were completely consumed by their need for each other.

Desiree knew, if it were humanly possible, they'd never leave the bed. And when they did, they'd just make love in other places. She'd never dreamed there were so many ways to love a man and that each one would be better than the one that came before it.

She felt like Eve, like Jezebel. She was temptress. She was siren. She was Jack's woman.

The worst part of it all was she didn't feel the least bit guilty. Or embarrassed. Or sorry.

The best part of it all was she didn't feel the least bit guilty. Or embarrassed. Or sorry.

She wondered if Jack spent his days thinking up ways to pleasure her, and she remembered the first time they'd made love and how he'd teased her and told her what he planned.

She refused to think ahead, to imagine what life would be like without him.

For Desiree, there was only here, and now.

Only Jack.

* * *

Jack spent so much time thinking about Desiree that he wondered if he were losing his mind. No woman had ever so obsessed him. He felt consumed by her. Haunted by her. He was besotted, like putty in her hands. All she had to do was give him a look from beneath those thick eyelashes, and his insides turned to mush.

He forgot why he was staying with her.

He had a hard time concentrating on the problem of Elise Arnold. Even when he talked to Jenny, he felt remote, as if Derek and Elise were people he used to know. As if the problem belonged to someone else.

"What's the matter with you, Jack?" Jenny said on Wednesday night. "You haven't heard a word I said!"

"Oh, sorry," he said and tried to keep his mind on the conversation.

What was he going to do? That was the question that kept pushing itself to the forefront of his mind, the question he kept shoving away.

He didn't want to think about tomorrow.

Because one of these tomorrows he would have to return to Houston.

He would have to leave Desiree.

So instead of thinking of the future, he buried himself in her sweet-smelling skin, held her, and kissed her, and stroked her, and lost himself in her warmth and softness. He tried, in every way he could, to give her exquisite pleasure, as if, because he couldn't give her commitment, he could make it up to her by the intensity and force of his lovemaking.

And the harder he worked to give her the ultimate in sexual gratification and enjoyment, the more lost he became himself, for he found himself achieving peaks of happiness and pleasure that were so absolute, he wasn't sure he could exist without them.

Jack the aggressor, the conqueror, became the slave.

On Friday night when Jack called Jenny, she still hadn't heard from Derek. "I did finally leave a message on his answering machine," she said. "But I didn't tell him what I wanted. I just said to call me."

"Let me know the minute you hear from him," Jack warned.

He heard her sigh. "Yes, Jack. I will. You've already told me that dozens of times."

Later that night, as Jack lay in bed with Desiree asleep in his arms, he wondered if he should tell Jenny he'd changed his mind. He looked at Desiree's face, childlike and trusting in sleep. Her breathing was even and slow, and he tightened his hold on her.

"Umm," she said, burrowing closer.

He kissed her gently. She sighed, still asleep. His tongue probed her slightly parted lips, slipped inside. He laid his hand against her breast, closed his eyes. Her breast filled his palm, and he gently kneaded it, rubbing his thumb over the softness of the nipple. He smiled as he felt the nub peak in his hand. He lowered his head, licked at the pebble-like hardness.

"Don't you ever sleep?" she mumbled, but she didn't push him away.

He smiled, continuing his ministrations. He loved the way she tasted. He couldn't get enough of her.

Soon he had her moaning softly. He worked his way down her body, breathing her musky scent, wanting to keep this feeling, this woman, here forever. When he reached the essence of her, his heart was pounding. He kissed her, holding her against him, using his mouth and tongue the way he knew she liked.

He wouldn't let her stop him. Usually she didn't want him to bring her too far this way. Tonight he was relentless. And he wasn't satisfied until she was writhing against his mouth, crying out as her body was wracked with spasms. Still he held her. Still he pleasured her. Still he loved her.

Only when she had collapsed, when her body felt boneless and completely pliant, did he allow himself to take his own pleasure. Even then he wouldn't permit himself to hurry. He entered her slowly and pushed as deep as he could. Then he held himself there for a long time. Finally, when he felt her tighten around him, he began to move.

And when he erupted, he felt as if something inside him had shattered, and he held onto her as tightly as he could. He called her name over and over, and when he was finally spent, he wrapped his arms around her and kissed her damp cheek.

He had made up his mind. Desiree was too important to him to take any chances with her life.

Tomorrow he would cancel the plan.

The first thing Saturday morning Jack called Jenny. "Look," he said before she could say anything, "I've been thinking. You were right. It's too dangerous to go ahead with this plan of ours. I've decided to call it off."

Jenny gasped.

"What's wrong?" Jack said, but he knew.

"It's too late, Jack. Derek called me last night, and I told him."

The minute Jack hung up from talking with Jenny he called Paul O'Malley, the investigator he'd hired. "Derek Arnold knows," he said.

"I'll get over to his place right away."

"Call me the minute he makes a move in this direction."

"I will," O'Malley promised.

Jack hung up the phone slowly. He stood there for a long moment, thinking. Then he walked into the kitchen.

The smell of frying bacon filled the air. Desiree stood at the stove, a spatula in her hand, still in her thigh-high sleepshirt, disheveled hair tumbling about her shoulders. She was humming. Something twisted in Jack's chest.

She turned when he walked in, gave him a radiant smile and leaned toward him. He dropped a soft kiss on her upturned lips, said, "Umm, that smells good."

There was a question mark in her eyes, and Jack knew he hadn't covered his concern well. He'd better be more careful. He didn't want her worrying, too. He smiled to show her there was no problem, and slipped his hands around her waist.

She sighed and rested against him for a moment. He breathed in the sweet, clean fragrance of her hair, buried his face in its softness for long moments. "You smell even better than the bacon," he said.

"Flattery will get you anything," she murmured, laughter in her voice.

"Anything?" The ache around his heart expanded. He hadn't known love could hurt this much. He caressed her, running his hands over her body to assure himself that she was there, in his arms, safe and warm and full of life.

"Keep that up," she said, "and your bacon will burn."

He squeezed her tight, kissed her neck, then released her. Grinning, he smacked her bottom. "You'd better not burn my breakfast," he growled.

"I'll burn something else if you're not careful," she said, laughing and grabbing for him.

He feinted, dancing out of her grasp.

Desiree turned back to her cooking, still laughing, and Jack thought how much fun she was. He'd never realized an intimate relationship could be so much fun. He appreciated her ability to tease him and play with him and make him feel special.

He walked to the coffeemaker and poured himself a cup of coffee, then leaned against the kitchen counter and watched her. Several times as she finished frying the bacon, she'd turn and wink at him over her shoulder.

"Desiree," he said. "I talked to Jenny, and she said she talked to Derek Arnold last night."

"Oh?" Her shoulders stiffened. She kept her face averted as she picked up the plate of cooked bacon and brought it to the table. When she finally looked at him, he knew exactly what she was thinking. "So this might be over soon."

He nodded. That was the other thing that was bugging him, the thing he didn't want to recognize, the thing he wished would just go away.

They both knew that once Derek Arnold made his move and they were able to resolve Elise Arnold's fate, there would be no reason for Jack to stay in New Orleans. The knowledge hovered in the air between them, burned in her dark gaze, quivered in her taut body. He could see how hard she was fighting to keep her tone normal, to keep him from seeing how upset she was by this news. He wanted to reassure her. He wanted to tell her that what existed between them would always be important to him, that he'd never forget her.

But his throat was too full to speak.

He knew those words wouldn't be enough.

And there were no other words he could say.

Desiree tried to pretend everything was okay. But she was filled with a terrible uncertainty, a sick fear that gnawed at her and grew as the day wore on. She did her best to hide her unhappiness, but she didn't think she was doing a very good job of it.

Oh, dear God. How would she survive it when Jack left her? This question beat at her until it was all she could think of. Ever since she'd made such a disastrous mistake with Mark, she had been afraid to trust her instincts; she'd been leery of getting too close to any man. Since Mark, Guy was the only man she had dated. And that was because he had been safe, and she knew it.

She'd gone dancing every Friday night and flirted and had a good time, but she'd never even considered any of the men she met as possible candidates for her heart or her bed. For a while, after Mark had run out on her, she had even tried to change herself, thinking she was at fault for the whole fiasco. She'd tried to tone herself down, wear more conservative clothes, subdue her lusty, physical nature.

She'd been miserable. Gradually, she'd come to realize that she didn't have to change her entire personality, that there was nothing wrong with her wearing colorful clothes or having fun. The only thing she had to be careful of was who she chose to spend her time with, who she chose to share her life.

And she had been careful.

She'd been so careful she'd been bored silly.

Until she met Jack.

Jack had brought a dimension into her life that she'd sorely missed. He'd brought excitement, adventure, passion and love. When she was with him, she felt wholly and completely alive. But she was scared silly. Scared that once he left her, nothing would ever make her feel alive again.

The phone rang at three-thirty that afternoon. Jack jumped to answer it. "It might be Paul O'Malley," he said.

Desiree nodded.

But it wasn't. It was Desiree's Uncle Justin, as Desiree was able to figure out from Jack's end of the conversation. He talked to her uncle for a few minutes, then held the phone out to her. His expression was thoughtful. "He wants to talk to you."

Desiree took the phone. "Hello, Uncle Justin." She wondered what he thought about Jack's answering her phone.

"Desiree, *chère,* I have remembered something, something I think might help Jack find Elise. He will tell you about it." He paused, then added, "I have been thinking about this for the past two weeks." His voice became choked up. "I am praying that Elise is still alive, that the good Lord will see fit to have spared her life. I...I know it will be hard, *chère,* but I will tell Lisette everything if I have to. I hope and pray that I will be granted another chance...a chance to know this child of mine..." His voice broke.

Desiree felt his pain and was ashamed of herself for being so wrapped up in her own problems she hadn't given much thought to how he must be feeling. Of course, Jack's news about Elise Arnold would have shaken her uncle. Of course, he had been worrying and praying. Given the kind of man he was, his warmth and goodness, of course, he had been suffering. "Uncle Justin," she said softly. "We're going to do everything we can to find her." She didn't say, *if she's still alive,* but knew they were both thinking the same thing.

"God bless you, *chère.* Please call me the moment you have any news."

Desiree slowly placed the receiver into its cradle, then turned to face Jack.

"He finally remembered the name of Michelle Sonnier's aunt," Jack said. "He said it took awhile, but something triggered the memory yesterday. The woman lives in Abbeville—or at least she did twenty-nine years ago."

"What's her name?"

"Marie Sonnier."

"You know, Jack, Abbeville is a really small town. If Marie Sonnier is still alive, if she still lives there, she'd be easy to find."

"*If* she's still alive. There are a lot of 'ifs' in this equation," Jack said.

"This is still the best lead you've got."

"Yes, it is. I wish it had come before. I—" He broke off, gave Desiree a worried glance.

"Are you sorry we let Derek Arnold know about me? Is that why you're acting so worried?"

Jack grimaced. "I thought I was hiding it rather well."

Desiree smiled. "I know you too well by now. I knew something was bothering you when you walked into the kitchen this morning, but I thought..." She didn't finish the sentence, because what she wanted to say, and couldn't say, was she thought he was feeling guilty about the fact that he would soon be leaving New Orleans and he didn't want her to know. "Are you going to go to Abbeville?" she said instead. She *had* to stop feeling sorry for herself. She'd gone into this relationship with her eyes open. She had decided it was worth the risk, so she'd gambled.

And lost.

"I can't go anywhere until we know what Derek Arnold's going to do. Besides—"

"What?"

Jack sighed. "Besides, there may be no reason to go to Abbeville. Maybe all this looking and questioning people is like chasing windmills. Maybe it's completely immaterial."

"Because Elise Arnold is dead," Desiree said.

"Yes, because Elise Arnold is dead."

Desiree chewed on her bottom lip, her own misery forgotten for a few moments. "For my uncle's sake, I hope we find out something soon. If she's dead, well, he's got to learn to live with it." Her face twisted. "Oh, I hope she's not. I hope Derek Arnold comes to New Orleans and does or says something that will tell us positively that Elise is alive. And I hope you can find her."

Jack sighed. "I hope so, too.

At six o'clock the phone rang again, and this time both Desiree and Jack jumped.

"Let me answer it," Desiree said. It was going to be bad enough once Jack left; she didn't think she needed the added complication of trying to explain to her friends and family what exactly he'd been doing there. Worse, she didn't want anyone feeling sorry for her.

Jack stood at her elbow. His blue eyes were anxious.

"Hello," Desiree said.

"Hi! It's me, your cranky old boss!" Julie said.

Desiree grinned. "Hi, Julie." She waved Jack away. "You're not cranky, and you're not old."

"Thanks. Listen, what're you and the gorgeous hunk doing tonight?" Julie was one of the few people who knew Jack was staying with Desiree—and why.

"We hadn't planned anything. We've been sticking kind of close to the house."

"Why? Has something happened?" Julie said eagerly.

Desiree knew their plot to trap Derek Arnold appealed to Julie's sense of the dramatic. "Not yet, but all the traps have been set."

"The husband knows about you, you mean?"

"Yep. He called Jack's sister last night, and she told him what we'd told her to tell him. So now we're waiting."

"Are you nervous?"

"A little," Desiree admitted. She lowered her voice so Jack wouldn't hear her. "Actually I'm too miserable to be nervous."

"Miserable? Why?"

"Because this situation will probably be resolved soon, and then Jack will leave me."

"Oh, Dee," Julie commiserated. "Maybe he'll surprise you. Maybe he won't leave."

"Yeah, sure. And I'm going to hit the sweepstakes next week." She laughed cynically. "Actually, I probably have a better chance of winning the sweepstakes than I do of keeping you-know-who here."

"You need to get out, forget your troubles, kiddo," Julie said. "Which is why I called, anyway. How'd you like to come and see me act tonight?

"Act tonight! You didn't tell me you'd gotten a part."

"I was keeping it as a surprise." Julie chuckled. "Actually, I was afraid I'd be so bad I wouldn't want anyone to see me, but...I'm pretty good! If you and lover-boy want to come, I'll leave tickets for you at the box office."

"We'll be there," Desiree promised.

Jack wasn't enthusiastic about going to see Julie in a play that evening. He really thought they should burrow in at Desiree's, but he could see that Desiree needed distraction, and Lord knows, he probably could use some himself. He was beginning to feel like a first-class rat.

The play was fun—a one-act comedy by a local playwright—and Julie was very good, he thought. She played a secondary role, but it was a meaty part, and she had some of the best lines in the production. Afterward, flushed with excitement and success, she asked them if they'd like to join her and some of the other actors.

Jack could see that Desiree, who was usually the first person ready to go somewhere and have a good time, wasn't really excited about the prospect, so he made it easy for her. "I think we'd better get home. I'm expecting a phone call."

Julie nodded, gave Desiree a quick hug and told them goodbye.

Desiree was very quiet on the way home. Jack wanted to say something, anything, that would take that look of pain out of her eyes, but he felt helpless. He'd always known there could be no future for them. He simply couldn't give Desiree what she wanted. What could he say? I'm sorry I hurt you. I'm sorry I have to leave you. You'll get over this. Hell, he wasn't sure *he'd* get over this.

So he said nothing.

That night there was a desperate edge to their lovemaking. When Jack kissed her, and touched her, he could feel the hunger and yearning in her response. He tried to bury himself in her, in the sensations and feelings their act of love evoked. He tried to forget that this might be one of the last times they'd be together like this.

He forgot about skill and technique and patience. Instead, his kisses were hungry and needy, and he couldn't wait very long before he was driving into her with a raw urgency that he couldn't control. And when their release came, within seconds of each other, she cried out his name and clutched him, her fingernails digging into his back.

Afterward, exhausted and damp with sweat, he gently turned her over, then gathered her close so that her back was fitted tightly up against the front of him. For a long time, he lay there listening to her breathing, his nose buried in her fragrant hair. He could feel her steady heartbeat, and he wondered what was going through her mind. Every so often he would stroke her, as if to remind himself that she was there, that nothing had changed.

But they both knew that before long everything would change. The most that Jack could hope for was that he wouldn't hurt Desiree too badly in the process.

Chapter Thirteen

When Desiree left for work Monday morning, Derek Arnold had still not made a move toward New Orleans. Jack talked to Paul O'Malley, who called from his car phone at six a.m., and Paul reported that all was quiet.

So Jack took Desiree to work, made her promise to stay in the building the entire day and told her he'd be parked at the curb at five o'clock when she quit.

Actually, he hadn't wanted her to go to work at all, but she had insisted. "He doesn't know where I work, Jack. How can anything possibly happen to me there?"

Jack shrugged. "I don't know. I'm just worried, that's all."

She had given him a sad smile, kissed him and said, "Don't worry. Everything's going to be all right."

Afterward Jack felt guilty. Hell, he should have been the one to reassure her, not the other way around. He kept thinking of how young and beautiful, how vulnerable she'd looked in her soft turquoise wool dress when she'd walked through the wrought-iron gates to her building.

He drove quickly back to her place. He wanted to be there if Paul O'Malley called. In his gut, Jack felt if Derek Arnold was going to do anything about the information Jenny had fed him Friday night, today would be the day he'd do it. He would have had all weekend to sit and think about it, and by this morning, he would have made up his mind.

Jack made himself a pot of coffee and sat at the kitchen table with his notebook. He looked at his notes about Elise, but they didn't interest him. Not this morning. His gaze wandered around the cheerful kitchen. Everywhere he looked he saw touches of Desiree's personality, her life with Aimee. Aimee's yellow plastic mug. Her high chair. The big red porcelain pig that held cookies. A pair of Desiree's silver earrings that lay forgotten on the kitchen counter. A crayon drawing hung on the front of the refrigerator with a magnet.

Other things reminded him of the past week: the open pantry, where he'd cornered Desiree one night, and where they'd ended up making love; the chipped sugar bowl sitting in the middle of the table and how she'd teased him about putting two heaping teaspoonsful of sugar in his coffee; even the stove and how he loved to slip up behind Desiree and snake his arms around her while she cooked. Even now, thinking about it, his palms remembered the exact texture of her firm breasts, how they seemed to fill his hands perfectly, as if they'd been made with him in mind.

Jack laid his head in his arms. He could hear his heart beating, keeping time with the kitchen clock. Suddenly, he just had to hear the sound of Desiree's voice. His head told him there was absolutely no reason to worry about her; she was perfectly safe at work. His heart told him to call her.

He walked to the phone in the hall, picked it up, pressed the numbers he'd already committed to memory. He waited impatiently for her to come on the line.

"Miss Belizaire's office," she said in her soft, throaty voice.

Something warm curled into Jack's stomach at the sound. "Hi," he said. "How's it going this morning?"

"It's a typical Monday. Very busy."

She sounded too businesslike. "Is someone there? Can you talk?"

"I can talk for a minute. Have you heard anything from Paul?"

"No." He laughed sheepishly. "I...I just wanted to hear the sound of your voice, that's all."

"Jack..."

He heard the wistful note and cursed himself for yielding to the weakness that had prompted his call. "I'm sorry, Desiree," he said, "I shouldn't have called. I won't call again unless I have some news."

"Okay. See you at five."

He hung up. He'd barely turned away from the phone when it rang. He snatched up the receiver. "Hello," he barked.

"Jack?" Static accompanied the greeting.

It was Paul O'Malley. "Paul? Where are you?"

"On Interstate 10. Trailing Arnold. He's on his way."

Jack looked at his watch. It was ten o'clock. "What time did he leave?"

"About nine. I waited to make sure he was actually headed towards New Orleans. I'm still not completely sure, 'cause we're just outside Beaumont. I mean, he could just be on a sales trip, but I gotta feelin' he's headin' your way."

Jack's stomach clenched. "That means he'll probably hit town about three o'clock, maybe four, depending on whether he stops for lunch."

"Yeah, that's what I figure. Anyway, I'll keep you posted. You gonna be at this number all day?"

"Yes. I won't budge until four-thirty, when it's time to go pick up Desiree."

"You got the number to my car phone, don'cha?" O'Malley asked.

"Yes."

"Okay, call me if anything changes. Although it might be hard to reach me since you won't know what area code I'm in."

"Why don't you just check in with me a couple of times instead?"

"Yeah, that might be better."

"And Paul?"

"Yeah."

"Don't lose him."

"You can count on me."

When they'd hung up, Jack took a deep breath, and called the law firm once more.

"Desiree," he said when she answered, "Paul O'Malley just called. Derek Arnold is on his way." He repeated everything O'Malley had told him, once again cautioning Desiree against leaving the office.

"But Jack, there's no reason for me to stay in at lunchtime. He couldn't possibly get here by then if they're near Beaumont now. Not unless he sprouts wings and grows a jet engine!"

"Humor me, okay? I'll just feel better knowing you're inside."

He heard her sigh. "Okay. Okay. I promise." She chuckled. "Honestly, you're worse than my brothers!"

"Desiree," Jack said, "I couldn't stand it if anything happened to you." Then, furious with himself for yielding to that damned weakness again, he added, "I'd feel guilty forever. I got you into this mess, and I aim to make damn sure you get out in one piece."

For the rest of the day he paced around. He couldn't settle into anything. He tried to watch television, but the picture remained a blur in his mind. He tried to read. The words were meaningless. He tried to nap. His eyes remained wide open. Finally he gave up. He changed into workout clothes and did push-ups until the muscles in his arms ached. Then he did sit-ups until he was gasping for breath.

Afterward he took a long hot bath, cleaned up the bathroom, put on fresh clothes and sat back down at the kitchen table. With notebook paper in front of him he began to write: *The first time I saw her, she was stepping down from the streetcar. Her yellow rain slicker...*

As the afternoon wore on Jack got more and more tense. He kept looking at the clock. Two o'clock. They should be near the city, maybe close to Baton Rouge. Two-thirty. He kept waiting for the phone to ring. Three o'clock. He tapped his pen against the kitchen table.

Why didn't Paul O'Malley call? Jack had been sure the private investigator would call him once they hit the outskirts of New Orleans.

He stood, stretched. Paced the length of the kitchen floor. Walked down the hall to the living room. Looked out the front window. He could just barely see the street from this angle. Nothing. Only bright sunshine, an occasional bird flitting from one branch to another. A large orange Queen butterfly sailed over a stubborn patch of periwinkle that had refused to die out for the winter.

He looked at his watch again. Three-fourteen. Damn it. Why didn't O'Malley call? Well, the hell with it. He'd try to call him. So Jack tried. With no success. He heard the phone ringing at the other end, but no one answered.

It was now three twenty-three. Jack's uneasiness grew. Why hadn't O'Malley called him? Something *must* be wrong.

He thought for a moment, made his decision. He called Desiree. "I want you to tell Julie what's going on and ask her if you can leave. Right now."

"But why, Jack?"

"I can't explain it. It's just a feeling I have. You'll have to trust me, Desiree."

"All right."

"I'll be there in twenty minutes."

When he saw her emerge from the courtyard, he felt weak with relief. He wanted more than anything to gather her in his arms, but he also wanted to get her home as quickly as possible.

He drove fast. Several times he reached over to touch her hand, giving it a reassuring squeeze, although who he was reassuring—himself or her—he wasn't sure.

At four-fifteen they pulled into the driveway. He didn't even bother to put the car in the garage, just hurried her into the house. Then, and only then, did he allow himself to hold her close. He could feel her heart beating. He could feel her soft breasts pressed up against his chest. He didn't kiss her. They didn't talk. He just held her.

Finally he let her go. Voice gruff, he said, "Go pack a few things. We're going to a hotel."

"Jack," Desiree protested, frown lines creasing her forehead.

"Don't argue with me, Desiree."

She opened her mouth to say something else, then closed it. Evidently she'd seen by his expression that his mind was made up. And it was. He might never be able to do anything about his feelings for Desiree, but dammit, he loved her. And he was through taking chances with her life.

She disappeared toward her bedroom. Jack was just walking out of Aimee's room, his own packed suitcase in his hand, when the phone shrilled. He darted into the hall, dropped the suitcase, grabbed the receiver.

"Yes?"

"Jack?"

Jack expelled the air he'd been holding in. Relief washed over him. "Paul! Christ, man, I've been going nuts waiting for you to call. Where are you? What happened?"

"Wait," O'Malley said. His voice sounded strained. "Lemme talk, okay?"

"I'm waiting."

"I lost him."

"What! How could you lose him! For God's sake, Paul, you're the best in the business! I trusted you!"

"I'm sorry, Jack. I underestimated the bastard. I didn't think he had a clue about me, so I guess I was careless. He must'a found me out, 'cause he stopped for gas just outside of Baton Rouge. Anyway, I pulled into the service station, too. And I had to get gas. I mean, it would've looked funny if I hadn't. While I was waiting to pay for my gas, he pulled his car around to the back of the parking lot, near the vending machines and men's room. I couldn't go right after him 'cause I had to pay first. I didn't want the attendant to get all worked up, thinkin' I was tryin' to get away without payin'. Anyway, by the time the guy in front of me got done—there was some mixup about his change—and I paid, several minutes had passed.

"I got in my car, drove around back. I didn't see Arnold anywhere. His car was there, though. I wasn't sure what to do, but I figured he couldn't go anywhere without his car. So I sat there and waited. I waited twenty minutes. Then I started to get nervous, tryin' to think what had happened to him.

"I got out of the car, walked around the building toward the men's room. I figured that was the only place he could be, unless he was hidin' in the woods, and why would he do that? I still didn't think he knew I was followin' him.

"Anyway, I went to the men's room, tried the doorknob. It was locked. I knocked. I figured if he was in there and I knocked, he'd just think it was someone wantin' to get in and he'd come out. He yanked the door open, and the next thing I knew I woke up with a splittin' headache and a knot on my head the size of a tennis ball. I was layin' in the weeds, about twenty feet from the back of the service station, and my pockets were empty. No I.D. No wallet. No money. No car keys. Hell, he even took my car."

Jack's heart thumped heavily, and his mind raced. "And this was when?"

"Well, we stopped around two. It was close to two-thirty when that bastard creamed me. I woke up a little after three."

"Christ, Paul, it's four-thirty. Why didn't you call me sooner?"

"It took me this long to convince the owner of the service station that I wasn't some nut case...plus I couldn't even remember your number."

Jack ran his hand through his hair. Arnold was probably already in New Orleans. Hell, he might even be outside this minute, watching the house. He might have even seen them come inside. Jack looked around, fear clutching at him. He could see the wide expanse of the picture window, and looking the other way, the windows overlooking the back-yard. His throat felt dry, and his palms felt clammy.

"Jack—"

Just the way O'Malley said his name caused Jack's breath to stop.

"There's something else." O'Malley waited one heart-beat. "He took my gun."

The words reverberated over the wire. Stark. Frighten-ing. Icy-cold fear slithered along Jack's spine.

A gun.

Derek Arnold had Paul's gun.

At this very moment, he could be within yards of the house, with a gun. Jack swallowed.

"The police finally believed me, and of course, they've got a description of the car and the license number and all that, so I'm sure they'll catch up with him."

"You were driving your Thunderbird?" Jack asked.

"Yeah. Dark green, looks almost black unless you're up close to it. Plates read 742 FQD."

Jack wrote down the numbers. "Where are you now? And what're you going to do?"

"I'm in the sheriff's office in west Baton Rouge. I'll call my wife. She can order a rental car for me. Have it deliv-ered here, or maybe one of these guys'll take me to the rental place to pick it up." He sighed. "Listen, Jack, I'm really sorry. I know I screwed up. Be careful." He hesitated, then said, "Do you want me to come to New Orleans?"

"No."

"My advice is, call the cops. The whole game's changed now that he's got a gun. In my opinion, the guy's a loose cannon, considerin' what he did to me."

That's what Jack thought, too. He snorted. "What am I going to say to them? That I think he's headed here? That I think he did something to his wife? That I think Desiree's in danger? I have no proof of anything. No case.''

"Then why don't you pack up the Cantrelle woman and take her somewhere safe? Forget about trappin' Arnold. It's too dangerous."

"That's exactly what I plan to do." His heart pounded as he replaced the receiver. He'd been in all kinds of dangerous situations during his career. He'd covered wars. He'd covered hostage situations. He'd covered mob scenes, and terrorist hijackings. Nothing had ever scared him so thoroughly.

Of course, during those situations, he'd only had to worry about his own skin.

Now he had something infinitely more precious to worry about.

He walked back to Desiree's bedroom. She was bent over the bed, just shutting a small suitcase. She'd changed clothes, put on jeans, socks and loafers, a bright orange sweatshirt. She turned, smiled. "Jack..." She frowned. "What's wrong? Was that Paul O'Malley on the phone?"

He nodded, quickly told her what Paul had said. He saw her face go still. "A gun," she said quietly.

"We have to get out of here, and fast," he said.

She didn't argue. She shut her suitcase, said, "I'm ready." Met his gaze steadily.

Jack took a shaky breath. If anything happened to her... "Desiree." It was a whisper, and he heard the fear in his voice. He reached for her.

She walked into his arms, raised her face, looked deeply into his eyes. Powerful emotions pummeled him. Fear for her safety. Love. "Whatever happens—''

"Nothing's going to happen," she said.

Her eyes were steady, full of trust. Her soft lips were parted, moist-looking. He cradled the back of her head, brought it forward and crushed his mouth to hers. He put everything he was feeling into the kiss. All the anxiety, all the torment, all the frustration, all the passion, all the love.

And she responded in kind.

They stayed fused for a long time. Jack lost himself in the deep recesses of her hot, sweet mouth. But finally he had to let her go. "Come on," he said roughly. "Let's get out of here."

Mouth swollen from his kiss, eyes shadowed but not frightened, she nodded. She grabbed her big tote bag, slung it over her shoulder.

He picked up her suitcase.

She walked out of the bedroom, and he followed her. His own suitcase was in the hall. He picked it up, too.

When she would have opened the front door, he said, "No. Wait. Let me go out and put these bags in the car. I'll look around first. You stay right here."

"Okay." Her dark eyes gleamed. Pink stained her cheeks. She opened the door and stood back to let him pass.

Everything happened so fast.

One moment Jack was stepping outside, looking around.

The next he was staring down the muzzle of a gun, and Derek Arnold was shouting, "You dirty, rotten son-of-a-bitch! Shackin' up with my wife! Who the hell do you think you are? Where is she? Come out here, Elise! Get your butt out here, or you're gonna be sorry!" His face was contorted with rage. "When I get my hands on you—"

Jack swung Desiree's suitcase. The gun exploded and Jack staggered back, his left shoulder stinging. From somewhere behind him, Desiree screamed. "Jack! Jack!"

Derek leaped at him, cursing and muttering. "Goddamn you, I saw you kissing her. I saw you through the window. How long has this been goin' on, huh?" He hit Jack in the face. Jack's shoulder felt as if someone had stuck a hot poker in it, but he managed, with the last of his strength, to heave his own suitcase up and into Arnold's face.

The next thing he knew he was lying on the ground.

When Jack fell, Desiree, who had been frantically trying to locate the can of Mace in her tote bag finally felt her fingers close around it. She flew out the door, spraying the can directly into Derek Arnold's eyes.

He screamed. He dropped his gun, clutched at his eyes, still screaming. Heart pounding, Desiree knelt over Jack. He struggled to sit up. "Desiree! Get back in the house. Where's Ar—"

Trembling with delayed reaction, Desiree said, "I sprayed him in the eyes." She inclined her head. "He's over there."

Arnold was half sitting, half standing against the trunk of a magnolia tree. He moaned and sobbed, his hands covering his eyes.

"Are you okay, Jack?" Her heart still felt as if it were trying to get out of her chest. She'd been so scared when she'd heard the gun go off. So scared. If anything had happened to Jack . . .

"I'm okay. It's just my shoulder."

His voice sounded weak to her. "Jack, here. Take this can of Mace in case he's able to try something else, although I don't think he's in any shape to do anything for a while."

"Wh-where are you going?"

"Inside. I'm going to call the police."

"Hurry," Jack said. "I'm starting to feel dizzy."

Blood had begun welling from his shoulder. She didn't want to leave him, but she knew she had to. She handed him the Mace, then ran to the house. She called the police, then raced back outside. Jack, clutching his shoulder, face white, looked as if he was about to pass out. But he was still holding the can of Mace, aimed at Arnold. She wanted to go to him. But she knew she couldn't. Not yet.

Desiree looked around and finally saw what she'd been looking for. The gun lay in the grass a few feet away. She walked over, picked it up. She didn't know much about pistols, but she did know how to shoot. She mentally thanked Norman for the lessons.

She walked over to Derek Arnold, who by now, had collapsed against the tree trunk. She spread her legs, raised the gun and pointed it directly at him. "Don't move a muscle," she said. "Or you're dead."

He whimpered.

Ten minutes later, Desiree heard the sirens. When a police cruiser, followed shortly by an ambulance, pulled into the driveway, dome lights flashing, Desiree finally let down her guard.

And as two officers and two paramedics rushed to her aid, she hurried to Jack's side.

"Oh, Jack, are you okay?" Tears blinded her as she knelt by him.

But he didn't answer.

He had passed out.

Chapter Fourteen

"Wh-where's Arnold?" Jack said.

Desiree whirled around, a big smile splitting her face. "You're awake!" Relief made her feel weak, and she clutched at the windowsill for a brief moment before quickly walking to Jack's bedside. "I thought you were going to sleep forever," she said tenderly. She pulled the bedside chair over close to the bed, sat and reached for his hand.

He clasped her hand, but she could feel how weak he was. "Am I in the hospital?" he said. He licked his lips.

"Yes, you're in the hospital. You were shot in the shoulder. Do you remember that?"

"Yeah, I guess. And I remember fighting with Arnold, swinging a suitcase at him." He frowned with the effort of concentrating, blue eyes cloudy. Then suddenly, they cleared, and he grinned. "I remember now! You sprayed him in the face with your Mace!" He laughed triumphantly, then grimaced. "Ow, that hurts." He licked his lips again.

"Do you want some water?" There was a pain around her heart, as if someone were squeezing it. Each time she thought about what might have happened...if Jack had been a few inches over...if the bullet had gone through his heart instead of a muscle in his left shoulder...if...oh, God. She would have died if something had happened to him. It was in that moment of fear, when she'd realized he'd been shot, that she'd known his leaving her to go back to Houston, back to his nomadic life-style, wasn't the worst thing that could happen to her. No, the worst thing, the impossible thing, the not-to-be-borne thing, would be knowing Jack was gone forever, that the light in his eyes would never shine again, that his heart would never beat again....

Something of what she was feeling must have shown in her face because he said, "What is it?" His grip on her hand tightened.

"Oh, Jack. I was so scared...." Tears trembled in her eyes, and she had to fight against the urge to bury her face in his chest and cry out her relief.

"Desiree," he whispered. "I'm all right."

She nodded, sniffing. She reached for her tote bag, extracted a crumpled tissue, blew her nose.

"Now, come on, tell me about Arnold," he said.

So she told him how the police had come and hauled Derek Arnold off, how a young officer had later come to the hospital to take her statement, how the lieutenant in charge had come still later to tell her that it looked as if Derek Arnold had really believed she was his wife.

"So Elise is definitely alive...." Jack said. He closed his eyes. "Damn. I wish I didn't feel so tired. I'm anxious to try to locate her aunt." He opened his eyes, looked at her. "What day is it, anyway? How much time have we lost?"

"It's Tuesday. But quit worrying," Desiree said. "Sleep. The only thing you need to concentrate on right now is getting stronger. Then we'll look for Elise's aunt."

The following day Jack's sister, Jenny, arrived. Desiree took one look at her—the same wonderful blue eyes, the concern and love in her worried expression—and knew she and Jenny would be friends.

And when Desiree impulsively hugged her, and Jenny, after only a moment's hesitation, responded in kind, Desiree's heart was almost too full to speak.

"Jack's told me a lot about you," Jenny said.

"You, too," Desiree echoed.

"I can't get over how much you look like Elise."

Desiree smiled.

"Is Jack going to be all right? I was so scared when you called. So afraid you weren't telling me the whole truth."

"He's going to be fine," Desiree assured her.

The two women smiled at each other, understanding without words that they each cared very much about the man in the room they were about to enter.

Desiree hung back, but she still had a clear view of Jack's eyes when Jenny walked into the room. She saw the leap of happiness, the love and trust that was obvious in the way they held each other's hands, the gentleness of the kiss Jenny gave him, the tender concern in her voice as they greeted each other. Seeing the way they felt about each other told Desiree a lot about Jack—that his facade of being a loner was just that—a facade..Obviously, his twin meant a lot to him, just as much as Desiree's brothers and sister meant to her. It was also obvious that Jenny felt the same way.

For some reason, this made Desiree feel more hopeful about her own uncertain future where Jack was concerned.

That night, after a long conversation with her parents and Aimee, Desiree and Jenny ate dinner together. Jack had urged them to go. "I don't want you two sitting around here all day and all night," he said. Desiree had still not gone back to work, and she thanked God she had stockpiled so much vacation time. She felt a little guilty about running out on Julie when they were so busy, but Julie had told her not to worry about anything.

During dinner, Desiree brought Jenny completely up to date on everything she and Jack had managed to ferret out about Elise Arnold. "What is she like?" Desiree asked. "All I have is Jack's version, but you and Elise were good friends, and you can give me a woman's point of view."

Jenny smiled sadly. "Elise is a special person. At least she was to me. Gentle, sweet, lovely, kind, generous. She's the kind of person who isn't capable of hurting anyone." Jenny's blue eyes darkened. "I guess that's why it made me so angry when I realized her husband was abusing her. If anyone didn't deserve that kind of treatment, it was Elise."

"You cared for her very much," Desiree said.

"Very much." Jenny toyed with her lime sorbet, her voice reflective. "To understand our relationship, you have to understand both of us. Like Elise, I had never made friends easily. In fact, other than Jack—and I suppose you know that twins share a special bond—and Kevin, my husband, I had never really had a close friendship. I'd had what I thought were friends—girls in high school, girls in college—but not the kind of friendship where you felt *safe*." She directed her intense blue gaze on Desiree. "Do you know what I mean when I say 'safe'?"

Desiree nodded slowly. "When you trust the other person completely...when no matter what you might tell them, they won't judge you, and they won't love you less. It's when they won't betray you."

"Exactly," Jenny said. "Elise and I were like kindred spirits. We recognized the same need in each other, and although it took time, we grew closer and closer. Elise began to confide in me, but unfortunately, she needed more help than I could even begin to give her. She needed counseling, professional expertise I didn't have, and I was afraid she'd never have the strength to break away from Derek."

"But she *did* break away."

Jenny nodded, her forehead knit in thought. "That's the way it looks now. I just hope . . . you don't think there's any chance Derek was *pretending* he thought you were Elise, do you?"

"You mean to throw us off the scent, or something?"

"Yes."

Desiree remembered the ugly fury in Derek Arnold's voice as he screamed at Jack, the obscenities he'd spewed, the hate in his eyes when she'd come at him. "I don't think anyone is that good an actor. No, he really believed I was his wife. There's no doubt in my mind about that."

Jenny's shoulders sagged with relief. "Thank God. I guess there was still some small part of me that was afraid to believe it. I guess all we have to do now is figure out where she is and try to get her word that Derek can no longer harm her."

Desiree went back to work on Thursday. Jack was released from the hospital on Friday. On Saturday he insisted that he, Jenny and Desiree drive over to Abbeville to try to locate Elise Arnold's aunt. Desiree and Jenny agreed, on the condition that Desiree would drive.

So Saturday, at noon, the three of them were in the Abbeville post office, and Desiree was sweet-talking the postmistress, a short, plump Cajun lady with salt-and-pepper hair and a missing front tooth. She was standing behind a barred window, and wearing a name tag that read: Estelle Dubois.

"Marie Sonnier?" the postmistress said. She nodded her head up and down. *"Oh, mais oui, chère,* I remember Marie Sonnier. But she hasn't lived here in Abbeville for a long time, *chère.* No, she's been gone at least ten years."

Desiree's heart sank. "Oh, dear..."

"But I'll bet Octave could tell you where she went, *chère.*"

"Octave?"

Estelle Dubois grinned. "Octave Arceneaux, our letter carrier." She turned, shouted, "Octave! Octave! Come up here. A pretty girl wants to talk to you." Her grin got wider. "Old Octave, he still likes the pretty girls!"

Jack, who was standing off to the side, chuckled. "Who doesn't?"

Desiree gave him a mock frown, her heart giving a little blip when she saw the expression in his eyes. She hurriedly looked away. Behind her, Jenny laughed softly.

A small, skinny man who looked to be in his sixties came shuffling slowly to the window. He looked at Desiree, his dark eyes lighting up.

"This here is Desiree Cantrelle from Baton Rouge way, Octave, and she's lookin' to find old Marie Sonnier. I told her you pro'bly could tell her where Marie is."

Octave nodded, his wispy hair falling across his deeply tanned face. "You a frien' of Marie's, *chère?*"

"I'm a friend of her niece's," Desiree answered.

"Well, ol' Marie, she's in a nursin' home up in Acadia Parish." He frowned. "Lemme see if I can remember 'xactly. She's stayin' in a home run by the Ursuline nuns. I believe it's in Evangeline, or right outside Evangeline. Marie, she used to have mail forwarded to her, but these past five, six years, nothin's come for her, so I don't rightly remember." He gave Desiree an apologetic look. "In fact, I don't rightly know if old Marie is still alive. If she is, she'd be mebbee eighty-seven, eighty-eight years old."

Desiree thanked him and thanked the postmistress. Then she and Jack and Jenny walked outside where they talked for a few minutes. "How many nursing homes can there be near Evangeline?" Jack mused.

"Let's call Evangeline information and see," Desiree suggested.

"Will they tell us that kind of thing?" Jenny asked.

"Let me try," Desiree said.

They found a pay phone, and Jack and Jenny waited in the car while Desiree phoned. Five minutes later, gleeful, she rejoined them. "Success! The only nursing home around there is the Ursuline Home for Women. It's right on Route 97."

Jack looked at his map. "It looks like it might take us about an hour to get there."

"Could we have some lunch first?" Desiree said. Her stomach had growled twice in the past ten minutes.

"Hey, you're the driver," he countered, eyes twinkling.

Desiree's silly heart gave another lurch. Oh, she was in a bad way if she couldn't even have a normal conversation or exchange a look with him without having that lovesick feeling sweep over her.

They ate lunch at a roadside café. Jenny and Desiree opted for spicy bowls of gumbo, but Jack insisted on red beans and rice. The waitress, a pretty girl with red hair and freckles, said, "I know you're a tourist."

"How do you know?" Jack said, winking at Desiree.

"Red beans and rice is what the natives eat on Mondays," the waitress said. "Not Saturdays."

After the waitress left, Desiree explained. "For Cajun women, red beans could be put on in the morning, simmer all day while they did the laundry, then be a good, filling meal to give their families that night. And even though modern-day Cajun women no longer stay at home and do their wash on Mondays, the tradition is so ingrained that all true-blue Cajuns, and most of the rest of the population of Louisiana, still have red beans and rice on Mondays.''

"I could get to like it here," Jack said, giving her a charged look.

There was that hollowed-out feeling again. Desiree shook it off. She'd better get used to him not being around, because her gut told her the closer they got to Marie Sonnier, the closer they got to Jack's leaving.

They found the Ursuline Home for Women easily, although getting there wasn't as simple as they thought it was going to be. Unfortunately, they had to take secondary roads most of the way, and they got caught behind several big open trucks loaded with sugar cane. Not only did they have to drive slowly until they could get around the trucks, but the roads were sticky with residue from fallen cane that had gotten smashed under the tires of passing cars.

So it was nearly three o'clock when they reached the large plantation-like setting of the nursing home. They drove through iron gates and up a driveway shaded by chinaberry trees wearing their brilliant yellow autumn foliage. It was a tranquil, lovely setting, and Desiree thought it might not be so bad to be old and sick if you could look out over this vista.

They parked Desiree's car and walked up the broad front steps to the veranda. There were several old women wrapped in lap robes sitting on chairs in the afternoon sunshine. There was one attendant who nodded to them as they walked by.

"Let me do the talking," Jack said as they entered the front door.

Desiree and Jenny exchanged glances. Jenny smiled, and Desiree smiled back. She knew Jack needed to feel he was once more in control. Ever since his injury, he'd been chomping at the bit. She wondered what he'd be like if he ever got really sick and incapacitated. His impatience and inability to remain inactive for long drove home the knowledge that Jack needed adventure, excitement, and most of all—challenge.

The two women hung back as Jack talked to the young woman sitting behind the reception desk. Desiree idly wondered if the woman was a nun. She was dressed in a plain blue skirt and white blouse and wore no makeup. Most telling of all, she didn't preen the way most women did around a man as attractive as Jack. Yes, she must be a nun.

Jack smiled, and the woman stood. She walked briskly down the corridor and disappeared into a room at the end. Jack turned to Desiree and Jenny. He beckoned them forward. "She says Marie Sonnier is here," he murmured as they approached. "But she has to check and see if it's okay for us to talk with her."

They waited a few minutes, and Desiree could see by the gleam in Jack's eyes that he was excited. Like a hunter spying his prey, she thought. Jenny, however, looked apprehensive.

"What's wrong, Jenny?" Desiree asked softly.

Jenny gave her an apologetic look. "I'm sorry. I know it's silly, but for some reason, I'm scared." She closed her eyes briefly, then said, "I'm praying we'll get some information about Elise. I just want to know she's all right."

A few seconds later, the young receptionist returned. She turned kind green eyes on them. "Mother Clothilde said you may speak with Miss Marie, but only for a few moments. She's very old, you know, and she's nearly blind."

They followed the receptionist down the hall, where she turned left and led them into another wing. Soon she pushed open a door and said, "Miss Marie. Some visitors for you."

A very frail, very wrinkled old woman sat in a wheelchair in front of a large window that overlooked the back of the property. Sunshine poured through the window and illuminated her face, which was feathered with hundreds of fine lines. Cloudy brown eyes turned in their direction, but Desiree could see that they were unfocused. "Visitors? Who are they?" she said in a shaky, high voice.

Jack spoke. "My name is Jack Forrester, Miss Sonnier. I work as an investigative journalist for World Press. My sister and I are friends of your great-niece, Elise Arnold. We've been looking for her for a long time, and our search brought us here to you."

"Come here, come here," the old woman said. "I can't see very well, you know." She made a sound like a snort. "I'm nearly ninety years old. I should be dead, but I'm not. People shouldn't live to be ninety years old."

Jack walked forward, followed by Desiree and Jenny. "Come closer," Marie insisted, frowning. "I want to touch you. Give me your hand."

Jack, with an amused backward glance at Jenny and Desiree, did as he was told. He held out his right hand and grasped Marie's gnarled fingers. She laid her other hand on top of his and rubbed it. "Tell me what you want with my great-niece," she ordered.

Desiree thought the old woman had a lot of spunk left in her for someone her age.

"My sister and I want to make sure she's safe. We also want to let her know her husband will never be able to hurt her again."

"Why not?" the old woman demanded.

Desiree stifled a giggle. She liked Marie Sonnier.

"Who's that?" Marie turned her head in Desiree's direction.

Jack shrugged. He motioned for Jenny and Desiree to come closer. "This is my sister, Jenny Wharton."

"Hello, Miss Sonnier," Jenny murmured.

"Speak up. Speak up!"

Jenny grinned. "I said hello, Miss Sonnier."

Marie insisted on going through the hand-holding ritual once more. "Now who's the other woman with you?"

Desiree stepped forward. "I'm Desiree Cantrelle."

"Cantrelle!" Marie's eyes widened, and she peered forward.

"Yes. And I think Elise is my cousin."

"Give me your hand," Marie ordered. Desiree put her right hand out. When the old woman grasped her hand, Desiree had the oddest sensation, almost as if there were a silent communication between them. When Marie let her hand go, Desiree felt a sharp sense of loss.

"Lucy? Lucy? Are you still there?" Marie said.

The young receptionist, whom Desiree had forgotten about, walked into the room from her position by the open door. "I'm here, Miss Marie."

"Make him show you some identification. I want to know these people are who they say they are."

Jack pulled out his I.D., and Jenny reached inside her purse. Desiree did the same, handing Lucy her driver's license. Lucy verified their identification.

Marie nodded, eyes narrowed. For long moments she remained still, lost in thought. The silence stretched. Faint noises, indicative of the nursing home's routine, drifted into the room as they all waited.

"You'll find her in Abbeville," she finally said.

Jack and Jenny and Desiree all looked at one another. Abbeville. They'd just come from Abbeville. "Where?" Desiree and Jack said in unison.

"She's living with the daughter of an old friend of mine—Cleoma Guidry. She's going by the name of Elise Guidry."

"Where do the Guidrys live?" Jack asked.

Marie closed her eyes, leaned her head against the back of the wheelchair. "Cleoma owns an antique shop. Only one in town. Ask anybody."

"She's very tired," Lucy said. "You'd better go now."

Jack nodded. "Thank you, Miss Sonnier. Thank you very much."

The old lady's eyes fluttered open. "Goodbye. God bless you."

Excitement gripped the three of them as they drove back to Abbeville, following the same painstakingly slow roads.

"The antique shop will be closed for the night," Jack said. "You know that, don't you?"

"But how many Guidrys can live in Abbeville?" Jenny said.

"Only about fifty or sixty," Desiree said.

Jack laughed. "So it might be a long night."

It was dark by the time they drove into the small town. As they drove down the main street, Jenny said, "Look! There's the shop!"

Sure enough, in white letters on a dark wooden shingle was printed: GUIDRY ANTIQUES.

They pulled up in front of the shop, and Jenny hopped out. She walked to the door, read for a minute, then walked back to the car. Smiling, she said, "Jack, write down this number."

Jack pulled out his notebook and she gave him a telephone number, explaining that that was the number to call in the event of an emergency.

"That must be the Guidrys' home phone, wouldn't you think?" she asked Jack.

They drove to the same pay phone they'd used earlier. "Let me call," Jenny said.

Desiree and Jack agreed. They sat in the car and waited, and Desiree wondered if he was as excited as she was. She doubted it. The thought of finally meeting her double, her unknown cousin, had to mean more to her than it did to him.

As if he'd read her mind, he reached for her hand. "How do you feel?"

"Nervous. Excited. Happy that it looks as if everything's going to end up okay."

Jenny was on the phone for a long time. When she finally came back to the car, her eyes were shining. "Let's go," she said as she slid into the back seat. "It's not far."

Five minutes later they were pulling up in front of a two-story brick house with a wide front porch. The front windows blazed with light.

Desiree and Jack followed Jenny up the walk. Before she even had a chance to knock, the front door was flung open. "Jenny!"

"Oh, Elise!"

Desiree hadn't gotten much of a look at her cousin. Now as Jenny and Elise embraced, she still couldn't see much of the other woman's face. But when they broke apart, and Elise stood back, saying, "Come in. Come in. Oh, Jack, hi!" Desiree got a good look at her, and even though she'd known she and Elise looked alike, still, the shock of seeing her cousin in the flesh was like a jolt of electricity going through her system.

Elise's eyes widened as her gaze settled on Desiree. "Oh, my God," she said, clasping her hand over her mouth.

"I—" she looked at Jenny "—I know what you said, but I didn't believe you. Why, we could be twins."

Jenny smiled. "Yes, you two look more alike than Jack and I do, and we *are* twins."

"Hi. I'm Desiree Cantrelle." Desiree smiled at Elise, wanting to put her at ease.

Elise gave her a shy smile and held out her hand. Desiree took her hand, then leaned forward and kissed her cousin's cheek.

"Why don't you all come into the living room?" Elise said, leading the way to a big room to the left of the foyer. An older woman with straight black hair and glasses stood when they walked in. She smiled.

"This is Cleoma Guidry, a wonderful friend," Elise said.

"Jack Forrester," said Jack, shaking Cleoma's hand. "My sister, Jenny. And this is Desiree Cantrelle."

Cleoma did a double take. "Blessed Mary, if you aren't the spittin' image of Elise."

"We're cousins," Desiree explained. She looked at Elise. "At least I think we are."

"Before we talk about that, Elise, please tell me what happened while I was in Spain," Jenny said. "I can't tell you how sorry I am that I wasn't there when you needed me."

Elise smiled sadly. "Oh, Jenny. I'm sorry to have put you through so much worry. But when I called and called, and you didn't call back, I just didn't know what to think. I...I don't think I was thinking very straight, either. I can't explain it. All I know is that suddenly I just couldn't go on the way I had been living—not for another day." She gave Jenny an anguished look. "Something inside me just fell apart, and I felt frantic. I knew I had to get away before Derek returned from his trip. I was terrified that when he got back he would kill me."

"Did he threaten to kill you?"

Elise twisted her hands, which had been lying in her lap. "He was always threatening to kill me, but the night before he left for that trip, he found a theater program that I had forgotten I had in my purse. He was furious, wanted to know when I had gone to the theater. Of course, I didn't dare tell him I was doing some work with the group, so I lied and said I had gone with you. He screamed at me, told me he didn't want me hanging around with you anymore. He called you names, then called me names. Finally, he started beating me. I . . . I kind of lost track of the time, but he beat me for a long time."

She gave a ragged sigh. She avoided everyone's eyes. "He left the next morning. Right before he left he told me he still wasn't finished with me, that when he got back he'd tend to me once and for all. He said when he got through with me, I'd wish I'd never been born."

Jenny reached for Elise's hand. "Oh, Elise . . ."

Desiree clenched her fists. She glanced at Jack. His jaw was clamped shut, and his eyes were icy with anger.

"I . . . I called you that day, and the next day, and the next. I waited as long as I could. I didn't know what to think. I . . . I'm sorry to admit this now, but Derek had me so brainwashed, I began to think you probably had changed your mind and didn't want to become involved with someone as worthless and weak as me."

"Oh, Elise, how could you think that?" Jenny cried. "You know I'd never feel that way!"

"I know it seems stupid, but you just don't know what kind of shape I was in," Elise said. She smiled wryly. "I'm so much better now, thanks to Aunt Marie and Cleoma." She turned her smile on Cleoma, who sat quietly. She turned back to Jenny. "I've been going into Lafayette three times a week for counseling. It's helped me tremendously."

"So how did you get here?" Jenny asked.

Elise explained that she'd squirreled away small amounts of money for years, and that the several hundred dollars she'd managed to save was enough to get her to Louisiana.

"How did you travel?" Jack asked.

"By bus."

He nodded. "I told you it was nearly impossible to trace someone when they ride the bus and pay cash for their ticket," he said to Desiree.

They talked for a long time. Then Elise turned to Desiree. "Why do you believe we are cousins?" she said.

Heart full, Desiree met Elise's gaze. She saw the uncertainty. She also saw the bright spark of hope. Desiree smiled gently. "Because I know your father."

"Uncle Justin?"

"Desiree? Is there news?"

Desiree smiled at the eagerness she heard in her uncle's voice. "Very good news."

"You've found her?"

"Yes."

"Thank the good Lord. My prayers have been answered."

"And Uncle Justin, I've told her about you."

For a long moment there was silence at the other end of the line. When her uncle spoke, there was a hesitancy in his voice. "Did you tell her how much I would like to meet her?"

"Yes. And she wants to meet you, too."

She heard his quick intake of breath. "I...I was afraid to hope."

She smiled. "I know you were."

"Where is she now? Where are you calling from?"

"We're in Abbeville. That's where Elise has been living. She . . . oh, why don't I let her tell you? Can you come here tomorrow?"

"Yes, *chère,* I will be there tomorrow. Just tell me where."

After they'd hung up, Desiree sat by the phone for a few minutes, gathering her thoughts. She knew her uncle was nervous, perhaps even frightened, but she had also heard the joy in his voice. She knew the next hour or so would be one of the hardest in his life, for now he would have to tell her Aunt Lisette everything. Desiree closed her eyes, said a quick prayer. Oh, she hoped everything would turn out all right. Elise and Justin and Lisette were all fine people who didn't deserve to be hurt anymore.

Cleoma Guidry insisted on Jack, Jenny and Desiree staying overnight with them. When Jack protested, saying they'd find a motel, Cleoma cut him off. "Absolutely not! This old house is practically empty. Why, I've got two more spare bedrooms—one for you, and one for Desiree—and I know Jenny and Elise have lots of catching up to do, so I'm sure they won't mind bunking in together."

So they stayed overnight. Desiree lay in the old-fashioned four-poster bed in one of the guest bedrooms and thought about Jack lying in his bed in the next room. Tonight, when she needed him more than she'd ever needed him before, they were separated by a barrier impossible to bridge. The past week had been so tumultuous, so laden with emotion, so fraught with tension and the knowledge hovering at the back of her mind—the knowledge that soon, so very soon, Jack would be gone.

Long into the night, Desiree's thoughts whirled, a chaotic mix of happiness that they'd found Elise, trepidation and fear for the reunion of Elise and Justin tomorrow, and a terrible loneliness that increased by the minute.

The next morning, Desiree felt sluggish and miserable. Even the thought of the reunion of father and daughter couldn't lift her spirits. And when she saw Jack, who was already up and drinking coffee in Cleoma's kitchen, she knew he'd passed the same kind of sleepless night. His eyes looked haunted, and he looked tired. Desiree felt a pang of guilt. He was still recuperating from his gunshot wound. He probably should still be resting instead of traipsing all over the countryside.

"How are you feeling this morning?" she said softly, walking over to him and laying her hand on his shoulder.

He covered her hand with his own, lifted his gaze. His blue eyes were filled with a longing Desiree recognized. The same longing was piercing her own heart. "I'm feeling okay," he answered. "How about you?"

She shrugged over the lump in her throat. Suddenly she couldn't bring herself to pretend. Swallowing hard, she turned away from the regret and sorrow, the I-wish-things-could-be-different-but-we-both-know-they-can't look so obvious in his expression.

When Elise and Jenny joined them in the kitchen, some of the strain Desiree was feeling eased. It was hard to feel sorry for herself in the face of what Elise had in store for her this morning. When Desiree saw Elise's hands tremble as she poured herself a cup of coffee, all thoughts of her own misery fled in the face of Elise's anxiety. She walked over to the kitchen counter where Elise was standing, put her arm around her cousin. "It'll be all right," she murmured. "You're going to like him very much."

Elise, who was facing away from the others, closed her eyes. "I . . . I've dreamed of this day for so long. But I'm so afraid. What . . . what if he doesn't like me?" she whispered.

"Bring your coffee. Let's go into the other room and talk," Desiree said quietly, giving Jack a meaningful glance over her shoulder.

He nodded, quick understanding flashing in his eyes.

When Desiree and Elise were sitting side by side on the Victorian sofa in the living room, Desiree took Elise's hand. "I'd like to tell you about your father."

Elise's dark eyes, bright with unshed tears, lifted to meet Desiree's. Bottom lip trembling, she nodded.

Holding fast to her cousin's hand, Desiree said, "From the time I was a little girl, Uncle Justin has always been my favorite person in the whole world, next to my parents and sister and brothers. He...he has a goodness of heart, a generosity and warmth, that people just immediately respond to." She looked deep into Elise's eyes. "You will love him. And he will love you. You'll see."

A lone tear rolled down Elise's cheeks, and she brushed it away.

Desiree took a long breath. "I know he's going to want to tell you about his relationship with your mother himself. But I'd like to tell you something about me, and Uncle Justin, that might help you when you meet him." So Desiree told Elise how she'd become pregnant with Aimee, the heartbreak, the misery, the shame that had followed. How Justin and Lisette had welcomed her into their home, how they'd loved her and encouraged her, how they'd helped her understand she wasn't a bad person because she'd made a mistake. She told her how understanding they were, how they didn't sit in judgment of her.

"They've always been like that," Desiree concluded. "As far back as I know. Whenever other people would talk about someone, make disparaging remarks, I always remember Uncle Justin and Aunt Lisette being the voice of reason, the ones who would caution against judging someone else. Uncle Justin's favorite expression is, 'until you've walked in his shoes, you have no right to condemn.'"

"My...my mother never condemned him," Elise offered. "And she raised me to keep my head high. She said there was no shame in the circumstances of my birth, that I was conceived in love and a sharing of spirits, and I should always remember that. She...she said my father was a man of honor, and that if it had been possible, he would have been with us."

"Your mother sounds like a wonderful woman," Desiree said.

"She was. I loved her very much."

"I'm curious about something, Elise. How much did your husband know about your background? Didn't he know you had an aunt who lived in Abbeville?"

Elise shook her head. "Derek was never interested in me. When we met, my mother was already dead, and I had always told everyone my father was dead—except Jenny, that is. When Derek and I went out, he always talked about himself, and I was such a mouse and so unsure of myself where men were concerned, that I just naturally let him. Anyway, when we got married, I couldn't very well change my story about my father, so I just never told him." She bowed her head. "Thinking about it now, listening to how that sounds, makes me realize what a sham my marriage was. I mean, if I couldn't tell Derek something so fundamental, what kind of relationship did we have?"

The question hung in the air. Desiree squeezed Elise's hand again.

"The subject of my Great-aunt Marie never came up," Elise continued softly. "I always knew about her, of course. When I was a little girl, my mother used to take me to see her, and I remembered how kind she was. I wrote to her after Derek and I were married, but by that time, she was going blind and couldn't write back, so I didn't hear from her. When she went into the nursing home, she did have one of the nuns write to me to tell me where she was. One thing she said that I didn't forget was, if you ever need anything, come to see me.'' Elise picked up her neglected cup of coffee, took a swallow, grimaced. "It's cold." She put it back on the coffee table, extricating her hand from Desiree's in the process.

"I never told Derek about the letter. He was out of town on a sales trip when it came, and I...I hid it in the bottom of one of my shoeboxes. At the time, I don't even know why I hid it. He hadn't started...beating me yet. Although..." She looked away. "He had abused me emotionally for years. I guess...on some level...I knew that." She sighed. "When I didn't hear from Jenny and knew I'd have to figure out something on my own, I remembered the letter. I took it out...and you know the rest."

Desiree slipped her arm around Elise's slender body. "From now on, things are going to be different. You'll see." She kissed her cousin's cheek. "You've found the rest of your family. You're one of us."

Shortly before noon, Justin arrived. In deference to the emotional turmoil they knew this meeting would produce, Cleoma, Jack and Jenny had left the house for a couple of hours. Elise had asked Desiree to stay with her.

So when Justin rang the front doorbell, Desiree answered the door. He enfolded her in a quick hug, then looked around. "Where is she?"

Desiree inclined her head toward the living room. He closed his eyes for a brief moment, then said in a firm voice. "I'm ready."

When they walked into the sunny living room, Desiree, for one crystal moment, saw Elise the way her uncle would see her: sitting quietly on the sofa, hands clasped loosely in her lap. Her shining dark hair was pulled back from her face, held there by a thin blue ribbon. She wore a matching blue dress made from some kind of soft, silky material that draped over her slender curves. Her face was pale, but composed, and her dark eyes looked like huge chunks of shiny marble. She rose slowly as they approached, her gaze fastened behind Desiree, on her father.

"Ma fille," Justin whispered.

My daughter. Shivers raced over Desiree's spine.

And then she was standing in the background, throat clogged with tears she tried to suppress, as Justin brushed past her, opened his arms wide, and Elise, like someone in a dream, floated into them.

Over Justin's shaking shoulders, Desiree saw the expression of pain, and love, and hope, that twisted Elise's face as she was clasped in her father's strong arms. Tears rolled down her cheeks, and then they were both crying and holding on to each other.

"Papa," Elise whispered.

Desiree couldn't watch anymore. She didn't belong here. This was a private moment.

Quietly, she slipped out of the room, then just as quietly, opened the front door and walked out onto the veranda. For something to do, and to still her quaking insides, she walked down the front steps and into the yard.

It was then she saw her aunt.

Lisette sat in the front seat of Justin's big sedan. For a moment, Desiree's eyes met her aunt's, then Lisette slowly opened the door and got out of the car.

"Aunt Lisette," Desiree said. She walked quickly over to the older woman, whose expression seemed sad and full of yearning. "Oh, Aunt Lisette. I didn't know you were here."

They hugged, and Desiree could feel the trembling in her aunt's body. What courage it must have taken for Lisette to come. "How is it going in there, *chère?*" Lisette said. "Will my Justin be okay?"

Desiree could hardly speak. She blinked back tears and nodded reassuringly. "Yes. Yes. Everything is fine."

Desiree put a reassuring arm around her aunt's shoulders, and they stood side by side, waiting in the brilliant autumn sunshine. "Are *you* okay, Aunt Lisette? This must have been quite a shock for you."

Lisette smiled sadly. "Oh, *chère,* I've always had a strange feeling about Michelle Sonnier. I drove my Justin into her arms, you know. I wasn't a good wife to him. I punished him because I felt so inadequate, so much of a failure when I couldn't give him a child. Every time..." She faltered, and Desiree could see tears glistening on her lashes. "Every time my Justin touched me, I felt guilty and miserable. For years, even though we managed to put everything that happened behind us, I've been haunted by the knowledge that I was the one who was to blame for everything. And now, I don't know, I can't explain it, but this child, this daughter of Justin's, has set me free." She smiled through her tears. "I feel almost reborn. It's the most wonderful feeling."

About five minutes later, the front door opened and Justin emerged. "Lisette," he called. "Come in." His voice rang with happiness. "You too, Desiree. Come back in."

Desiree let Lisette go ahead of her. Her heart was pounding as if she were a major player in the drama unfolding, and she could only imagine how nervous her aunt must feel, how Elise and Justin must feel. Would they be able to handle this? Would it really be okay, as she'd assured her aunt?

She needn't have worried.

Lisette and Elise looked at each other for perhaps five seconds, then Lisette moved forward. She smiled. "You are every bit as beautiful as I imagined you to be, *ma fille*," she said.

A kind of radiance slowly spread over Elise's face, and with shining eyes, and a tremulous smile on her lips, she walked into Lisette's arms.

Just at that moment, the grandfather clock in the hall struck the noon hour, and as the sound of the chimes permeated the room, Desiree knew this family had been reborn.

Chapter Fifteen

Jenny was leaving New Orleans Monday morning. Desiree said her goodbye to Jack's sister on Sunday night.

"Chin up," Jenny whispered as they hugged.

Desiree tried to smile. She had had a hard time keeping a smile on her face once they'd left Abbeville. Even thoughts of the wonderful reunion between Elise, Justin and Lisette didn't help. As they drove back to New Orleans, all three seemed lost in their own thoughts.

Jenny tried to initiate conversation. She talked about Elise and her future. "Isn't it wonderful that your uncle and aunt want Elise to come and live with them? I'm thrilled for her. This is what she needs. To belong to someone. To feel a part of a loving family unit."

Desiree and Jack agreed, but neither pursued the subject, and after a few more tries at conversation, Jenny subsided into silence, too.

And then they were at Jenny's hotel, and it was time to say goodbye.

"I'll pick you up at eight-thirty in the morning," Jack said before getting back into Desiree's car. "That should get you to the airport in plenty of time."

"Are you sure it's okay for you to drive?" Jenny asked.

"I'm fine. Don't worry about it." His tone didn't invite argument.

Desiree felt as if someone had put a rock into her stomach. She and Jack didn't talk after they left Jenny. They rode the rest of the way to Desiree's cottage with a strained silence between them. The rock in her stomach grew heavier with each passing mile.

When would Jack leave? Would this be their last night together? Was he planning to tell her goodbye tonight? By the time they reached her house, she was so afraid, her body felt numb.

The tense silence continued as Desiree pulled her car into the garage, as they walked together to her house, as she unlocked the front door. Jack turned on lights, and Desiree headed immediately for the bathroom. Once inside, she locked the door, slipped down the toilet lid, sat on the seat and let the tears that had been bottled up for hours slide down her face.

She wept silently. She didn't want to make a scene. She didn't want him to feel guilty or sorry for her. She certainly didn't want him to stay with her out of pity or some misguided sense of loyalty. Even though she didn't know how she'd go on living once he left, she knew if he stayed with her for any of those reasons, he would grow to resent her.

Eventually he would hate her.

Finally she stopped crying. She washed her face with cold water, looked at herself in the bathroom mirror. God, she looked terrible. Her face was blotchy-looking. Her eyes looked red.

She washed her face again, then carefully applied makeup, more than she usually wore. She brushed her hair, looked at herself again. Well, she might not look wonderful, but she looked presentable. Maybe he wouldn't know she'd been crying. Just as the thought formed, there was a soft knock on the bathroom door.

"Desiree? Are you all right?"

She gritted her teeth, forced herself to answer brightly. "I'm fine. I'll be right out."

When she opened the door, she could see him in the kitchen. He was leaning against the kitchen counter. His head was bowed. She took a deep breath, squared her shoulders and walked into the kitchen. "Well," she said, "are you hungry? Do you want a sandwich or something?"

He looked up. Lines of weariness were etched around his eyes. "I'm not hungry. But you go ahead. Fix yourself something."

Desiree shook her head. "I'm not really hungry either."

He straightened up, walked toward her. His eyes were filled with tenderness as he gazed down at her face. He raised one hand and slowly stroked her cheek.

Desiree closed her eyes, savoring the gentle touch. Her heartbeat was slow and steady. The kitchen clock ticked loudly.

"Let's go to bed," Jack murmured, slipping his arm around her and pulling her close.

She nodded, the ache around her heart too acute to speak.

That night their lovemaking had a poignancy that Desiree had never felt before. For her part, she knew this might be the last time, or at least one of the last times she and Jack would be together, and her passion was tempered with pain, her ecstasy with anguish, her fulfillment with fear.

They made love slowly and with great gentleness, then lay together in their favorite spoon position and drifted off to sleep. They didn't speak, as if by avoiding words, they would avoid the inevitability of their parting.

Jack took Jenny to the airport Monday morning, then went to the hospital to have his shoulder checked.

The doctor who checked him said, "You're healing up nicely."

"Is it okay for me to drive back to Houston?" Jack asked.

"Don't see why not, especially since this wound is in your left shoulder—and you're right-handed."

Jack walked out of the hospital and into the bright December day. He got into his car, but instead of turning the key in the ignition, he just sat there. The same thought pounded through his brain. There was no longer any reason for him to stay in New Orleans.

No reason except Desiree.

But he'd been over and over their situation. He loved her. He thought she loved him. Those were the two positives. But Desiree wanted so many things he could never give her. And she deserved those things. She deserved a man who would make her first in his life, a man who would build her a secure future, a man who could put down roots and be contented.

What it boiled down to was that Jack wasn't good enough for her. And he knew it. Desiree was the finest person he had ever known. With the exception of his sister, Desiree was the only woman he'd ever known who was completely giving and unselfish, completely loving and generous, completely open and honest. She was a wonderful woman and a wonderful mother.

She deserved the best.

And she'd never get the best if Jack kept cluttering up her life.

He *had* to leave. To be fair to her, he shouldn't prolong this episode between them. Oh, he knew she'd be hurting when he left, but she'd get over him. A woman as beautiful and sweet and passionate and exciting and terrific as Desiree would soon be beating potential suitors off with the proverbial stick.

At the thought, Jack's guts twisted.

How could he stand thinking about Desiree with another man? He tried to push the thought out of his mind, but unwanted images refused to disappear: someone else touching her, someone else kissing her, someone else burying himself in her sweetness, her warmth.

Jack hit the steering wheel with the heel of his right hand. He swore out loud. *Don't be a jerk. Get out of her life. Get out of her life now!*

The day inched along. But finally it was five o'clock. Finally it was time to clean off her desk. Finally it was time to go home.

But when Desiree got there, she found herself dreading seeing Jack. Dreading hearing what she knew she would soon be hearing. She pulled into the driveway, left her car running, went to open the garage door.

Suddenly her heart slammed against her chest.

Jack's Miata wasn't there!

Fear barreled through her. Her throat closed up. Her hands shook. *No. No. No. No. He's just out running an errand. There's nothing to be afraid of. He's not gone. Of course he's not gone. He would never just leave.* Somehow she managed to pull the car into the garage. Somehow she managed to walk back to her house. Somehow she managed to get the door unlocked.

The minute she walked in she knew.

But still she clung to a thread of hope. "No, no, please God, no," she whispered as she headed straight for her bedroom. She looked at her dresser, devoid of Jack's cologne, his hairbrush, his deodorant. Vainly trying to keep from crying, she flung open the closet. "No, no!" she wailed. "No." The tears gushed out of her eyes, poured down her face. All his clothes were gone.

He was gone.

Her heart pounded like a wild thing, and she was shaking so badly she could hardly walk. She staggered to the bed, collapsed onto the side. "No," she whispered brokenly. "Oh, Jack. Oh, Jack."

Then she saw the folded piece of notebook paper sitting propped next to the phone on her bedside table. She reached for it. She was crying so hard she could hardly read it.

Dearest Desiree,
I know I should have waited until you came home, but I wanted to avoid what I knew was going to be painful for both of us. I have gone back to Houston. I will never forget the time we spent together. I will never forget you. You are the most wonderful woman I've ever known, and I hope you'll find the happiness you deserve.

Sobbing aloud, Desiree crumpled the note in her hand, then threw it against the wall. She threw herself across the bed, beating her fists against the mattress. "Damn you, Jack Forrester. Damn you. Damn you forever."

She cried until there were no more tears left. Then, like an old woman, she dragged herself up and into the kitchen. Her head was pounding like someone had taken a hammer and driven nails into it. She gulped down some aspirin, then turned out the lights. She went back into her bedroom, stripped off her clothes, throwing them around indiscriminately.

Then she crawled into bed and lay there huddled under the covers. The darkness closed around her, and she wondered if she'd ever stop feeling the pain.

"Jack, you've been like a bear with a sore paw for the last week," Rebecca Post, one of his co-workers, said. "What in the devil is bothering you? You're not angry about my getting the Moscow assignment, are you?"

Jack looked up. Rebecca, an attractive journalist with whom he'd worked many times in the past, stood in front of his desk. Her hands were shoved into the pockets of her khaki slacks and her green eyes were filled with curiosity.

He grimaced. "Of course I'm not angry about your assignment."

She gave him a reflective look. "Then what's bugging you? It's not like you to grouch at everyone like you've been doing." She pushed her straight blond hair back from her face.

He sighed. He knew damn well what was wrong with him. He was going through withdrawal, the most painful, excruciating withdrawal anyone could ever experience. He missed Desiree. He missed her so profoundly that it was like a piece of him was gone. There was a great emptiness inside him, and try as he might, he couldn't seem to get past it.

He'd been back in Houston for a little over a week. He had thought that the pain of leaving Desiree would fade, little by little.

It hadn't.

Instead, each day the pain had intensified, until now it was like a great, gaping wound, throbbing and pulsing with a life of its own.

He couldn't eat.

He couldn't sleep.

He couldn't concentrate.

He wished Gerald Crampton would give him a new assignment. Anything. Just to get him out of here. Maybe if he was sent to some remote jungle or some godforsaken desert or some place equally miserable, he'd be able to put thoughts of Desiree where they belonged: in the recesses of his memory where they could be trotted out occasionally to remember as a wonderful interlude in his life, but nothing more.

But Gerald Crampton had said, "There's nothing doing anywhere right now, Jack. Besides, I want you to go to London right after New Year's. I want you to cover the summit meeting the president has planned. That's only about ten days away, so it'd be crazy to send you somewhere else now." He'd bitten down on his cigar. "Just enjoy the Christmas holidays with your family, and relax, for Christ's sake."

Relax.

As if he could.

As if he wouldn't sell his soul to relax. And forget.

But each waking moment, and all of his dreams, were filled with images of a laughing, dark-eyed, dark-haired woman. A woman who could turn his blood into fire and his bones into water. A woman who could take him to the highest peak with a simple touch. A woman who could send him to the deepest recesses of hell.

Which was exactly where he was now.

* * *

"Desiree, what's wrong, *chère?* Are you sick?"

Desiree looked at her mother. "No, Mama, I'm fine."

"Sure, you're fine. That's why you won't eat my cookin', that's why you mopin' around the house all day long, that's why you don' want to go to the *fais-dodo* with your brothers and sister."

"Mama, just because I'm trying to lose a little weight and don't feel like dancing tonight doesn't mean I'm sick," Desiree said tiredly. "I've been working hard lately. I need rest."

"I've never known you to pass up a night of dancin' *chère,* unless you was sick... or in love."

Desiree swallowed. She could feel her eyes filling with tears. God, she was weak. If she couldn't even survive a little motherly questioning without breaking down, how did she hope to survive the rest of her life?

Arlette sat down at the kitchen table. *"Chère,"* she said softly. "What happened with you and Jack?"

The gentle question, the love shining in her mother's eyes, were too much for Desiree. She flung herself into her mother's arms, weeping like a child. "Oh, Mama, what am I going to do?" she cried. "I thought it was going to get easier, but it hasn't."

"Jack, I'm tired of looking at your long face," Jenny said. "I thought we were supposed to be finding something for you to give to Mother." It was midafternoon the day before Christmas Eve, and Jack and Jenny were standing on the second level of the Galleria, overlooking the ice skating rink. All around them last-minute shoppers rushed by, laughing and talking. Christmas carols sounded from the loudspeaker system, and the very air was charged with excitement and festivity.

Everyone, it seemed, was into the Christmas spirit.

Everyone, that is, except Jack.

Jack didn't answer. He knew he was acting like a love-sick idiot. He just couldn't seem to help himself.

Jenny sighed. "Jack, look at me."

He turned. His sister's blue eyes were filled with compassion. She smiled gently. She looked particularly lovely today, he thought, and wished he were better company for her.

"If you love her, why did you leave her?" Jenny asked.

He shrugged. His chest felt tight.

"Talk to me," Jenny urged softly. "Maybe I can help."

"No one can help." Nothing could help. The only thing that could help would be having Desiree here, right now, and that was impossible.

"Try me."

He sighed heavily. "Okay. Let's go get a drink or something. Then we can talk."

Over coffee in one of the small restaurants, Jack said, "I've never been in love before."

Jenny smiled. "I know."

"I'm not sure I like it."

She chuckled. "I know that feeling, too." She reached across the table, touched his hand. "Come on. Tell me what went wrong."

His gaze met hers. "Nothing went wrong, not the way you mean. I just had to leave her, that's all. And it hurts. It hurts like hell."

Jenny's tone was sympathetic. "Why did you have to leave her?"

"It's obvious, isn't it? I'm not marriage material. I traipse all over the world. My home, if you can call it that, is a one-bedroom apartment in Houston. Desiree has a three-year-old-daughter, and she wants a regular family life—a home, a husband who's there at night, and more kids."

"And you can never give her that."

"No. At least not that way."

"Don't you ever want to get married, Jack? Haven't you ever considered it?"

He shrugged again. "Sure, I've thought about it. I mean, hell, I'm not crazy about always being alone, but I've never met a woman I wanted to marry before Desiree, and she wouldn't be happy sharing my kind of life."

"You asked her?"

"No."

"I see."

"No, you don't see." But a tiny spark of hope flared inside him. "Maybe I *should* have asked her," he said slowly.

Jenny stared at him. "No, I'm sure you're right, Jack. You're much better off finding someone who just wants a casual relationship, someone who just wants to have a good time. You'll be happier that way."

"I *won't* be happier that way."

"Desiree needs stability, security, family life."

"I could give her all those things."

"But you travel all over—"

"Maybe Desiree wouldn't mind that."

"No, Jack. You were right to leave her. I mean, after all, how much security and stability can a person have traveling all over the world. Just because the two of you would be together, just because you love each other—"

Jack stared into his sister's wise eyes. "Do you really think there might be a chance for us?"

A slow smile spread across Jenny's face. "I certainly think it's worth a shot, don't you?"

Christmas Eve had always been one of Desiree's favorite days in the whole year. She liked it even better than Christmas Day. Her family had all kinds of traditions for Christmas Eve. Arlette always put a big ham in the oven and to go along with it she'd fix fresh green beans and jambalaya, and of course, a big pot of gumbo. The turkey and trimmings were saved for Christmas Day.

After dinner, the family always gathered around the tree, and the adults opened the gifts they'd given to one another. The children were allowed to open the gifts from their aunts and uncles. Then the entire family, including the children, went to Midnight Mass.

Christmas morning, each family spent at their own homes, where Santa had always visited. This year, Aimee was so excited about Santa coming, she could hardly sit still.

Desiree tried to be happy, tried to enter into the spirit of the holiday she'd always loved so much, but she was having a hard time. Her mother kept sending her anxious glances, and Desiree knew her misery showed.

Right now, she and her mother were working in the kitchen. Soon the rest of the family would be there.

"Be careful of your dress, *chère,*" her mother said. "You better put an apron on."

Desiree sighed. She reached for the apron, tied it over her red dress.

"Stir that gumbo, will you?" her mother said.

Desiree reached for the wooden spoon.

The doorbell rang.

Arlette said, "I wonder who that could be."

Desiree shrugged. One of the neighbors, probably. It wasn't the family. They'd just walk in.

From the living room she heard her father talking and Aimee's excited squeal, then the sound of another male voice.

She stopped stirring. She forgot to breathe. The other voice sounded like . . . no. Impossible.

"Desiree, *chère,*" her father said as he entered the kitchen, a big smile splitting his face. "Someone is here to see you."

And then Aimee, holding onto Jack's hand, led him into the kitchen. Jack—dressed in a white turtleneck sweater, dark gray jacket and gray jeans. Jack—with an apprehensive expression on his face. Jack—who looked as if he wasn't sure what kind of welcome he'd get.

The wooden spoon clattered to the floor. Desiree stared at him, completely incapable of speech or coherent thought. In her wildest dreams, she'd never imagined a more unlikely scenario.

Jack smiled tentatively. "Merry Christmas, Desiree."

"Jack," she whispered. What was he doing here?

"René," Arlette said. "Why don' you help me with the gumbo? You come and stir, and Desiree—she and Jack can go into the livin' room." She turned to Aimee. "And you, *chère,* you stay here with your grandmama and grandpapa."

"But, Grandma!" Aimee protested.

"Listen to your grandmama," René said firmly, his tone brooking no argument, and Aimee reluctantly let go of Jack's hand.

Jack bent down and hugged her. "I'll see you later, honey."

"Promise?" Aimee said.

"I promise."

Then Jack straightened and reached for Desiree's hand. "Come on," he said softly. Like someone walking in her sleep, Desiree let herself be led into the relative privacy of the living room, which was lit only by the twinkling colored lights of the big Christmas tree in front of the picture window.

Desiree trembled as he turned her to face him. But the next minute, she was in his arms, and he was holding her close. "Oh, God, Desiree, I've missed you so much," he murmured against her hair.

Her heart was going like a demented thing. She lifted her face. His blue gaze fastened on hers. She was afraid to hope.

His hands cradled her face, and he dipped his head. When his cool lips met hers, something fell apart inside Desiree, and a sob erupted. She pushed at him. "No." she said brokenly. "No. I can't take this. Jack, why have you come? I don't want you here unless..." She could feel the tears, and she didn't want to cry. She didn't want to make a fool of herself.

"I love you, Desiree. I love you. That's why I'm here. These past two weeks without you have been the worst kind of hell. I found out I don't want to live my life without you. And I came here to tell you so. To see if there's still a chance for me. For us."

Oh, God. She was still afraid to hope. Still afraid he'd change his mind. "I . . . oh, Jack."

He pulled her back into his arms, lifted her chin. With his thumb he wiped away her tears. "Oh, my love, please don't cry. I'm sorry I hurt you. Can you forgive me?"

She nodded. The tears still flowed. She couldn't seem to stop them.

"Desiree," he murmured, "I have to know. Do you love me?"

"Yes. Yes, I love you. I've always loved you. Didn't you know that?"

He kissed her then, a long, deep, drugging kiss that had her head reeling and her heart pounding. She wound her arms around his neck, clinging to him as if she'd never let him go. Finally, they drew apart. He smiled down at her. "You're so beautiful, do you know that?"

She smiled, too, and the last of her fears and uncertainties vanished.

"Let's go sit over there," Jack said softly. He motioned to the sofa.

When they were sitting side by side, his arm around her, he leaned down and kissed her again. "I'll never get enough of kissing you," he whispered against her mouth. Then he drew back and his eyes were sober.

A tiny fear jabbed at Desiree, but his words dispelled it as quickly as it had come.

"Desiree, will you marry me? Will you marry me and travel with me? Could you be happy making our home wherever my work takes me, at least until Aimee's a little older?"

A great joy filled her heart. She wanted to shout. She wanted to sing. She'd taken the greatest gamble of her life, and she'd won. Still, she couldn't resist teasing him. After all, he *had* put her through the most miserable two weeks she'd ever known in her entire life. "Well, I don't know," she said with a soft chuckle. "It all depends on how many trips home to Patinville you'll let me take in a year."

He grinned. "As many as you want."

"Three?"

"Of course."

"Four?"

He gave a mock frown. "Now, don't push your luck! I may be in love, but I'm not a complete pushover!"

She tried to keep her face serious. "How about kids? How many kids do you see us having?"

He laughed and captured her upturned mouth in another breath-stopping kiss. "How many kids do you want?" he muttered when he let her up for air.

"Oh, about six," she said.

"God, you drive a hard bargain." He gave her a hard kiss full of promise, then stood, pulling her with him. He reached into his jacket pocket. His eyes were shining as he handed her a small velvet jeweler's box.

So happy she could hardly think, Desiree snapped open the lid. A beautiful diamond solitaire sparkled with all the lights of the tree. "Oh, Jack, it's so lovely."

Just then Aimee came racing into the room. "Grandpa said I could come in now!" she announced happily. Her brown eyes gleamed with excitement. "What's that?"

Jack grinned at her, then removed the ring from the box and slipped it on the ring finger of Desiree's left hand.

"Oh, Mommy," Aimee said, eyes wide. "A ring! It's so pretty!"

"This ring means your Mommy and I are engaged."

"'gaged?" Aimee said, frowning.

Jack laughed. "Yes, engaged. That means we're going to get married."

Aimee's eyes got even wider. "Really?" she squealed. "Does that mean you'll be my daddy?"

"Would you like that?"

"Uh-*huh!*" Aimee beamed. "I love you, Jack Rabbit!"

Jack's eyes gleamed suspiciously bright, Desiree thought, as he bent down and scooped Aimee up in his arms. He kissed her cheek, and as Desiree's gaze met his over Aimee's head, happiness clogged her throat.

"I've got something pretty for you, too, honey," he said, setting Aimee down again. He reached into his other pocket, pulling out another jeweler's box.

To Desiree's great delight, there was a miniature version of her diamond engagement ring in this box, and when Jack took it out and put it on Aimee's pudgy finger, Desiree thought her heart would burst.

Aimee dashed off into the kitchen. "Grandpa! Grandma! Guess what? Jack Rabbit's gonna be my daddy! Look at the ring he gave me! We're 'gaged!''

Jack and Desiree both laughed, and then he pulled her into a fierce embrace. Just before his lips met hers, he said, "Six kids, eh? Don't you think we'd better get started?"

* * * * *

COMING NEXT MONTH

HE'S A BAD BOY
Lisa Jackson

"Mavericks"

Jackson Moore wasn't a sinner or a saint, but he'd given schoolgirl Rachelle Tremont a taste of paradise eleven years ago. Could paradise be regained?

LUKE'S CHILD
Christine Flynn

Luke Montgomery's entire life revolved around work—until he discovered he had a six-year-old son! Suddenly Luke had to prove to Emily Russel, his boy's adoptive mother, that he wasn't going to hurt young Cody. . .

A HOME ON THE RANGE
Judith Bowen

Lucie Crane was a woman running from lies and Boone Harlow was a man of the West, a rancher who valued truth. Did the truth threaten the only home Lucie had ever known?

COMING NEXT MONTH

FROM FATHER TO SON
Kayla Daniels

Rick West had learned one thing from his hapless dad—avoid women that make you *feel*. Dana Sheridan couldn't imagine what she'd done to alienate Rick, but his unfriendly attitude wouldn't stop her. . .

THE CAT THAT LIVED ON PARK AVENUE
Tracy Sinclair

A missing millionaire. . . Was the drop-dead gorgeous lawyer, Jake Waring, a criminal mastermind? How was detective Sabena Murphy going to solve this crime?

BUILDING DREAMS
Ginna Gray

That Special Woman!

Ryan McCall was venemous about the opposite sex, but somehow his pretty, petite next-door neighbour managed to touch him. It wasn't because he was a sucker for a pregnant lady though. . .certainly not!

Silhouette Special Edition

It takes a very special man to win

THAT SPECIAL WOMAN!

She's a friend, a wife, a mother—she's unique! And beside each Special Woman stands a wonderfully *special* man. It's a celebration of our heroines—and the men who become part of their lives.

Look for these exciting titles from Silhouette Special Edition:

May BUILDING DREAMS by Ginna Gray
Heroine: Tess Benson—a woman faced with single motherhood who meets her better half.

June HASTY WEDDING by Debbie Macomber
Heroine: Clare Gilroy—a woman whose one spontaneous act gives her more than she'd ever bargained for.

July THE AWAKENING by Patricia Coughlin
Heroine: Sara McAllister—a woman of reserve who winds up in an adventure with the man of her dreams.

August FALLING FOR RACHEL by Nora Roberts
Heroine: Rachel Stanislaski—a woman dedicated to her career who finds that romance adds spice to life.

Don't miss THAT SPECIAL WOMAN! each month—from some of your special authors! Only from Silhouette Special Edition!

COMING NEXT MONTH FROM

Silhouette

Desire

provocative, sensual love stories
for the woman of today

THE MAN WITH THE MIDNIGHT EYES BJ James
THE SILENCE OF ANGELS Karen Keast
JAKE'S CHRISTMAS Elizabeth Bevarly
NOT *HER* WEDDING! Suzanne Simms
BEWARE OF WIDOWS Lass Small
IT HAD TO BE YOU Jennifer Greene

Sensation

romance with a special mix of
suspense, glamour and drama

COOL UNDER FIRE Justine Davis
PAROLED! Paula Detmer Riggs
AFFAIRE ROYALE Nora Roberts
WHAT LINDSEY KNEW Ann Williams